He saved h‹

Once upon a time, Kane Harte rescued Anastasia Patrick from hell. He took her away from a killer, protected her, and maybe even came perilously close to loving her. But then she was given a new life. A new name. A new home. And there was no room for Kane or the darkness he carried in her new world. So he walked away. Didn't look back. Fine, maybe he looked back a little. Or a lot. Maybe he dreamed of her every time his eyes closed. Sue him.

She falls for bad guys. It's a quirk. A flaw? Whatever.

When her ex turned out to be a killer, Anastasia "Ana" Patrick knew she was in trouble. But enter the FBI—or rather, enter the super scary, slightly shady, and undeniably hot Kane Harte. He protected her, he gave her a new life—new name, new home, new *Ana*. And he also broke her heart. That would be the previously mentioned issue she had with bad guys. She fell for the dangerously secretive Kane, and he walked away.

He shattered her heart but gave her safety. Not exactly a fair exchange…

Now her safe world has been wrecked. Danger has found Anastasia—Ana—once again, and she has no choice but to flee on her own. The killer from her past has escaped prison, and he's coming after her. Ana runs, desperate to get away, and she finds herself barreling straight into the arms of the protector she never expected to see again.

Kane Harte can kill a man in a hundred different ways. He can also break a woman's heart without batting an eye.

She won't fall for him again. Absolutely, Ana will *not* make that mistake again. Once burned, twice super cautious. But she needs a hero, and Kane excels when it comes to handling deadly trouble. She will control herself around him—there will be no giving in to the crazy desire she still feels for Kane—and, uh, sure, when the Feds decide that she has to be the bait to lure in the killer, Ana will play by their rules. Not like she has a choice, not if she wants to stay alive...

He won't keep his control. He won't play by the rules. And he will take what he wants.

Kane is done. He did the whole good-guy routine once before and walked away from Ana. Not happening again. This time, he'll give in to his need, his obsession, and he will never, ever let go. The Feds want to trap the killer after Ana? Fine. He'll trap him, but Kane will be the one calling the shots and setting the stage. Kane and Ana will play lovers—they will *be* lovers—and they'll draw in the killer. Kane will eliminate the threat to Ana, and he will do whatever it takes to possess the woman who has haunted his dreams for far too long.

Kane made a mistake when he let her go the first time. Now, he's going to fight like hell for his second chance with Ana. Nothing will stop him from claiming Ana. Not the Feds. Not her

killer ex. And not his own bloody and dark past. "Heartless" Kane Harte will put his life and heart on the line for his Ana. Touch what belongs to him? Try to hurt her? He will make you pay.

When He Fights

A Protector And Defender Romance
Book 3

Cynthia Eden

HOCUS POCUS
PUBLISHING INC

For everyone who has ever just wanted to tell the rest of the world to go away for a bit while you escape into a book...

Happy escape time. I hope you have the best adventure.

Prologue

ONE. ONE MOTEL ROOM. ONE BED. ONE MASSIVE bodyguard who had been her protective shadow for the last month. Following her every move. Watching her with his intense, glittering, hazel eyes. Sharing her meals. Learning her secrets. Talking with her in that deep, sexy, rumbling voice that made her knees weak.

And this was it. Her night. Their night. Her *one* chance to—

"All the other rooms were taken. Sorry, there's only one bed."

Ah. Yes. There it was again. The voice that made her quiver in ways that she should not. Because her life was on the line. Danger surrounded her. Sex should be the absolute last thing on her mind.

Exhaling slowly, Anastasia Patrick turned to face the utterly protective badass who'd followed her into the motel room. He'd kicked the door closed. Locked it. Now Kane Harte stood in front of that door like the massively immovable object that he was.

Anastasia swallowed. He wore a black t-shirt. One that

1

stretched and struggled to fit around his truly massive shoulders and biceps. A valiant battle. Kane always wore t-shirts. And she did not object. How could she? Why on earth would she?

The tight t-shirts just make him look hotter.

Dammit. She was not supposed to be lusting after her bodyguard. She was not supposed to be fantasizing about him. She was not supposed to be...falling hard for him.

Yet she was. Oh, she was.

And tonight, this was going to be her *one* night to make her move. Because maybe the attraction that threatened to rip her apart wasn't one sided. Maybe Kane felt the same intense, almost insanely powerful attraction, too. Maybe it wasn't just adrenaline and fear fueling her. Maybe for the first time in her life, she wasn't falling for the bad guy.

She was going for the hero.

"I'll sleep on the floor," Kane added. He strode past her. Dropped their bags to said floor. "No big deal."

"Uh...you don't have to do that." Her words sounded way too high. And sharp.

He glanced over at her with a frown. Stubble lined his hard jaw, and Kane had his battered baseball cap pulled over his head. Beneath that cap, thick, dark hair waited. Gorgeous hair.

Not that Kane was *gorgeous*. Not exactly. He was far too big and bold and dangerous-looking to be described as gorgeous. The man was truly massive in size. She figured he had to be an easy six-foot-four. And she couldn't even guess at his weight. Every ounce of the man was pure muscle.

He towered over her own five-foot-four height, and the first time she'd met him, his size had made her nervous. Unsure. Now, though, it just made her feel safe. Correction, Kane made her feel safe.

Hard, square jaw. Sharp, slanting cheekbones. A long blade of a nose. And the most intense hazel eyes she'd ever seen...all of those features added up to *dangerously attractive.* Drop-dead sexy. But not gorgeous in the traditional sense.

Then again, who cared about the traditional sense? *Kane is hot. I would love to climb him like the mountain he is.*

"Ana?"

Oh, but she did adore it when he said the shortened version of her name. The name rolled and rumbled and almost sounded like an endearment.

And she realized she should be saying something. Oh, right. The bed. "You can share with me," Anastasia blurted.

If possible, his face tensed even more. But, in that one moment, she saw desire—no, lust—flash in his eyes. A primitive, almost savage desire.

Yes, please. Her breath caught.

"I don't think...that's a good idea," he gritted out.

Oh. Well... "Why not?" Whoops. Maybe she shouldn't have asked but...*Dammit, why not?* "Honestly, it seems like a great idea to me. It's a king-size bed. Obviously, it was designed for two people, and it has to be way more comfortable than the floor." A floor that did not look particularly clean. Not like they were at a five-star resort. They were on the run, staying at hole-in-the-wall locations as Kane tried to keep her out of sight.

Hiding was necessary because...

Her ex wanted her dead.

Her ex. A man who she'd discovered—much to her horror—just happened to be a powerful mob enforcer. And a hitman.

She'd rushed to the FBI with her discovery. They'd

wanted her to wear a wire, to go back in and get evidence. They'd promised her a new life. Promised her safety if she worked with them.

She'd done everything they wanted but...

Her ex had discovered the truth. Now he was coming after her. The authorities couldn't find him. He'd seemingly vanished. An easy enough task considering all of Logan Catalano's shady connections.

The Feds were afraid that he planned to kill her. Thus, her hyper-protective bodyguard and hiding in off-the-beaten-path motel situation. Anastasia was also concerned about the same dire ending for herself—and, thus, her not arguing at all when she'd had to go on the run with her new bodyguard.

Fun fact? She wanted to keep living. She liked living. Sue her.

"I don't mind sleeping on the floor," Kane told her.

The lust was gone from his eyes. One thing she'd quickly learned about Kane was the fact that the man was great at concealing his emotions. Hello, stoic expression. But she'd seen that flash, and she now knew that there was a weak spot in his armor. "Is that what you want?" Oh, yes, her voice had gone breathy. She couldn't help that. Grabbing onto her courage with both hands, she closed the distance between them. Stopped right in front of Kane. Tilted her head back and stared into those wonderful eyes of his. "Why don't you tell me what you really want?" Husky.

His jaw hardened. "Ana."

"Kane." She put one hand on his chest. *Ohmygosh.* So hard. So strong. So sexy.

"This isn't a good idea."

"What isn't?" Did he understand—at all—how difficult

this was for her? She was taking a risk, but Anastasia thought he was worth it. Honestly, he might be worth *any* risk.

"If I get in that bed with you..." Kane's words trailed off.

"What will happen?" The heat from his body reached out and curled around her even as his rich, masculine scent tempted and teased her.

"I'll fuck you."

Her mouth dropped. Oh, yes, sweet victory, he'd just said the words...*Out loud.* Finally, the man had given voice to the simmering need between them. She'd felt that need almost from the first moment. Tried to ignore it. Tried to fight it. And then she'd just given up. She felt an instant attraction to Kane. Felt an amazing chemistry that made her body practically burn for him. And he was saying he felt the same way.

"Good." Anastasia shot onto her tiptoes. Her hands curled around his shoulders as she tried to pull him and his delectable mouth closer to her. "That's exactly what I want you to do."

His hands clamped around her waist. "No."

Yes. In so many ways...yes. "Why not?" Her gaze searched his.

"Because you're scared. Because you're living on the edge. Because you're not thinking clearly."

"Kane?" Her heart slammed hard in her chest.

"Yeah?"

"Shut up and kiss me."

And he did. Those powerful hands of his lifted her like she weighed nothing and he held her and his mouth crashed onto hers. *Implosion. Explosion.* Whatever. Her whole body seemed to ignite as a white-hot lust raced through her veins. Her mouth was open. His was open. His tongue thrust into her mouth, and he tasted and he took. Her nipples tightened and her sex quivered, and she knew she was getting wet and super turned on and it was all from a kiss.

Her nails bit into his shoulders. A moan broke from her. She let go of all control and kissed him like the desperate woman that she was.

Kane.

He'd been in her dreams. In her mind. In her fantasies. And, ever-so-sneakily, he'd worked his way into her heart.

Her legs wrapped around him. Seemed like a normal move to make as he held her with that effortless strength of his. Kane was moving them. Taking a few, quick steps even as he kissed her as if his very life depended on the task. Then she felt the hard, flat surface of the wall against her back. He pinned her between his body—his heavily aroused body—and the wall.

Kane was built along massive dimensions, and the cock shoving so hard against her was equally massive.

But his hold was careful on her waist. He'd always been so careful. Meanwhile, she just wanted to rip the man's clothes away and climb all over Kane.

"No." He'd torn his mouth from hers. "I can't. We can't." His breath shuddered out. He didn't back away. Kept right on pinning her to the wall.

Her legs kept right on being wrapped around his waist. Her nails were still in his shoulders, pressing through the t-shirt. "Kane?"

"You don't want this."

Oh, her arching hips said she did. "I want you." Just so they were clear.

"It's fucking displacement. Gray warned me this shit would happen." A hard exhale. "You don't want me. You want the safety that I offer."

Um, she wasn't turned on right then because of *safety*. "I know what I want."

"Ana..."

Longing poured through her. "I think I'm falling in love with you, Kane." A stark admission made as she continued to have her legs wrapped around his waist.

At her words, his eyes blazed and he...

"No." Very firm. Kane pulled away. Lowered her at the same moment.

Her sneaker-clad feet hit the floor.

"You don't love me," Kane denied. Definite.

Her heart kept racing, but a chill skated over her skin. "You tell me what I want. What I don't want. You tell me when and who I don't love." Her arms curled around her stomach. "I think I'm the expert when it comes to knowing how I feel."

"*Ana.*" He reached out for her but...stopped himself. Instead of touching her, his hands flattened on the wall behind her. "You have been living on fear and adrenaline. Your emotions are all over the place. I'm a safe fucking harbor for you. But what you *think* you feel for me? It's temporary. When the danger has passed, when you have your new life and this is all just a bad dream, you will regret me."

She could never regret him. "I want you. I'm falling for you."

His eyes glinted. "You don't know me."

"I—"

"You know what I've told you about myself. Bits and pieces of my life. You *think* I'm safety, but I'm not. I'm as fucking dangerous as your ex, and the last thing you need is to get involved with someone like me. Because you're wrong. I'm not a safe harbor. I'm a nightmare. One that you won't be able to escape, not if you give yourself to me. Not if we cross this line." His head came in closer to hers.

She could not look away from his eyes.

"I fuck you? If I do that, I won't let go. When the time comes for me to give you up, for you to go on to that new life, *I won't let go.*"

Why was that such a bad thing? "Maybe we could have a life together."

"Because you like to fuck monsters?"

His words *hurt.* She flinched, unable to help herself.

"Dammit! Ana, I'm—" He shoved away from the wall. From her. Took two steps back. No, three. Four. Stood there with his hands fisted at his sides. Kane pulled in a deep breath. Then another. "You don't know what I want to do to you."

She'd thought he wanted to fuck her. Instead, he seemed to be putting up new walls between them.

"There are rules," Kane stated as he rolled back those broad shoulders of his. "Rule one is that I don't fuck the witness. I protect her."

Right. Witness. That was her.

"I don't keep the witness. There is no place for her in my life."

Brutal. She blinked quickly because a watery film had just obscured her vision.

"There is no place for me in hers," he continued flatly.

Because he didn't want a place. She would have gladly made a place for Kane in her life.

His gaze never wavered from hers. "Fucking would change everything."

She wasn't so sure it would. Anastasia was afraid it might change nothing. That they'd have sex. Insanely amazing sex. And he'd still walk away when the time came.

"I've been keeping my hands off you." His hands were currently clenched. "It's taken every ounce of my self-control, but I've done it. I watch you. I ache for you. But I know that I am *not* supposed to have you. You aren't meant to be mine."

Why not? No, she wouldn't ask. She was already getting enough of a rejection.

"I'm sleeping on the floor," Kane announced.

Right. The better to not fuck her. She stared at him. He stared at her. Time tick-tick-ticked so slowly past.

"It's not real," he said. "What you *think* that you feel? It will go away. It's happened before."

Oh, now that just hurt even more. "You often have witnesses who fall in love with you?" *Who you fuck? Or, uh, don't fuck?*

"Close proximity. Forced proximity. Danger. Adrenaline. It's a witch's brew that plays with your emotions and channels your lust." He side-stepped. His hands unclenched. "It's not real."

So why did it feel like it was?

He grabbed an empty ice bucket. "Going to get some ice," he suddenly muttered. "Ice, some sodas. And, ah, you didn't have any dinner tonight."

She had no appetite.

"Maybe I can find one of those candy bars that you like so much in a vending machine."

Really? He was gonna consolation prize her with the promise of a candy bar? A candy bar did not equal sex, and she was just so hurt. Rejected. Because Kane didn't get it. The way she felt for him wasn't just about safety. Or some confused, displacement BS.

It felt more real than anything she'd ever experienced in her life.

"I'll be right back." Then the man basically double-timed it out of the motel room. The door clicked closed behind him.

Sure. He'd practically run away.

Why not?

She looked back at the bed.

One motel room. One bed.

One broken-hearted and thoroughly rejected Anastasia.

"Fuck, fuck, fuck," Kane breathed as he stood in front of motel room one-oh-three. He looked down at his hands under the hard glare of the exterior light near the room, and sonofabitch, his fingers were actually shaking a bit. Shaking because he wanted Ana so very much.

He gripped the stupid ice bucket tighter.

I wanted to take her right there, against the wall. I wanted to drive hard and deep into her and feel her come around me. I wanted to make her scream. I wanted her nails raking down my back.

I never, ever want to let her go.

He stalked away from the motel room. Headed for the ice machine. He damn well needed to cool down because the truth was that his body was always in overdrive anytime she was near him. He was supposed to be protecting her, for shit's sake. Not wanting to constantly strip her and make her scream as she came for him.

He rounded the corner. Saw the machine. Heard the whir of the motor.

He'd done the right thing. If he crossed the line and slept with her, there would be hell to pay. He'd only taken the protection gig as a favor for his buddy Gray, but the Fed would be furious if Kane screwed up the case.

Or screwed her.

He shoved the bucket under the dispenser. Hit the button and watched as chunks of ice tumbled out.

I did the right thing. Because he would never, ever be right for Ana. No matter how much he wanted her. She was going to get a new identity soon. A new life. She didn't need a bastard like him dodging her steps.

And he'd told her the truth. At least, partially. If he took her...

I don't think I can let her go.

The ice kept tumbling down into the small bucket. The machine was loud as hell. Clanking. Gurgling. Grinding. His gaze darted to the left. A vending machine waited. Half-stocked.

He started searching for Ana's favorite candy. The woman loved peanuts and milk chocolate.

And Ana said she loved me. That she was falling for me.

The ice overflowed from the bucket and poured down to the floor.

THE MOTEL ROOM door opened behind her. A soft creak of the hinges. Anastasia exhaled slowly and squared her shoulders. Five minutes had passed—just five—but she'd gotten herself under control. She'd swiped away those pesky tears. After all, crying never did anything but gave her a headache. She didn't want Kane to see her tears. Didn't want him to know that her guts were twisted and her heart broken.

She pasted a smile on her face and swung around. "I

was thinking we could watch one of those cheesy horror films that you like so—" Anastasia stopped.

Because that wasn't Kane standing in the open doorway.

It was her ex. Logan Catalano stood there, wearing a wrinkled dress shirt, faded khakis, and grinning at her. "Found you."

She stumbled back a step.

Logan tucked the key card into his pocket. "Told the front desk clerk I'd been locked out of my room. For twenty dollars, he gave me a new key, no ID required." He crossed the threshold, put up the *Do Not Disturb* sign, then he shut the door. Locked it. The main lock, and the small, secondary lock on the door. "Waited for the new boyfriend to leave. Then I came inside."

Kane wasn't her boyfriend.

I wanted him to be.

Logan bent down, reached toward his ankle, and when he rose, a knife was gripped in his hand. "Did you say something about a horror film, sweetheart?" The sharp blade of the knife gleamed. "Because you don't have to watch a show. I'll let you be a real-life scream queen. Right now." He lunged for her.

She did scream. As loud as she could. She screamed and she ran, but he was in front of the door so the only place she could run toward was the bathroom. Anastasia dove for the small bathroom, thinking she could get inside and lock him out. She could stay safe in there until Kane came back. Kane *would* come back. She knew it with certainty.

But she didn't make it to the bathroom. Logan grabbed her from behind. His fingers fisted in her hair, and he caught her, only to then slam her forehead into the bathroom's door-frame.

She *felt* the thud through her whole body. Her breath shuddered out even as a pain-filled whimper slid from her.

"I'm so pissed at you, Anastasia," he growled. His mouth was at her ear, his breath blowing over the shell.

Anastasia. He'd always called her by her full name. Maybe that was one of the reasons she'd started to hate that name. Maybe it was why she liked Kane's shortened version so much better. Ana was...

A new person.

A new life.

The knife was at her throat.

"I'm so pissed that I am going to make you *beg* me for my forgiveness."

A droplet of blood slid down her neck.

Tears pricked her eyes. Those stupid tears again. Tears wouldn't save her. Fighting would.

But he whipped her away from the doorframe and threw her toward the bed. She hit the side of it. Fell down to land in front of the small nightstand. Anastasia shoved her hair out of her way and looked up at her attacker.

He smiled at her. Classically handsome. Bright green eyes. Golden skin. Dimples. And his hand—his right hand with the swirling tattoos was wrapped around the knife. "I won't cut that pretty face," he promised her. "But you will beg."

He rushed toward her.

She leapt to her feet. Ignored the dizziness and the throbbing in her head and she grabbed the lamp from the nightstand. She threw it at him. It just bounced off his chest. Bounced and then fell to the floor where it *shattered*.

"Keep it down in there!" Something banged against the wall. Sounded like the fist belonging to the person in the room beside her.

Her eyes widened. "Help!" The people in the room next door could hear her. *"Help!"* She jumped onto the bed and raced across the covers. If they could hear her, then they could help her.

Logan tackled her. They both slammed into the bed. She went down, face-first, with him on top of her.

His laughter taunted her. "No one is going to come help you, Anastasia. I've got you."

The knife pressed to her side. The tip of the blade cut into her.

"You are going to be so sorry," Logan swore as the knife dug deeper.

The motel room door flew open. Hit the wall. A very distinct crash. *"Ana!"* A roar. The true, deep bellow that sounded as if it had just come from a massive beast.

Her head whipped toward the door. A shudder swept over her even as a smile pulled at her lips. *"Kane."*

Kane was back.

Kane was there.

Everything was going to be okay.

He was already running across the room. A second lock on the door hadn't kept him out. He'd just kicked in the door or beaten it in or something, and he was—

Logan yanked her up. Put the knife to her throat. "I will slice her from ear to ear."

Kane whipped out a gun.

She blinked.

"I will shoot you in the fucking head," Kane promised flatly. "Before you are even done cutting her, you'll be dead."

"Um, wait!" Anastasia cleared her throat. The movement had the blade lightly slicing her. *They all needed to calm down.* She'd love to avoid the *cutting* her part. Surely, that could be possible, yes?

"*What in the hell happened to your forehead?*" Kane snarled.

It did hurt terribly. Had it already bruised?

Probably.

Logan hauled her off the bed, but they slipped when the covers tangled around their legs, and she went down, hard, and, in that moment when she fell, Kane fired his weapon.

The gunshot blasted.

The knife clattered down beside her. Anastasia covered her head, and she screamed. Logan torpedoed over her as he ran straight at Kane. But Kane fired a second time. And she heard the thud of the bullet sinking into flesh.

Her hands began to lower.

Logan fell right in front of her. Her screams echoed around her. She was on the floor, with her knees beneath her, with her hands near her head, and he was on the dirty carpet just steps away. His head turned. He stared at her. Those bright, bright green eyes stared at her with fury. With hate.

With fear.

And Kane put his gun to Logan's head.

* * *

POLICE LIGHTS SWIRLED in a sickening flash. Anastasia stood in the motel's parking lot, watching as the federal agents and the local cops swarmed like bees.

FBI Special Agent Grayson Stone glared as Logan was loaded into the back of an ambulance. Grayson had been the agent in charge of the case, the one who'd arranged for Anastasia to have protection. To vanish with Kane.

He'd also been the one to originally ask her to wear a wire and collect evidence on her homicidal boyfriend.

Grayson barked orders left and right. Two agents jumped into the ambulance with Logan. The siren shrieked. Grayson slammed the doors closed, and then the ambulance raced away.

She kept standing, pretty amazed that her legs were succeeding in their effort to hold her upright.

"Ma'am." An EMT. "We really would like to take a look at that bump on your head."

Her forehead. Yes, she'd made the mistake of touching that bump a few moments ago. A giant goose egg that hurt like a bitch.

"You could have a concussion."

She could. Definite possibility.

But she didn't move. Just watched the other ambulance rush away.

Grayson closed in on her. "You okay?"

No, she wasn't. "He was going to slice me with his knife. Make me beg." Her breath shuddered in. Out. "He would have killed me if…" Her words drifted away.

She'd just spotted Kane. He'd been taken away by some of the Feds after they arrived on scene. She'd been sure they were questioning him. But now he stalked toward her with steady, unshakable purpose.

"But Kane broke down the door," she finished.

"Kane almost killed our perp," Grayson said.

You have no idea. Because Kane *had* put the gun to Logan's head. He'd been about to pull the trigger. And—

Kane shouldered past Grayson. Went right to Anastasia. "Why the hell aren't you already at the hospital?" His hand curled under her chin. He tipped her head back. "That's major swelling and bruising. We need to make sure the bastard didn't give you a skull fracture."

The EMTs had not mentioned a skull fracture. Great, new fear unlocked for her.

"We were trying to get her into the ambulance," the EMT to her right groused.

"Try harder," Kane ordered. Then he just swept her into his arms and started carrying her toward the ambulance that waited a few yards to the left.

"Kane!" One arm curled around his neck as Anastasia clung to him.

He kept marching. Didn't stop until he put her down right inside the ambulance. With a glare on his face, he told her, "You're going to the hospital."

He started to back away.

She caught his arm. "Thank you for saving me."

"You shouldn't have been alone. He never should have gotten that close."

Her grip tightened on him. "Thank you for saving me," Anastasia repeated.

His eyes glittered at her. "I could have made sure you never had to fear him again."

Her heartbeat was far too loud. The EMTs were there. Grayson had followed them. And Kane was just casually talking about how he could have killed Logan for her. If she hadn't stopped him, if she hadn't leapt forward and thrown her arms around him and told him to stop. Begged him to stop. "That's not who you are," she whispered.

"Yes, sweetheart, that's exactly who I am."

He pulled away. Backed away from the ambulance even as an EMT guided her to sit down on the stretcher inside the vehicle.

"And that's why you need to have a different life," Kane told her, voice clear and flat.

She...

"On it," Grayson said. "Rest assured, I am on top of the different life situation." He cleared his throat. "Kane, I believe your work is done. Thanks for stepping in. Thanks for protecting and serving."

Kane grunted. His eyes—those swirling hazel eyes—did not leave Anastasia.

"Ahem." Grayson maneuvered closer to Kane. He slapped a hand on Kane's shoulder. "Also, know that I will owe you one big-ass favor in the future."

"I'll collect," Kane vowed.

The EMTs were poking and prodding at her. She was struggling to keep watching Kane.

"I think this should be goodbye," Grayson mused. "I'll go with her to the hospital. Get her checked out. Make sure that we have all our loose ends tied up. Really great job catching the killer, Kane. I knew I could count on you. You never let me down, and you don't cross lines. Not like plenty of other assholes I can name."

No, Kane hadn't crossed lines.

He'd just saved her.

Grayson let go of Kane. "I have her from here on out."

That was it? Kane was just...just leaving her while she sat in the back of the ambulance? And she should say something. Anastasia knew she should. Part of her wanted to recklessly call out...

Don't leave me!

But, no, she couldn't. She couldn't do that. She just had to stay in that ambulance and feel her stomach knot. Feel the shivers that slid over her body and the racing heartbeat that shook her chest. If Kane hadn't broken through that door, would she be dead?

A tear spilled down her cheek. "Goodbye," she whispered.

Grayson hopped into the ambulance with her. "You're going to testify. You're going to send Logan away for life." He shouldered an EMT out of his way. "You're going to be safe."

Safe.

Because she was going to get the promised new life. The new identity. A new town. A new name. A new job.

Once the testifying was done. Once Logan was locked up. Once...

Kane turned away. He—he didn't even say goodbye to her.

Another tear slid down her cheek.

The ambulance doors were slammed shut.

"Ana?" Now Grayson seemed worried. She should look at him and not just stare at the closed ambulance doors. "Ana, are you okay?" Real concern deepened his words.

"We're trying to examine her." The disgruntled mutter from an EMT.

Anastasia swallowed. Her head turned toward Grayson. "I'm never going to see him again, am I?"

Understanding flashed on his face. Then, jaw locking, Grayson shook his head. "No." A soft exhale. "Believe me, it's for the best."

It didn't feel like the best thing.

Grayson leaned toward her. His voice dropped as if the words were for her ears only, and he said, "If you see Kane again, it's because danger is coming after you. Hell is calling, and he's the answer to the call. If you see him..."

Her hands fisted.

"If you see him again," Grayson told her, "then you are in deep, deep trouble."

The siren screamed on.

* * *

HE TENSED when the siren wailed. Kept his spine straight and his gaze locked dead ahead.

The scene was chaos. Madness.

And Ana...

Ana was leaving him.

Ana...beautiful, sweet Ana. With a smile that had—for all too short of a time—lit up his world. Ana, who had offered him her gorgeous body. Ana, who had kissed him as if her very life depended on the task.

Ana...who had stopped him from putting a bullet into her ex's brain.

Ana...who had seen the monster who lived and breathed inside of Kane.

There was a reason that "Heartless" was his nickname. "Heartless" Kane Harte. He didn't love. He didn't feel. He just didn't care.

Except...

The ambulance carrying Ana had left. He turned around. Slowly. He could feel her absence in the very air around him.

Goodbye. Her voice, drifting through him.

Sonofabitch.

She should have been mine.

Chapter One

PRISON ESCAPE.

Ana's heart slammed into her ribs as her gaze got trapped by the TV screen. Or, by the reporter's words as the perky blonde stood in front of the penitentiary and looked intently, soulfully, into the camera.

"Five days ago, convicted killer Logan Catalano escaped custody during a psych transport. Authorities are still searching for the murderer, a man with long ties to the mob and believed to have been linked to as many as fifteen mob hits over the—"

The chocolate milkshake fell from Ana's fingers and hit the floor, sending the once delicious shake pouring across the tile.

"Authorities consider Catalano to be armed and dangerous. If you have any information on his whereabouts—"

"Butterfingers!" A child's excited voice.

Ana blinked. She looked down at the mess around her feet, then over at the grinning redhead with freckles on her face and an adorable gap where her front teeth had previously been.

"You have butterfingers!" the girl exclaimed again. The tiniest hint of a lisp tagged on her words as she pointed at Ana. And the milkshake. The grin faded from the girl's features. "So sorry." A long sigh. "That is a waste of ice cream. Are you sad now?"

Ana's heart shoved hard into her chest. The pounding felt like a jackhammer as she grabbed for napkins and began to clean up the sopping mess. It was a hellishly hot summer day in Gulfport, Mississippi. She'd stopped by the ice cream shop for a sweet treat and, instead of enjoying her favorite shake, she'd just gotten terror shoved down her throat.

Logan is out. The authorities don't know where he is. I am going to lose my mind.

By the time Ana tossed away the dripping napkins and the remains of her shake, the teen behind the ice cream counter had already changed the TV channel. A big, flat-screen TV filled the wall to the right. The shows typically kept customers entertained—or just distracted—while their milkshakes were being prepared. The shakes could be truly colossal affairs, with candy bars and even full cupcakes stacked on top of them. It took a while to make such cool perfection, and the little kid with the missing front teeth was correct. *A total waste of ice cream.*

Normally, Ana would be severely mourning that ice cream loss, but, at the moment, she was too utterly terrified to mourn. "I'm incredibly sad." A response to the girl who stared at her with unblinking eyes. *Sad, terrified, about to lose my mind. All of the above.*

The kid went back to licking her triple-scoop ice cream cone while Ana beelined it for the door. The bell over the door jingled happily as she rushed outside. The killer sun momentarily blinded her even as the humidity hit her like a punch to the gut. With her breath choking in and out, Ana yanked her phone from her bag and made her way down the sidewalk at double-time speed. She dialed a number that she was only supposed to call in emergencies.

A number she'd memorized long ago.

This is totally an emergency.

The line rang once. Twice.

She paused at the edge of the sidewalk. Checked the road. Bounded into the crosswalk when she didn't see any oncoming cars.

"Hello?" His crisp, cool voice. No identification, but then, he didn't need to identify himself. She recognized FBI Special Agent Grayson Stone's voice.

Since he hadn't bothered to identify himself, she didn't bother to identify herself, either. "He escaped?" Ana cried out. "He escaped and you didn't think to—*ah!*" Her words ended in a terrified scream.

"Anastasia!" Grayson thundered.

She ignored him, for the moment, and glared at the truck that had *just* come to a stop, missing her by inches. Her left hand slammed down on the hood. "Walking here!" Ana snapped. She hit the hood again, for good measure.

Oh, crap. Had that sounded too New York? It felt too New York. And she wasn't supposed to be New York any longer. She wasn't Anastasia Patrick. She was Ana Marie Wayne. She lived in Gulfport, Mississippi. She loved crawfish and gumbo. She belonged to a book club, she taught yoga and music therapy sessions, and she was not the same woman any longer. Not.

"Ana, are you okay?" Grayson demanded.

The teens in the truck shouted apologies to her. She hurried out of the crosswalk even as her right hand kept gripping the phone to her ear. As if she'd needed that extra terror right then. Her poor heart couldn't take much more. "No, I am not okay." Though she had made it to the sidewalk on the other side of the road. Her rental house waited up ahead. A true beauty of a house, right across from the beach. Big, twisting oak trees—limbs decked out with Spanish moss—shaded the sidewalk. "I just had to learn in a freaking ice cream shop that my ex has escaped prison!" Hushed and rushed words. "Why didn't you tell me? Why didn't you *call* me?" A courtesy call would not have killed the man.

"It's all right, Ana—"

"There is no world where this is all right!" She rushed around to the back of her house. Unlocked the door. Barreled inside. Disarmed the alarm—then reset it because...*Logan isn't in prison!* She flew up the stairs, and, even as she kept the phone pressed to her ear, she grabbed her go bag. Oh, yes, she had a go bag at the ready. A necessary precaution since she'd always feared this moment would come.

"I didn't call you right away because I didn't want to worry you."

She came to a dead stop in the middle of her bedroom. The room she'd carefully painted a sky blue. The room she'd furnished with estate sale and thrift store finds. The antique rocking chair. The hand-stitched quilt on the brass, four-poster bed. The art she'd created and hung on the walls. This was her place. She should have been *safe* here. "Consider me very worried, Grayson. Very worried."

"I thought he'd be picked up within a day or two." Grayson's halting response. She heard voices in the background behind him. "Didn't want to risk exposing you unnecessarily."

"The news report said he'd been out for *five days*."

"Yeah, the story has grabbed national headlines now."

Her eyes squeezed shut. "He doesn't know where I am." That was something. That was what she needed to focus upon.

"I was...actually just about to call you." A huff of breath. A sigh? "Someone hacked into my files."

She shook her head.

"I have reason to believe your location has been compromised."

Her eyes flew open. She threw the strap of her go bag over her shoulder and bounded for the bedroom door.

"I'm sending a guard for you," he said, his voice all casual and unalarmed. *Unalarmed.* Like he'd told her takeout was on the way. "You're going to be safe. You're going to be protected."

Her feet flew down the stairs.

"You don't need to panic."

Too late. She was in one hundred percent panic mode. "You just said Logan knows where I am!"

"He *may* know. I don't have complete certainty that he's aware."

Bullshit. "He knows. I sent him to prison. He wants me dead. There is every reason to panic." She bounded off the stairs and flew for the back door once more.

"Just stay put," Grayson urged her in his flat, everything-is-under-control FBI voice. "Your guard will be there soon. He promised to arrive before nightfall. He has your address."

Before nightfall? That was like—at least three hours away. He wanted her to sit and wait for three hours on a guard to arrive? Did he know all the horrible things that could happen in three hours?

"Lock your doors," Grayson ordered her. "Set your alarm. Stay in your house."

Impossible. She was already outside. She'd slung her go bag in her Jeep. "I've got a better idea."

"*Ana…*"

"I get the hell out of my house. I jump in my ride." She jumped in the Jeep. "And I run like a murderer is on my trail. Oh, wait, he is."

"I have a guard coming—"

"I'll call you when I'm in a safe place," she barreled over his words. "Or maybe I won't. Because if Logan has someone hacking into the FBI's system, perhaps it's better if you don't know where I end up." Her fingers would not stop shaking as she cranked the vehicle. "Goodbye, Grayson."

"Wait! I have a plan. Just listen to me for a second. I am in—"

She didn't listen. There were no more seconds to waste. Ana was in full-fledge panic mode. She hung up. She whipped her Jeep into reverse and shot out of her drive. A moment later, she was zipping down the street. Her Jeep bounced. She bounced. And the fear that had never fully let her go swirled in her veins.

She remembered—all too vividly—the last time that Logan had found her. The way he'd tossed her onto the bed. Pressed a knife to her. The threats he'd made.

And then…

Oh, God, and then she'd been in the courtroom. Testifying against him. His eyes—scary and soulless—had pinned her. She'd known that if he ever got free, then she would be a dead woman.

Now he's out. And he's coming for me.

She'd feared this would happen. For the last two years, she'd had nightmares. She'd woken up in a cold sweat countless times. She'd jumped and shuddered at every shadow or creak of sound in her house. Fear had never left her alone.

And now...

He's coming for me.

Her ex had escaped jail, and he was coming to kill her.

Where in the hell was a hero when she needed one?

* * *

"She's running."

Kane Harte nearly crushed the phone in his hand. "What?"

"Yeah, sorry, but you really need to move faster."

Kane straddled his motorcycle. He'd stopped for gas and a check-in with Gray, and he had not wanted this news to be what he heard. "I am hauling ass. You just told me about the escape *yesterday*."

"And Ana just found out about the escape because it made the national news, and now our girl is on the run. Move faster."

First, she wasn't *our girl*. She was a woman, and she sure as shit did not belong to Gray. "Did you tell Ana I was coming for her?" Low. Rough.

"Um. I did mention that a guard was coming."

"And?"

"Ana said she wasn't waiting. That she was running. And she's running right now, and if you don't get to her soon, she's going to vanish and probably die because I don't have a way to track her." Words that verged on the edge of being out of control.

Gray was never, ever out of control. Too tightly wound? Absolutely. A general prick most days? Damn straight.

But one thing you could say about Gray was that he was never, ever out of control.

"She was leaving her place right then," Gray informed him. "No doubt driving out in the Jeep she owns now."

The Jeep, huh?

"If she gets away and she's out there on her own..." A long sigh. "Logan has reach. You know he has reach. I know he has reach. He'll find her. He'll kill her. And we'll be lucky if we can recover the parts of her body that he leaves behind."

Rage flared inside of Kane. *That shit is never happening.* "You're an asshole." Because he knew Gray was trying to rile him up. To push Kane to the edge. A dangerous mistake because Gray wouldn't understand what could happen when Kane went over that edge.

"Oh? I'm the asshole? Nice try, but I'm not the one who broke the woman's heart before."

What. The. Hell?

"I didn't want to bring you in on this. She specifically asked that you never be told her location, but desperate times and all that—and...are you just seriously sitting on that damn bike somewhere? Could you get moving? Did you miss the *move faster* part earlier?"

Oh, he could get moving, all right. "I'll take care of her."

"Did you hear me? She's on the run. As in, now. Kane, you have to do something—go *find her.*"

"I didn't break her heart."

"What? Yeah, you did. She cried in the ambulance ride. And I am not telling you the shit she told me back then. You can't pry it out of me. Kept it quiet for two years, and I'll go right on holding the woman's secrets." A deep inhale. "I need her alive. You understand?"

He understood plenty. "I'll call you when I have her."

He hung up the phone. Swiped his fingers over the screen. Kane studied the data there before he hopped on the motorcycle and made a few quick calculations. Then he sped down the road. Turned right.

Glanced around. Nodded.

And...

Braked. In the middle of the empty intersection.

He removed his helmet. Moved to stand in front of the bike. Another check on his phone showed that he was in the right spot. So he crossed his arms over his chest. He braced his feet apart. And maybe, just maybe, he even started a countdown.

Ten.

Nine.

It had been two years since he'd last seen Ana. Or at least, two years since she'd last seen *him*. An important distinction because perhaps he'd had to sneak out and put his eyes on her. To make sure she was all right, after all. Like any concerned friend might do.

Eight.

Seven.

And maybe she'd been in his head. In his damn dreams. Tormenting him. Showing him what he could've had if he'd just kept kissing her. Touching her on that long ago night.

Six.

Five.

A Jeep rounded the corner up ahead. Baby blue. As it lurched closer, he could see the line of what looked like small ducks tucked near the front windshield. A freaking army of ducks standing at attention.

Four.

Three.

Maybe...maybe he'd actually arrived in Gulfport before

the sun rose. Because he'd been frantic when he got the news from Gray that she was in danger. And maybe he'd tagged her vehicle so that he could keep track of her while he figured out how to approach her.

Two.

One.

Only she was the one coming to him. Approaching him fast.

Her Jeep slammed to a stop. The brakes squealed as the vehicle shuddered about fifteen feet away from him.

Not a busy road. The road leading from the back of her rental house and snaking away from the beach strip was never really busy. That was one of the reasons why he'd chosen this spot.

The Jeep had braked hard. Some of the ducks had fallen. Taking his time, Kane decided to sit on the motorcycle. He pulled out a baseball cap from one of the saddle bags because the sun really was killer out there. He slapped the cap on his head, crossed his arms over his chest, and waited for his prey to finish coming to him.

In seconds, Ana jumped out of the Jeep. Slammed the door. She rushed toward him wearing yoga pants and a sports bra—jeez, that was *all?* The pants hugged her hips, the bra made his mouth water, and, okay, fine, she had on sneakers, too. Sneakers that swept her quickly forward as she ran to him. For one crazy, wild moment, he actually thought she was going to run to him and throw her body against his as she held him tightly and told him how incredibly happy she was to see him again.

"What in the hell are you doing here?" Ana demanded, and her sultry, husky voice did not seem happy at all. Nope, instead, she seemed way, way too pissed.

He kept his falsely relaxed pose and quirked a brow at

her even as hunger, no, lust tightened every muscle in his body. Two years had passed since their heated kiss. Since the night that she'd nearly died in front of him.

Two years.

She'd haunted him every moment. Filled him with regret. Made him wish that, hell, yes, he'd crossed the line and taken what he wanted so desperately.

If he'd kept kissing Ana that night, she wouldn't have been alone when Logan came for her. She would never have been terrified. She would never have gotten a knife shoved into her side—yes, he'd seen the blood that day. The blood on her side and the giant bruise and goose egg on her forehead. If he hadn't stopped kissing her that night, Ana wouldn't have been hurt. Kane would have been with her, and Logan would not have been able to attack while she was alone.

"You can't just—you can't just stop in the middle of an intersection! Do you have a death wish?" Her hands went to her hips.

No hug from her. Check. No big, I-missed-you scene. Got it. She'd gone straight to the death wish portion of the greeting. That was fair. "Do *you* have a death wish?" His voice came out harder than he'd intended. But, what the hell? His voice tended to *always* be hard. It had been that way since puberty hit.

She gasped and took a quick step back.

He thought about lunging off the motorcycle, grabbing her, hauling her into his arms, and kissing her.

Nope. You're supposed to be the bodyguard, remember? Gray is gonna have all his FBI directives again.

But...fuck the directives.

This time, Kane would take what he wanted.

He was looking at what he wanted.

"Kane. You can't be here."

Oh, but I can be, and I am. He smiled at her and heard the swift inhalation of her breath. "Nice to know you remember me."

"You are a hard man to forget." Another step back. "Kane..."

"Hello, Ana." *I've missed you.*

She shook her head. "What are you doing here?"

"Same as before, sweetheart." He should not have used the endearment. Oh, well. Kane figured he was about to do a whole lot of things that he should *not* do. Screw it. He'd be making his own game plan this time.

She blinked her big, gorgeous golden eyes at him.

"I'm here to protect you," he said. *Protect you. Fight for you. Eliminate your bastard ex.*

And...yeah, he was also there...

To claim you, baby. Because this time, I'm crossing the line.

Kane had one big rule that he liked to follow in life. He never, ever made the same mistake twice.

Chapter Two

A GIANT, IMMOVABLE OBJECT BLOCKED THE ROAD. AND she wasn't talking about the big, gleaming Harley.

Kane Harte reclined on his bike like he didn't have a care in the world. He wore a white t-shirt, one that was super stretched because of his massive arms and shoulders. Seriously, had the man gotten *bigger* in the last two years? It sure appeared that way. He had a dark ball cap pulled low over his brow, and a short and—dang it—sexy beard covered his hard jaw line.

He lounged and kept those arms crossed over his chest and...

"Do you just hang around in intersections all the time?" The only thing she could think to say because he'd pretty much shocked Ana straight to her core. How was he in Gulfport? How was this happening? Two years had passed without a single word from him. Two. Years.

And three days.

Not that she'd counted or anything. Some dates were just hard-core burned in a woman's memory. The date he'd left her? The date that she'd almost died?

Impossible to forget that.

"I was waiting for you." Deep. Dark. Rumbly. The kind of voice that would make a woman quiver in all the right places.

She ignored the quiver. *Not going down that path right now.* Her chin notched up. "And you knew I would be coming this way because...?"

He stared at her.

"Because you're psychic?" Ana threw into the silence. "Because you just had some massively wild hunch? Because—"

"Gray called me. Told me you were running. I couldn't let you leave. It's not safe for you to run on your own."

She waited for more. Only there was no more. "*How* did you know I was coming this way, *now?*" There were a dozen ways she could have fled from her house. How had he known that she would be on this particular road, heading for this intersection?

He sighed. His hands finally dropped from his massive chest. He reached down, unzipped one of the pockets in his cargo pants, and he hauled out a phone. "I tagged you, sweetheart." His fingers swiped over the screen, and then he turned the phone back toward her. She saw a small, glowing dot on that screen.

She was the dot? Oh, no. "*Stop.*" An angry snarl because she was at her limit. Too much had happened in way too short of a time.

My ex escaped prison.

He's coming after me.

And Kane Harte is blocking the road so I can't escape.

He'd also...tagged her? Since when? Anger burned in her gut. "How long have you been tracking me?" Had he been, ah, tagging her the entire time? For the last two years?

"Got in town before the sun rose. As soon as I learned that Logan had escaped and was after you, I came here."

Her breath shuddered out. "You knew where I was?"

"I've known exactly where you were since the moment we parted ways."

No, no, that made zero sense. "Grayson said my location was private. Confidential. I left everything behind when I moved here. New name. New life." Her parents had both died when she was in college. She'd had no close relatives. No family that would look for her. She'd vanished after Logan's trial.

He glanced around the empty intersection. "We should probably take this conversation somewhere else before some bozo decides to come plowing through and hit my bike."

"Well, your bike is parked in the middle of the road so... yeah, you should move it." She motioned toward him, waving her hand broadly. "Crank it up. Drive away. Go. Hurry. Wouldn't want that precious bike to get damaged. It looks really expensive."

He did not move. "I knew you were living in Gulfport. I was the one who suggested the location to Gray."

Her jaw nearly hit the ground.

"You told me that you liked the beach. That you wished you could see it every day. Well, you have a rental house with direct beach views, so I figure that's pretty close to your dream, isn't it?"

She got a really bad, twisting feeling in her gut.

"I knew you were living here, but I didn't tag you until I arrived in town. Gray had asked me to stand in the shadows until I got word from him. I was worried you'd flee before that word came from him. Couldn't risk you going out on your own, so I tagged your vehicle while you slept."

Rage almost choked her. Two years. Two years of

dreaming about him, and he'd known the entire time exactly where she was. And he'd just...*tagged* her Jeep while she slept.

"A few minutes ago, I received a call from him telling me that you were coming in hot. He doesn't want you leaving town."

"So you made yourself into a roadblock. Sure. Why not? Totally logical." No, it was not. Not in any world. And she was done. So very done. Ana turned on her heel and marched back toward her waiting Jeep. A car was heading toward the stop sign near her Jeep. A red Mustang. She could see the frowning face of the driver. "I'd suggest you move," she tossed over her shoulder at Kane.

Kane is back. Kane knew where I was the entire time.

Behind her, she heard the snarl of the motorcycle's engine as it fired to life. The loud sound had her heart racing even more. She hurried to the Jeep and jumped inside. The Mustang whizzed by her and snaked through the intersection.

Kane had already moved his ride.

He...

Drove toward her vehicle. Spun the bike and brought it back so that he could pause right next to the driver's side. "We need to talk," he informed her.

"I need to run," she informed him right back.

"Not an option."

The hell it wasn't. Her go bag was in the seat beside her. It was stocked with clothes, a wig, and cash. She even had a fake ID in there that she'd picked up from a slightly shady guy during her last visit to New Orleans. She was ready to vanish.

Except for the pesky *tag* that he'd placed somewhere on her Jeep.

"Gray wants you to stay put," Kane told her.

Gray—Grayson. His good FBI buddy. "What if I don't particularly care what Grayson wants?" Her head turned. She'd left the Jeep door open, mostly just because he hadn't given her time to shut it before he'd rolled up. "You going to force me to stay?"

"I just want to talk," he told her. He sounded all reasonable, even with that deep and dangerous voice of his. "Give me twenty minutes, that's what I'm asking. Let's go back to your place. Get inside—you know, where we're not in danger of getting smashed by other drivers and where we won't be overheard with what is a pretty confidential conversation—and then we can talk. We can make a plan."

"And if I don't like what you have to say? What happens if I don't like your plan?" She wet her lips.

His gaze dropped to her mouth. Lingered. Heated.

Whoa. Hold up. Heated?

He pulled out a pair of sunglasses and slipped them over his eyes. Now all she could see was her own slightly desperate expression staring back at her. Okay, fine, her expression was more than slightly desperate.

And he hadn't responded to her questions. So she gave an answer. "If I don't like your plan, I leave." There. Done. "You remove the tag from my Jeep, and I drive away. You let me vanish."

He nodded. "If you don't like the plan, we'll drive away."

Her shoulders sagged in relief. Great. Fantastic. She would—uh, oh. Back up. He'd said *we'll*. As in, plural. "Wait—"

"I'll follow you back to the house. Not exactly safe for us to keep lingering here. So haul that sweet ass, and let's go." An order.

He revved the motorcycle's engine again.

Her eyes narrowed. Glaring at him, Ana snapped, "It's fantastic to see you, too, Kane. You look great. So glad the last two years have treated you well. Always fun to run into an old friend who...oh, just happens to basically be *stalking* you. Lovely surprise on this beautiful day. Lovely." She jerked the Jeep's door closed. Glared at him.

He made a motion with his hand. A turn of his fingers. As in...*turn this vehicle around.*

She made a motion with her hand, too. As in...*fuck you.*

But she cranked her Jeep. Ana quickly repositioned her lucky duck army—her nickname for the cute, plastic ducks she'd started collecting once she became a Jeep owner. Once the ducks who'd tumbled at her sudden and fierce braking were resettled, Ana released a long breath. Then, for the moment, she turned around and headed back to her place. Blind panic and soul-crushing fear had sent her fleeing before. She could take a breath. She could give him twenty minutes. She could hear him out.

Then, when they were done talking, she could leave his sexy, muscled ass behind. Because there was no "*we*" in this situation. There was just her. And it was her life on the line.

Had he come off stalkerish? Probably. Correction, definitely.

As Kane shoved down the kickstand on his Harley and stared at the house that waited about twenty yards away, he realized that he could have handled things differently with Ana. Used a hell of a lot more tact. This had not exactly been the reunion he envisioned. Yeah, dammit, he'd envisioned a few reunions over the last two years. They'd mostly involved her running straight into his arms. Kissing him frantically.

Fucking him right then and there.

If a guy didn't have dreams, how was he supposed to get through the days?

She slammed the Jeep's door. A black bag hung from one delicate shoulder. "Are you coming in or what? We gonna have this big talk in my backyard? Or..." Her delicate jaw hardened. "Should I say *your* backyard?"

Oh, shit. She'd figured that out, had she?

"Because see, I have this really bad suspicion that I am staring straight at my mysterious landlord. Grayson told me that a friend of his owned the place. A person he trusted completely."

"Gray is typically not big on trust," Kane said as he left the motorcycle and stalked toward her. What would she do if he kissed her?

Her gaze shot chips of golden fire at him.

Right. She'd probably slap him. A kiss might just be worth a slap, though.

"He trusts you completely. Have I been living in your house all this time? Have I been paying rent to *you*?"

He'd actually been keeping her rent in a savings account for her. "Told Gray that you didn't need to pay a damn thing," he groused.

"Screw that. I pay my own way." She spun away and bounded up the porch steps.

He followed, after making sure that the perimeter appeared secure. When he crossed the threshold and entered the house...

Home.

His gaze swept over the rooms as he trailed her through the place. She'd painted the walls. Refinished the wood floors. Brought in all kinds of furniture pieces that were just —interesting. They didn't match, but yet, somehow, they did. As if that made sense. Some antique pieces. Some modern. All felt warm. Welcoming.

All felt like...

Ana.

"I knew it was too good to be true. I mean, first off...the view is killer." She gestured toward the floor-to-ceiling windows at the front of the house. A view that showcased the sandy shores that waited right across East Beach Boulevard.

The house was on a corner lot. Not on stilts. Not that house and not the others near it. They all sported giant yards dotted with massive oak trees that had twisted and bent, but never broken during the previous storms. The house was on a slab, elevated by the terrain, above the flood zone and far enough back that it *should* be safe from rising waters. All the houses on this stretch *should* be safe. Provided a too-powerful storm didn't sweep into the area.

Should be. Should be safe.

Because wasn't that the way life worked? You *should be* safe. As in...Ana should have been living her perfect dream. With her killer view. She should have never needed to know fear again. Except her bastard ex had managed a full-on Houdini routine.

He must have had help. Gray's suspicion. Kane's, too. They both wanted to track down that help. Especially with the leak at the FBI about her location. Hacking? Nah. Full-on *leak*.

"The view is killer," she repeated, "and the rent should have been astronomical. But I got a great deal." A snort. A kinda adorable one. Or maybe he just found way too much about her to be appealing and adorable. "I was desperate, so

I didn't question fate. I was suspicious, though, when Grayson said the owner didn't care if I painted the place. If I refinished the floors. When he said I could do anything I wanted, I thought—well, that's unusual. Not typical at all with a rental, but, hey, I went with it." She huffed out a breath. Braced her legs apart and faced him. "It's your house. You've known I was here all along. And you never once reached out to me."

He stepped toward her. Caught himself before he *rushed* at her. "You left your old life behind."

"You didn't even say goodbye." An accusation.

She'd been whisked away in an ambulance. Taken to a hospital.

"You didn't even look back," Ana muttered.

Those words cut him to the bone. He'd looked back. He'd freaking traveled to Gulfport over and over and stayed in the shadows. Watched her as she jogged along the sidewalk in front of the beach. As she did yoga at sunset. As she went to the ice cream shop that served the colossal milkshakes that she loved.

Fucking stalker, that's me. As if that truth wouldn't send her screaming from him. Kane sucked in a deep breath, then let it out slowly. "I wasn't part of your new life."

"Yet here you are." A nod. "Because...what? Surprise, surprise, my old life is trying to drag me under again."

Yes. His gaze swept over her. Mostly because he was desperate to drink her in. *Ana.* Delicate but determined. Golden skin. Brown hair with faint, red highlights. Shorter hair. Barely brushing over her shoulders. Cut in layers that framed her face perfectly. Her eyes were still big and wide and soul-stealing. Unpainted but full lips. Soft. Tempting. Cute little nose.

Toned body. High breasts. Legs that he knew—from

personal experience—would feel great wrapped around him. *They were only wrapped around me once, but they felt great.*

"Grayson told me that he was sending me a guard. I might have hung up on him before he got to explain exactly who that guard would be." A negative shake of her head. "I have no idea why you drew the short straw and got assigned to me again. I'm sure there are dozens of agents or marshals or—or whatever—that he could send to me. We will just ask him for a replacement."

Yes, there probably had been plenty of other individuals who could have been assigned to her protection. But, they wouldn't have done the job the same way Kane would.

Because, for him, it was personal. And Gray—tricky bastard that he was—knew that important fact. "Other agents aren't me." The other agents wouldn't protect her the way he would. "I'm familiar with you. I know your secrets."

She rocked forward onto the balls of her feet. "You knew me two years ago. You don't know me now."

His gaze slid away from her. Again, this was probably not the time to confess that he was kept updated on her life. An emailed update arrived from Gray like clockwork every month. To buy himself a bit of time as he tried to figure out how best to handle Ana, Kane strolled toward the large harp positioned near the left, front window. "Switched to the harp, huh?" Something he'd actually already known. He'd known exactly when the harp had been delivered. He'd arranged for the delivery guys because he'd wanted to make sure that not just anyone got in her house. His fingers trailed over the long strings, and music filled the air. "Do you like it better than the violin?" Because, once upon a time, she'd been a violin virtuoso. Performing routinely with the New York Philharmonic. Not that he'd seen her on the stage. By the time he'd come into her life, she'd given up performing for avid audiences.

Correction, she'd been forced to give it up. Because her ex had been determined to kill her.

"It's not that I like it better." Her fingers sort of fluttered at her side. It was a move he didn't even know if Ana realized she'd just made. Like a phantom stroking of her fingers over harp strings. "Just different."

"I'm glad you're playing music again."

She swallowed. "There are some things you can't give up. For me, it's music." She looked down and frowned at her hand, as if she'd just caught the movement. Her fingers fisted.

He knew Ana could play pretty much any instrument. Back when he'd been protecting her and taking her in and out of shady motels, she'd told him that, as a child, she'd been able to perform nearly any song after just listening to it once.

Since he couldn't even play *Jingle Bells* on a piano if his life depended on the task, Kane had been more than impressed by her skills. She was truly phenomenal, and walking away from music? He'd often feared that it must have ripped out her heart.

But...

"I teach music therapy," she suddenly told him. "I mean, I do music therapy or I..." Another clearing of her throat. The hand she'd fisted released as she crept toward him. "I help people who need a way of communicating. Work with lots of different groups and ages in the community. Music is transcendent, you know?" A bright smile lit her face.

And he couldn't breathe. Because he'd forgotten just how truly beautiful she was.

But her smile faded all too fast. "The harp is different from my violin." Now she was brisk. "But different is good, and I enjoy playing it." A sigh. "I also enjoy teaching yoga classes. I started yoga to help calm my mind, and now it's pretty much an addiction for me."

"I figure there are worse things out there that a person can be addicted to in this world."

Her stare held his. "Yes." Softer. "There are." She'd taken a few more steps toward him. Now she stopped. Tilted her head back. "I think we agreed on a twenty-minute discussion."

He didn't remember actually *agreeing* to just twenty minutes.

"You were going to tell me why I shouldn't run, when my demented ex is on my trail. A man who killed for the mob. Who routinely made bodies disappear. And to think, I once thought he was Mr. Perfect."

"No one is perfect."

"Why can't I run?"

His gaze got locked on her mouth. Those soft lips.

"Kane?" Husky. "Why can't I run?"

A sharp knock sounded on her back door. She jumped at the sound, and her hands immediately flew out and locked around his arms. Her eyes had gone very, very wide.

"You expecting company?" he demanded.

A quick, negative shake of her head.

The knock sounded again. More demanding this time.

"Stay here," he ordered her as he spun away and headed toward the rear of the house. He automatically reached back and hauled up the gun he'd tucked into the waistband of his jeans.

"This is why I should have run!" Her steps rushed

behind him. "And you came into my house with a gun? I didn't even notice it until now!"

Not noticing it had been the point. Thus, the reason he'd hidden it at the base of his back and pulled down his shirt to cover it up.

"Kane..."

He rounded on her.

"Kane, what if it's a neighbor?" She grabbed his arm. Her fingers darted over him, and he felt the fluttering touch charge through his body. Every single cell. He was suddenly honed in and one hundred percent focused on her. Ana licked her lips. "You can't greet my neighbor with a gun!"

The knocking came again. Even harder than before. Almost like the person was trying to beat down the door.

"That doesn't sound like a neighbor," she whispered. Fear flashed on her face.

And then—

He heard the back door opening. Flying inward. A door that he'd locked, and hell, no, it wasn't a neighbor. Whoever had just entered the back of her house had *broken* in. Without another word, Kane took off running for the back door.

A man had already hurried inside the house. His back was to Kane as the guy quickly shut the door, flipped the lock, and then he—

"Bastard," Kane growled as he slammed to a stop. The gun was still gripped in his hand.

The man turned toward him. Slowly. With his hands up. A smart move. But the guy flashed a cocky grin his way. "Hi, there, Kane." His gaze flickered to the gun. "How many times do I have to tell you, friends don't point weapons at friends?"

Kane's teeth snapped together.

"I knocked." A shrug from the man. "No one answered. Figured I'd better let myself in with the spare key I happen to possess, just in case something bad might be happening." Keys dangled from his fingers. His head cocked to the left as he peered to the side of Kane. "Hello, Ana. You hung up on me before I could say—"

"*Grayson,*" Ana snapped the FBI agent's name like the curse that it was.

"Before I could say," Gray continued determinedly, "I am in the area. Right in Gulfport." He smiled at her. Then at Kane. "The gang is all back together, how about that?"

Kane growled at him. Then, he lowered his gun and, biting off each word, he gritted, "Ana wants to know why she can't leave town."

"Oh." A grimace from Gray. "Sorry but...I'm afraid it's because you're going to be bait."

"*What?*" Utter shock and horror from Ana.

Kane put the gun down on the gleaming, white marble countertop in the kitchen.

Then, when Ana tried to lunge past him and attack Gray, Kane wrapped his arms around her waist and hauled her back against him. He held her easily in the air. Her legs kicked, and her hands fought at his unbreakable grip. "Sorry, sweetheart," he said, meaning both the apology and the endearment. "But I can't let you kill him."

Chapter Three

GRAYSON SLAPPED THE KEYS DOWN ON THE COUNTER and held his hands, palms out, toward Ana. "I'm not here to fight."

She heaved and twisted but Kane was not letting her go. He didn't hurt her. The man had complete control of his strength, and no matter what she did, she couldn't seem to break free. Her feet dangled in the air because he'd lifted her up, and she kicked back at him, aiming for his shins, but Kane didn't even grunt at the impact. "Why do you have keys to my house?" she snapped at Grayson.

He winced. Looked vaguely guilty. "In the event of an emergency, I thought it best to have backup keys and to know your alarm codes."

"This isn't an emergency!"

"Well, how did I know that?" His hands fell back to his sides as he appeared disgruntled. "I mean, I talk to you on the phone. You seem panicked. You don't let me fully explain. I call in Kane, and he basically hangs up on me. Then I'm at your back door, I see your car and his motorcycle, but neither of you respond to my polite knocks."

Polite? It had sounded as if the person on the other side of the door had been trying to pound his way inside her home!

"So I got worried." A roll of one shoulder. Grayson wore a crisp, white shirt, black pants, and gleaming, black dress shoes. His dark hair was shoved back from his face. "Being the concerned friend that I am, I decided to let myself in the house to make sure you were both all right." His gaze dropped to take in Ana's heaving body and her kicking feet. "How about you promise not to try ripping off my head? If you make that promise, I bet your new bodyguard will let you down. Sound like a plan, hmm?"

"Fuck yourself," she enunciated clearly and precisely. Like any refined lady would. "And, Kane, if you don't let me go right this minute, you will be sorry."

"Can't let you kill him." Kane's breath blew over the shell of her ear.

A tremble slid through her.

"He's annoying," Kane added, "but he's useful." His breath teased her again, and, oh, damn, had she just felt a lick of his tongue against her? Surely not.

Surely. Not.

"I get that you're stressed," Grayson announced.

"Oh, you get that? Fantastic." She rolled her eyes at him. "Give yourself a couple of cookies."

"I have a plan."

"Do you?" she challenged.

He nodded.

"I have one, too," she revealed to Grayson and to Kane because they should both be aware of it. "My plan involves me not being used as bait. It involves me not finding a knife shoved into my side because my freak ex gets to me again and pins me to a bed and tells me that he won't cut my face but the rest of me is fair game and—"

Kane put her down. Her feet touched the floor, but before she could launch for freedom, he'd spun her around. His head lowered. He got really close. All up in her space.

As if he hadn't been in my space before.

"That will *never* happen again," Kane vowed. "I will not let him *ever* put a knife to you, and if you hadn't stopped me before, he'd be cold in the ground right now. We wouldn't even be having this conversation."

For a moment, she could not breathe. The past was between them in that instance. She could see Kane as he held the gun to Logan's head. Kane had wanted to pull the trigger. She'd known it. She had never seen such hate and fury on Kane's face before that time. But Logan hadn't been armed by that point. He hadn't been fighting back. And...

I couldn't let Kane become a killer. Not for me. Not because of me.

"It will never happen again," Kane promised. "I *don't* make the same mistake twice."

Her head moved in the slightest nod.

"Great!" A loud and pleased exclamation from Grayson. "This is what I am talking about."

She peered over her shoulder at him.

Grayson fired a happy smile her way. "Motivation," he elaborated. "Kane has it. He will do anything to keep you safe. Sure, I could bring in a new guard—or even guards, plural—to keep you safe, but would they have Kane's motivation? His drive? His...personal interest?"

"*Gray.*" A sharp warning from Kane.

Grayson pursed his lips. "I don't think they would," he said after a brief pause, answering his own set of rambling questions. "I think Kane is the perfect man for the job, and I also think that, deep down, you're happy to see him, Ana."

Happy wasn't quite the right word. But then again, she didn't exactly hate seeing him so...*dammit*. She was all messed up. "I won't be bait." There. Ana stepped away from Kane and Kane's tempting scent. Like, masculinity in a bottle or something. Rich and sandalwoody and just...sexy.

She exhaled. Put a bit more space between them. The better to not drink in his scent. Ana positioned her body between Grayson and Kane. "Not bait," she repeated.

"Let's not use the B word," Grayson offered. "Let's think of this situation more as...the FBI helped you quite extensively in the past. You wanted a new life. We gave you one. And now, it's time to pay back the debt."

Her brows shot up. "Excuse me? I *paid* that debt when I wore a wire and got all the evidence for you. And then when I testified against Logan—and against the mob guys I'd seen him with back in New York. Let's not forget all that." Logan wasn't her only enemy. She'd spilled all that she'd seen and heard. Plenty of people had been caught in the FBI's web—uh, her web—and sentenced to prison.

She'd needed a new life so that she could keep breathing after all of that.

"Logan could have fled the country." Grayson began to amble around her kitchen. Poking and prodding at things. "And, it's a possibility that he actually *did* leave. We should not overlook that scenario."

"If you believed that possibility, you wouldn't be here right now." She darted a look at Kane and found his hazel eyes locked and loaded on her. "Neither of you." Because Kane would never have come back into her life.

He was the walk-away-and-never-look-back type.

Not   the...*I'm-dying-without-you-and-I-need-you-to-make-my-life-complete* type. Unfortunately.

"Logan has a great many connections in this world." Grayson's voice had turned musing. "But, according to the psychiatrist who worked with him, he also has quite a fixation. On you."

"Some girls just have all the luck," she muttered. Goosebumps rose on her arms.

"The psychiatrist believes that Logan will seek you out. Considering the, ah, hack at the FBI, I also believe he is seeking you out. He's a moth. You're the flame. I'd like for you to draw him in until he gets burned."

"Or until *I* get burned," she said. She still had the scar from her last encounter with Logan.

"Not happening," Kane promised in that rumbly voice of his.

Each time he spoke, she felt the impact of that deep voice flooding through her body. When he actually touched her...*hello, hypersensitivity.* She quivered. She yearned.

She had serious problems.

Two years had passed. Two years. And three days. She should be over him. No, she *was* over him. Way over. So over that...

She hadn't been with another man in two years.

Two years. No lover. Since leaving Logan, the closest she'd come to being intimate had been when she'd basically thrown herself at Kane.

Crap. Ana shoved back a heavy lock of hair that had tumbled over her left eye.

"How about we sit down?" Grayson had stopped near her kitchen table. "We can talk like rational adults. No one will attempt to physically attack anyone else. We'll discuss just how we are going to work together in order to trap a wanted criminal."

Sure, they could do that. "Or I could run out of the door, hop in my Jeep, and vanish."

Grayson stared at her. His face subtly changed. His jaw hardened. His gaze sharpened. His expression stopped being quite so warm and became calculating. Assessing.

"You've made friends in this town, haven't you?" Grayson asked her. "After all, you've been here for two years. You've put down roots."

She had. One of the reasons she wanted to flee from Gulfport was because she didn't want any of her new friends getting pulled into the madness that had been her previous life.

"Logan has intel that will tell him where you are. Here." Grayson motioned around him. "We both know that Logan Catalano is an apex predator. He will be able to get close to the individuals you consider to be friends. He will make them talk. Make them tell him everything that they know about you."

"They won't know where I've gone." Ana was suddenly very, very cold.

"Do you think that will matter to him?" Grayson closed in on her with his slow, deliberate steps. "Or do you think that he'll still slice the throat of your next-door neighbor, that sweet widow? Eighty-three-year-old Shirley Hosier? Or that he'll just let your dolphin training buddy, Felicia Vickory, go right about her business? You and Felicia hang out together once a week for dinner. You think he'll let her walk away or do you think he might decide to hold her head under water and to stop her from breathing at the Gulfport Aquarium where she works because Logan doesn't give a shit who he hurts? And, honestly, making the people you care about suffer would probably make him feel a whole lot of pleasure. Oh, hey, and let's not forget your best friend Zuri—Zuri and that restaurant she loves so much. She's the manager there, right? It'd be a shame if she got cut with one of those giant butcher knives that are kept in the kitchen—"

"*Enough.*" A roar from Kane. Suddenly, he was between her and Grayson.

Her breath heaved in and out.

"*Don't* scare her," he snapped at Grayson.

Too late. She was suitably terrified. And incredibly pissed off.

"She needs to be afraid. She knows exactly what her lover was."

A deep growl came from Kane.

"If she walks away, if she runs away, he'll take his rage out on the people who were close to her. We all know it." Grayson was adamant. "He will kill anyone in his way. The man can't be allowed to stay on the loose. We have to catch him. We have to lock him up again. We have to find out how the hell he orchestrated his escape in the first place. Who helped him. What other ties he has. *We have to trap him.* And Ana is our best shot at doing all of that."

She couldn't see Grayson because Kane's big body blocked her view of the other man. That was good because if she couldn't see Grayson, then Grayson couldn't see her. And since Kane wasn't looking over his shoulder, he wouldn't see her, either.

Ana swiped her hand over her face, wiping away the tears. "I would love to be bait," she declared, making her voice bright. Perhaps even semi-enthusiastic. "I was wondering what I could do this week. Didn't have lots of plans and was worried I might be bored. Being bait is the perfect item to put on my to-do list. Thank you both so much for this opportunity."

Kane's shoulders stiffened. Then he whirled toward her. His eyes narrowed into chips of glaring fury. His big hands closed around her shoulders. A careful, soft touch, despite the rage in his stare. "Are you *crying*?"

"Absolutely not." Absolutely, yes. She blinked quickly. "Shall we move on to the planning portion of this event?" Still bright. Still fake. All she really wanted to do was run to her bedroom, yank the covers over her head, and curl into a ball. Was that so much to ask? But she'd kept the mask in place. There was no point in letting Kane and Grayson see her crumble.

Sometimes, nightmares just wouldn't end.

Not unless you made them stop.

"You should have let me kill him," Kane rasped.

She stiffened in his hold. The past was right there again —all big and bloody and scary between them. For a moment, Ana could not speak at all.

"Ahem!" A loud throat-clearing from Grayson. "We don't talk about murder in front of federal agents. We don't talk about killing people in front of law enforcement personnel. That is rule one. Rule two—*we aren't killing anyone.*"

Kane's fury still glittered in his eyes, sharpening and hardening the hazel.

"We are setting a trap. We are catching an escaped criminal. We are *not* killing him." A pause. Then Grayson added, "The only way you'd be able to respond with lethal force is if you were defending yourself. You don't get to preplan an attack because that is literally called *premeditation.* Here in Mississippi, premeditated murder is a capital offense—it's first-degree murder. You know what you can get for that? Other than, of course, *life* in prison? You can get a lethal injection. Death pumping through your veins. You can get hell via nitrogen hypoxia. You can select the old favorite of electrocution. Or, hey, if you're feeling really, really classic and crazy, you can throw back to a firing squad, though I don't know if that one has been used since—"

She'd flinched. Over and over. As each method of punishment was stated way too bluntly by Grayson.

Lethal injection. *Flinch.*

Nitrogen hypoxia. *Flinch.*

Electrocution. *Flinch.*

And...firing squad? *Flinch.* Was that even still a thing or was Grayson just trying to terrify her? Because she had no intention of getting the death penalty, and she certainly wasn't going to have Kane go down for premeditated murder.

"He's trying to scare you. Don't worry. I can handle myself." Kane squeezed her shoulders.

"I am very worried," she whispered back. "My ex is coming to kill me."

"Yeah, but he'll have to go through me in order to reach you." Low. "That's not happening. I won't be leaving your side at all. From here on out, consider me your shadow."

She gazed up at him. "You're a very big and obvious shadow."

He smiled at her.

That smile of his stole her breath.

"*Is anyone listening to me?*" Grayson asked, annoyed.

Kane let her go. Stepped to the side. She got a clear view of Grayson's disgruntled expression.

"Are you listening?" he fumed once more. "Or are the

two of you way too busy whispering sweet nothings to each other?"

"Sweet nothings?" she repeated. "Is that a thing?"

Grayson's lips thinned.

"Just getting into character," Kane allowed.

Wait, wait, wait. What character?

"Gray told me some of his plan earlier," Kane revealed. "The new cover story for us." His hands curled and uncurled at his sides, but his voice was deceptively mild. "I'm down for it."

"Fantastic." Her gaze swept over Grayson's figure. "What's the plan?" The sooner they got started, the better. Because the sooner they faced this nightmare, then maybe the sooner they could end it.

Grayson hauled out one of the chairs at her kitchen table. He sprawled in it and tapped his fingers lightly on the tabletop as he waited for her and Kane to join him at the table. "The last time, you went into hiding."

Yes, she was *still* in hiding. Slowly, she sat down, too. Her fingers didn't tap against the tabletop. Instead, her fingers strummed lightly at her side, as if she was playing her harp. She caught the nervous movement and quickly stopped.

Kane took the chair beside her. He made zero nervous or stressed gestures. Just sat.

"You were off the radar. Bouncing from shady motel to shady motel. Switching cities." Grayson's fingers tapped again. "He still found you."

As if she needed the reminder.

"You don't run this time. You don't hide. You keep on with your life, as if everything is normal. You go about your routine. You go to work. You see your friends. You—"

"Put a fun target on my back because I'm right out in the open?"

He didn't deny the charge. "You let Logan see you. You let him get close. And when he comes for you, Kane will stop him."

"Damn straight." Utter certainty from Kane.

Her gaze whipped to him. "Don't *you* have a life?" Ana blurted the question. "Like...a family? A, um, girlfriend?" Or, heaven forbid, "A wife? Someone who hates for you to just up and vanish like this?"

The silence in the room was deafening.

Jealousy twisted in her gut. A jealousy that she had zero business feeling. Not like he'd ever sworn undying devotion to her. Not like he'd been in her life for the last two years or anything and she...

Oh, damn. Her eyes widened with a bit of horror.

"No girlfriend." Flat. "No wife."

Her breath whispered out.

"No ties at all that would stop me from moving into your life."

Grayson's hands flew up as he gave a little clap. "Great. Then there is no problem. You'll move in here, you'll take the role of her boyfriend, you'll be seen in public with her, and you can—"

"Ahem." She cleared her throat. Very, very delicately.

Both men swung their heads toward her.

"Not a real boyfriend," Grayson hastened to say. "Purely a cover situation. When Kane poses as your boyfriend—lover, current hookup, whatever you want to call him—"

Her eyes narrowed on Grayson.

"It will give him a reason to be close to you. He can

accompany you around town. Stay in the house with you at night, and it won't arouse any suspicions. It will be the easiest cover story, trust me." A rough laugh. "I mean, I'm coming off a case where the cover story was an actual marriage, so just dating is a million times easier than that ruse."

She didn't laugh back. She did clear her throat again. "There's a problem." A small one. Or maybe not so small.

For nearly two years, she hadn't gone out with anyone. She *had* no actual lover. But, uh, recently...well, she'd...

Grayson blinked. "There's no problem. I assure you, this will work. You may have to do some brief PDAs in order to sell the ruse to friends and coworkers, but surely you can manage to hold hands with Kane or to kiss him on the cheek. Not like I'm asking for some major make-out session."

Ana shook her head.

"You can't hold his hand? Not even to catch a killer?" Grayson demanded.

"That's not the problem." Though it was pretty problematic that each time she touched Kane, a sensual surge pulsed through her entire body. No one else had ever made her feel that way. Just Kane. Just "Heartless" Kane Harte. A nickname Grayson had revealed for Kane long ago. Grayson had seemed to think the name was so very fitting.

She hadn't. She'd been sure that Kane had a heart. Maybe one that he just kept carefully hidden from the rest of the world.

"What's the problem?" Kane wanted to know.

Right, so...Beneath the table, her sweaty palms pressed against the soft fabric of her yoga pants. "I have a boyfriend." A new development. And maybe boyfriend wasn't the right term. *But I am dating someone. Casually dating him. Okay, we've been out a handful of times with very minimal kissing at all. And...*

Kane didn't move. Didn't blink. Didn't seem to breathe. She could actually feel the moments ticking away. One second. Two. Three. Four. Five. Six.

Was someone going to speak?

"That wasn't in my latest intel report on you," Grayson muttered.

"It's new." Very new. Not serious. She'd only recently decided to dip her toe back into the dating pool after a whole lot of urging from her friend Zuri. "We've only gone out on a few dates."

Kane shot to his feet. His eyes seemed to *blaze* at her. "Do you love him?"

"Uh, no, no, I do not." She jumped to her feet, too. Slapped her sweaty palms down on the table and leaned toward him. Glared right back at him. Why was he so mad? He was the one who'd ghosted her for two years.

And three days.

"I do not love him." She thought Turner Mitchell was nice. That was all. "But I have gone out on a few dates with this man, so don't you think it will be weird if I'm suddenly living with a different boyfriend? Hmmm? Don't you think *that* might be suspicious?"

"Are you fucking him?" Kane demanded.

Her mouth dropped. Just dropped. Ana was surprised it didn't slam into the floor.

"Time out!" Grayson was on his feet now, too. "Hey, Kane. I've got a stellar idea. Let's take a walk outside and get some air."

Kane did not move. "Are. You. Fucking. Him?"

"What does that matter?" She was not, in fact, fucking Turner, but for some reason, Ana didn't make that confession. Anger twisted and seethed inside of her as her hands pressed harder to the table. "You don't know me. Not anymore. You have zero say in what happens in my life. Who I fuck or who I do not fuck..." Making the full disclosure that she had not fucked anyone in over two years was just not happening right then. A woman had her pride. "If I am fucking Turner or not—how does that matter? *Why* would it matter?"

"It matters," he snarled right back. "Because I am trying to decide if I have to kill him or not."

Her breath left her in a rush. A squeak of sound because surely, he had not just said those words to her.

"*Outside!*" A roar from Grayson. "We are going outside right now. Understand? And we are not killing anyone." He grabbed Kane's shoulders. The two men were pretty close in size. *Pretty* close. Not the exact same. Kane was still bigger. In the shoulders and in general height.

But Grayson was clearly furious, and he shoved Kane hard. He kept shoving until they were at the house's rear door.

Then Grayson tossed Ana a broad smile. One that never reached his eyes. "Things are completely under control," he assured her. "Kane is not going to kill the guy you're dating. No worries at all."

He pushed Kane outside.

The door slammed.

And Ana realized that she did, in fact, have plenty of worries.

Chapter Four

"I AM GOING TO KILL HIM. IF HE'S FUCKING HER, HE'S A dead man." Kane's breath shuddered in and out. In and out. He paced to his bike, spun on his heel when he reached the motorcycle, and stalked right back to a watchful Gray. "*Dead*."

"Yeah, so, first, calm down."

Kane snarled at him. He reached his friend and, immediately, Kane turned on his heel and began to march back for the bike.

"Second, and, you know, stop me if you've heard this before, but...*don't threaten to kill people in front of a Fed. Even if the Fed is your BFF.*"

Kane had reached the motorcycle. His back teeth clenched so hard that his jaw ached. He'd waited too long. He'd stayed away too long. And, dammit, what the hell had he thought would happen? That she would put herself in some freaking sexual isolation for two years? Just because *he* hadn't fucked anyone since he'd last seen her, that didn't mean she hadn't gotten involved with someone else.

I will kill the sonofabitch. Kane spun away from the motorcycle.

"I think I should give you a third because you didn't listen to items one and two, did you? Okay, here we go. Third, she didn't say she'd fucked him."

Kane stopped mid-stalk.

"I mean, Ana didn't say she *hadn't,* either, so I'm not saying go get your hopes up. I'm saying...well, go back to items one and two. Calm down and stop threatening to kill the new guy." Gray shrugged. "We both know you're not gonna kill some stranger just because he's sleeping with Ana."

Uh, no. They did not both know that fact. Gray was seriously underestimating the rage and dark jealousy flowing through Kane's veins. "You told me that I had to pull her out of hell."

"Yes. You did that for Ana once before, and I want you to do it again. Look, a cover story change is not a big deal." Gray advanced toward him. "So you don't play the role of her boyfriend. Whatever. You can be her cousin."

The man was not serious.

Gray's voice turned thoughtful. "Maybe even her stepbrother."

"Are you shitting me right now?" Her *brother*?

"This could work." Now Gray was fully enthusiastic. "A family member would have the same all-access pass to her life. And she could keep the current boyfriend she has and go about her business. Perfection in motion."

"The hell it is." He stood toe to toe with his friend. "I'm not her cousin, and I'm not her fucking *brother*."

"Stepbrother," Gray corrected. "Because the two of you look nothing alike. No one would buy that you're biological siblings."

Kane couldn't speak. A low growl built within him.

"I thought you had this under control." Gray's voice dropped. "You let her go. You stayed away for two years. I don't get it. If you wanted her so badly, how the hell did you walk away in the first place?"

Because I had to do it for her. She was just getting away from one twisted sonofabitch. She needed to stand on her own. To make sure she wasn't just tied up with adrenaline and fear and...

"You didn't trust her, did you, Kane?" Even softer. "She offered you a life with her on a silver platter. Maybe it was every dream you ever wanted."

Ana *was* every dream that he'd ever wanted.

And she was dating someone else. *Sonofabitch.*

"You figured she'd change her mind. Is that what happened? Or maybe you just didn't realize how badly you wanted her, not until she was gone."

"I knew how badly I wanted her the moment we met." Flat.

Gray jerked in surprise.

Oh, what? Had his friend thought that Kane would keep denying the truth? Not happening. "I wanted her the minute I saw her. But you had assigned me to protect her. The job was to keep her alive. Not to lust after her. Not to fuck her." *Not to fall in love with her.* He shut down the thought as soon as it whispered through his head. "She was being hunted by her ex-lover. She was scared and desperate, and Ana needed someone she could trust. So I became that someone. I didn't cross lines." Except for the last night. And then...

I wanted to do so much more.

Kane's chin lifted. "She'd been with a monster already. She needed a shot at a normal life. I'm many things, but normal isn't exactly how most would describe me."

"You're dangerous."

Kane grunted.

"Territorial. Possessive as hell of things that belong to you."

Another grunt. Because Gray was not wrong in his description.

"You're a vicious fighter."

Again, true.

"You've killed, and you've hunted and you've done the bloody, violent jobs that no one else could handle in this world."

All reasons why he should not have crossed lines with Ana.

"But you don't kill innocent people. So I know that despite the BS swagger you're throwing around, you won't kill the man Ana is fucking. *Not* that I think she's fucking him," Gray rushed to add. "If she was fucking him, though, I think you'd just want her happy. You'd back off. You wouldn't destroy the man."

Kane just stared at him.

"You wouldn't," Gray denied.

Aw, that was cute. It sounded as if Gray was trying to convince himself of that very important fact.

"Dammit, just *don't,* okay?" Gray groused. "Don't kill him. Do go back to having ironclad control. You don't want to play her stepbrother, then fine, we'll figure something else out. The point is that I need a protective detail that can remain very, very close to her. There was chatter earlier from my sources that made me think an attack on her might be imminent. Even before Ana called me—FYI, she saw the story of Logan's escape on the news, and that's what led to her panic—but even before the call, I was going to contact her. Because red flags are waving. Something is about to go down, and protection has to be close." He glanced around. The area behind the house was dead quiet. "If you can't handle this, then I need to know, immediately. You can ride out right now, and I can stay with her until another guard can be brought in. But if you're leaving, then go. She needs help, not some domineering asshole who is going to threaten to wreck the whole case."

Kane's heart drummed too fast and hard in his chest.

"Don't see you riding out," Gray noted.

"Fuck yourself."

Gray laughed. "You're gonna protect her."

"I did it before, didn't I?"

"You're gonna keep your control."

Maybe. That part was still up for debate. "I can do the job. I can eliminate threats to her."

"And you are *not* going to kill the guy she's dating?"

Kane rolled back his shoulders. "I'm not going to pretend to be her freaking stepbrother or cousin."

"Well, she already has a boyfriend, so you can be her platonic friend who—"

"I'm the ex who is here to fight for her." Oh, hell, yes, he was. Warming to the new role, he continued, "The ex who never got over her and will do anything to win her back." He shouldered past Gray. Strode for the house. For Ana.

"Yeah, okay," Gray agreed from behind him. "That might work."

* * *

"Ana, I know it's last minute, but I just got tickets to the concert at that rock casino in Biloxi tonight," Turner Mitchell told her.

Turner. The man she'd gone out on two and a half dates with in the last month. Turner, a nice guy who owned a taekwondo studio down the corner from the Gulfport Aquarium—the aquarium where she taught her yoga classes. He'd flirted with her for about three months. Had asked her out several times before she'd finally agreed to coffee. She counted the coffee as their half date. Then they'd gone to dinner. And dancing.

Two and a half dates.

Unfortunately, after finally getting back into the dating game, there had been zero chemistry between them. He'd touched her, held her hand, kissed her, and she'd pretty much felt like she was in cold storage.

Ana had already planned not to keep seeing him because, well, what was the point when she hadn't felt like the relationship was going anywhere? She'd wondered if, because of everything that had happened before, perhaps she just couldn't respond the same way any longer. After having a lover who turned out to be a brutal killer for the mob—a man who'd come after her and nearly killed her, trust was a major issue. Without trust, intimacy just didn't seem possible for her.

Then Kane had appeared, he'd touched her, and that sensual surge had flooded through her veins.

So maybe it's not about trust and intimacy and...dammit, maybe I just am not attracted to Turner. I don't respond to him the same way that I do Kane.

Or maybe she just was still hung up on Kane.

Perhaps it was some freaking hero complex situation. Kane had saved her life. She'd gotten obsessed with him.

*Liar, liar...*A low voice whispered through her mind. *You were obsessed even before he saved you.*

She ignored the voice. Gripped the phone tightly and tried to figure out how to respond to Turner.

But it was just—she hadn't been able to fully relax with Turner. To let go. And maybe it was because she was lying about her life or maybe he just wasn't the one for her.

No maybe about it. Definitely not the one.

"The tickets were given to me by a friend," Turner told her. "Thought we could take in the show tonight."

At the rock casino. Right. Check. A line of casinos waited down the way in Biloxi, Mississippi, about a twenty-minute drive away from her home on the shoreline. Each casino had a different theme, and the one Turner was talking about had been decked out in extreme rocker style. The casino had an attached hotel and a large theater for shows.

Her phone had rung shortly after Kane and Grayson went out for their air. As if their talk had summoned him, the caller had been Turner.

And he wasn't quite her boyfriend. Maybe she'd exaggerated that part. As far as fucking him? Nope. Definitely had not happened. Would not happen.

"I remembered you saying that you liked the band." He rattled off the name.

She frowned. She *did* like that band, but for the life of her, Ana couldn't remember telling Turner that fact.

"So when I got the tickets, I thought, hey, Ana would love these."

"Ah..." She needed to think of an excuse, stat. One that did not involve her saying...*Can't go. Sorry. A killer may be coming after me.*

The back door opened. She turned to see Kane filling the doorway.

"I'm the ex who is here to win you back," he told her with a grim nod.

She nearly dropped the phone. It did slide and wobble, but her fingers clamped around the device even as her eyes widened. "I'm not available tonight," she rushed to say into the phone. Had Turner overheard Kane's words? She'd certainly heard them, all loud and clear. "An...an old friend came to town," she explained quickly.

Kane walked into the kitchen.

Grayson followed on his heels, shutting and locking the door. "Platonic friend for the win," he said.

Kane shot him a glare.

"My friend is visiting now," she told Turner as her gaze darted between Kane and Grayson, "so I can' t make it. Sorry."

"Oh." Turner's disappointment was clear. "That's okay," he rallied. "There will be plenty of other shows. I'm sure we can catch one of those."

Ana wasn't about to make any promises. "Thank you for the invitation." Very polite. "I hope you have a great time." She tossed out a few other pleasantries before ending the call. Her fingers still had a too-tight grip on the phone when she lowered it to her side.

Kane's expression could still have been cut from stone.

"That him?" Kane wanted to know.

"Yes, that was Turner. He had tickets to a concert tonight. Wanted to see if I was available."

"You're no one's last-minute choice."

She knew her eyes had to be huge. "What is happening here?"

He closed in on her. All big, intent, and, yep, that hot gaze of his seemed possessive. "Your ex is back in your life."

Was he talking about her murderous former lover? Because she'd gotten that point, yes. Logan had escaped and was apparently hell-bent on her destruction. The news every woman longed to hear. Not.

"Me." Kane's hand touched his chest. "I'm the ex who is back and ready to fight for my second chance with you. *Me.* That's the story we're spinning. The reason I'm back in your life. You can share it with that Turner jerk and with anyone else who might be asking."

Her gaze immediately flew over to Grayson. Now his words made sense. She nodded. "I'll choose the platonic friend role, thanks."

Kane reached out. His fingers curled under her chin.

A shiver skirted over her because—of course—that flood of sensual energy pulsed right through her at his touch.

Kane leaned toward her. His heat and that tempting, masculine scent swept out to wrap around her as he rasped, "Sorry, sweetheart, but I don't think that role is gonna work for me."

She pressed up onto her tiptoes. Their mouths grew dangerously close and, voice husky, Ana told him, "Too damn bad."

Chapter Five

SHE HADN'T INTENDED TO BE IN A BEACH-SIDE BAR with Kane as midnight trickled ever closer. The band played from a stage nearby, while couples swayed—some barefoot—in the sand. Laughter flowed in the air, the drinks kept pouring, and stars glittered overhead.

Ana and Kane were at a tall table on the edge of the patio. The blare of the music almost drowned out the pounding waves. Almost. When she strained, Ana could hear the water as it crashed into the shore.

"You could try to look happier," Kane advised her.

She could. Or she could just keep right on doing what she was doing. And what she *was* doing? Nursing a cute, little blue drink with a pink umbrella perched in it. "We're not on a date," she told him, very deliberately, as her gaze darted toward the band and then to the couples swaying. "We are two platonic friends who are having a drink and unwinding after a long day." Her fingers fluttered in the air. A nervous habit she'd picked up. Strumming strings that weren't there. She caught the act and tried to still her phantom playing. Had Kane noticed? Hopefully not.

"We're just friends," she repeated as she tried to sound confident and in control.

Though, actually, what they really were—they were two individuals who'd had to get the hell out of the house because Grayson had brought in a crew who were supposed to be going hard on a fast and intense security installation. She'd already *had* security at the house, but Grayson had wanted to step up the game. Extremely step it up. And his crew had needed work space, so...

After Grayson's briefing session with her had ended, she'd changed clothes. Ana now wore jeans, a loose top that dipped a little off her left shoulder, and comfy sandals. She and Kane had taken a short walk down the beach. They'd gone to the bar so she could be seen in public. Part of Grayson and Kane's master strategy to lay the groundwork that her life was totally normal and that she was simply visiting with an old friend.

"You care about him?" A growl.

Her gaze whipped to Kane, and surprise, surprise, that intense stare of his was on her. A candle flickered in the middle of the table, and the light seemed to match the gold buried in his hazel eyes. "About who?" Ana asked, blankly. *You? Yes, yes, I cared. Was convinced that I was in love with you two years ago.*

"The bozo who asked you to go see the concert."

"Bozo?" Now she did smile. "What kind of insult is that?"

"Fine. The lucky fucking bastard you've been seeing..."

Her smile wiped away. He'd called Turner a bastard, but adding the "lucky fucking" part didn't exactly seem insulting. It seemed envious.

"Do you care about him?" Kane wanted to know.

To buy herself time to respond, she reached for her

71

drink. The glass felt cool beneath her fingertips, and she slid the umbrella out of the way so that she could get a better sip of the sweet brew. It slid through her, refreshing but with a kick at the same time, and her eyes darted to the crowded dance floor as she...

Well, speak of the devil.

She put the glass down. So hard that it clinked against the table.

"Ana? Do you care about him?" Low and intense. "Because if you do, I...fuck, I won't get in the way, I won't—"

"He's a bastard." Flat. "I thought he was nice, but I believe I was mistaken. There was zero chemistry between us. I was planning to break things off before you swept back into my life."

"Uh, say again?"

"And he's standing about ten feet away with his tongue shoved pretty far down the throat of his current dance partner, so I'm just going to assume that he has already moved on. He clearly had a backup date ready tonight, and this development certainly makes things easier." Did it, though? Because, despite her bright words, things felt very awkward. And embarrassing.

And a bit hurtful.

Kane slowly turned his head. Stared at the dance floor.

"He's wearing the blue shirt," she supplied. Turner also still had his tongue shoved down the throat of the woman with him. Tongue in her throat. Hands on her ass.

"You were fucking *him*?" Kane's voice had reached a dangerous, intense degree. It was also a wee bit too loud. She thought about flying across the table and putting her hand over his mouth to shush him.

"That weak-looking asswipe? You were fucking *him*?"

Definitely too loud. Heads turned their way. She *did* have to half-lunge over the table and put her hand over his mouth.

He frowned at her.

"I did not fuck him." A whisper. "Jeez, let's not attract too much attention, all right? *I did not fuck him.* I kissed him, like, once, maybe twice, and there was zero chemistry." Now the truth just tumbled all out because...

Seriously? It just tumbled out. Screw the because part. Her feelings were all over the place. "I wasn't even gonna see him again," Ana grumbled, and she felt her cheeks heat. "Then you stormed back into my life, and I didn't exactly want you to know that I'd just been living in the no-sex zone. So, yeah, there's that." Her hand was still over his mouth. She was still practically crawling over the table top. "Not like I want you to *mistakenly* think that I've been hung up on you for all this time."

Or to think that she still longed for him.

Dreamed about him.

Wondered where he was. If he was happy. If he was—

His tongue snaked out and licked against her palm. Sensual electricity flooded through her. "Kane...?"

His gaze smoldered.

She should pull her hand back. Yep, one hundred percent, and...

He licked her again.

She shivered. She also did start to pull her hand back because she knew when a situation was getting out of control and this one most certainly was. Time for a quick retreat.

"Ana!" Surprise. Shock.

And...

Things had just gone from bad to worse.

With her hand still just an inch or so from Kane's lips, her head whipped to the right.

Turner Mitchell gaped at her. There was no sign of the woman he'd been holding so tightly just moments before.

"Ana?" Turner stalked closer, and the closer he came, the angrier he looked. His light brown hair had been shoved back from his forehead. "Ana, I thought you were visiting company tonight."

"She *is*," Kane replied before Ana could actually get words out of her mouth.

She did manage to fully snatch her hand back. Finally. So, win.

Kane rose to his feet and moved to stand between Ana and the forward stalking Turner. "I'm the company she's visiting." He towered over Turner by at least four inches. "Speaking of company, where did yours just go?"

Turner side-stepped so he could lock eyes on Ana again.

She used that opportunity to hop out of her chair because an exit felt like a good idea. "We should go," she told Kane. She grabbed for his hand.

He stiffened. Looked down at her hand, then immediately swallowed her fingers in his bear-like grip. "Sure thing, sweetheart."

Right. Of course, he'd use an endearment right then. Why not?

"*Sweetheart?*" Turner sounded as if he'd just choked on the term.

Ana would have felt guilty, truly, she would have, because he *had* seemed like a decent guy but... "Turner, I know you're here on a date. I saw you two, um, dancing."

"I'm not on a date!" Turner denied instantly. "You didn't see anything!"

Really?

Kane laughed. Only it was not an amused sound. More mocking. Way more mean, too. "You had your tongue in the redhead's mouth and your hand on her ass. If that wasn't a date, then it sure was an intense hello session."

Turner yanked a hand through his hair. "I can't screw this up with you, Ana!" His hand fell to his side, only to immediately rise as he pointed at Ana. "You have to let me explain."

"She doesn't have to do anything," Kane snapped back. "She owes you nothing."

Turner's handsome face—he was handsome, in a pretty boy way—flushed. "Look, you steroid-eating bastard—"

"Ouch," Kane murmured. "Someone is getting awful personal. And not nice at *all*." His head turned toward Ana. "Bad choice," he told her.

She glowered up at him. Had she not said she was going to end things with Turner? And he'd been charming... before.

Before this night.

Before I saw his true colors.

Wasn't that one of the things that had held her back for the last two years? She'd been so wrong before about a lover and, too late, the truth had been revealed.

Bad choice.

Back when she'd met Logan, Ana *might* have been slightly drawn to bad boys. But she'd more than gotten her fill of them, thanks.

"Not really into steroids," Kane continued as he rolled back his shoulders. "Just into putting in the work. No pain, no gain, am I right?"

Turner fired him a look of disgust. A look he then turned on Ana. "You were supposed to be with a friend tonight! You blew me off."

"I am her friend." Kane whistled and kept right on holding her hand in that bear-like grip of his. "Platonic friend, huh, Ana? My name's Kane."

She'd deal with him in a moment. First, Ana stepped toward Turner. "We are not in some deep, committed relationship."

"No, you are not," Kane stated decisively from behind her. "Don't see a ring on her finger."

She pulled her fingers—all ringless—from his grasp.

"We went out a few times," Ana continued in a polite but firm voice. "It was not serious. The connection was not there."

"It *is* there," Turner argued. Not polite. More snarling.

"In what world?" Her face scrunched. "And, please, don't pull some big, messy scene with me. You found a backup date." The concert must have already ended, and they'd come to the bar. Ana made a vague motion with her now free hand toward the dance floor. "You two seem to have great chemistry, and I wish you well." She did. There. Done. End of drama. "Have a good night, Turner." She turned to leave.

He reached out. Grabbed her wrist. He was much smaller than Kane, but Turner's grip *hurt*. She sucked in a sharp breath at the flash of pain when he seemed to grind the bones in her wrist together.

"Oh, you do not want to do that." Kane's tone had gone lethal. "Let her go, now."

"Back off," Turner thundered. "I don't care how big you are, I am a third degree *decided* black belt, and I'm not scared of your size. I can take you down just like I take down anyone else."

"Let *go*," Ana told Turner. "You are hurting me."

Would he have let go on his own? Ana wasn't sure.

Because as soon as that one word—*hurting*—left her lips, Kane attacked. He moved wicked fast for someone so big. By the time she could even blink, her hand was out of Turner's rough hold, and Turner had just gone crashing into the table she'd sat at only moments before. The table toppled. Turner toppled. When he crashed to the floor, so did her drink. It spilled onto him, and the umbrella fell into his lap.

"You don't hurt her. Not ever." Kane loomed over the fallen man. "Third degree, my ass. Amateur, you do not want the hell I'll bring to your door."

Everyone was looking at them. Even the small band had stopped playing. How utterly wonderful. "It's all under control," Ana called out as she whirled to face the crowd. "He slipped. Accidents happen. Go on about your business."

She heard a scuffle behind her. Wincing, Ana looked over her shoulder.

Kane had his fingers curled around Turner's neck.

"Oh, jeez." She bounded for Kane. Tapped him on the shoulder. "Let go."

"He charged at me," Kane defended. "I just stopped him before he could make contact."

Fair. But they had too many eyes on them. "Let go. You've made your point."

He kept holding a squirming Turner. "What point might that be?"

Seriously, the cops would be called soon. The bouncer was even starting to make his way over to—no, scratch that. The bouncer had just done a double-take when he saw Kane, and the bouncer was hurriedly backing away. Sighing, Ana explained, "The point that you're the toughest badass in the room. I get it. Now let Turner go."

"He hurt you."

She flexed her wrist. "I've been hurt worse."

Kane's head turned toward her. "I don't want you *ever* hurt."

She swallowed. The look on his face was just so—so intense.

"Turner!" A squeal from a lady with long red hair, a white crop-top, and super small jean shorts. The woman Turner had been kissing moments before.

"Let him go," Ana pleaded again.

Kane did.

The woman ran toward them. She threw her arms around Turner. "Baby, are you okay?"

Turner glared at Kane, ignored the woman, and, with his eyes on Ana, he said, "Ana, you have to believe me. I have no idea who this lady is."

The lady in question let out a loud gasp. "I'm the woman you've been sleeping with for the last three months!"

Wait, *what?*

The redhead elbowed him in the ribs. When he doubled over and groaned, she sashayed away, but not before telling Kane, "Have fun. Beat the hell out of him if you want." She didn't look back.

Ana raised her brows. She looked at Kane. Then they both looked at Turner.

"Fuck," he groused as he rubbed his ribs. His gaze flickered over Ana. "We're over, aren't we?"

Ana nodded. "Definitely over. You and I. And you and the redhead, too. Just so you're aware." Because the redhead had already strode over to start chatting it up with the band's lead singer.

Turner hissed out a breath.

"And, hey, guess what, asshole?" Kane drawled.

Turner fired him a glare.

"I'm not Ana's platonic friend. Not some visiting company. I'm the ex who is here to win her back. Thanks for making the job easier."

Turner took a swing at him.

Kane easily dodged the blow, but he did swing a punch of his own. One that connected and sent Turner crashing into the already broken table once again.

* * *

THEY MARCHED BACK into her house. Ana hadn't spoken during the return trip to her place. Kane figured that was a bad sign.

But, hey, things could be worse. He could be playing the role of her platonic friend.

Thanks for fucking things up, Turner. And, FYI, you never had a chance with Ana. She was way out of your league.

Gray looked up at their entrance. He'd been huddled near the security panel with two men in blue shirts. "We're not quite finished—"

"I'm going to bed," Ana interrupted quickly. She did not look over her shoulder at Kane. The words seemed to be for Gray. And maybe the two guys helping Gray. "I will be in no one's way, and no one will be in my way." She kept striding forward. Then paused. Turned toward Gray and the two men. She sucked in a deep breath. "Thank you very much for your assistance." Her voice was gravely polite.

Kane arched a brow as he watched her.

She'd lifted her chin. Squared those delicate shoulders. "I appreciate all that you are doing, and I know you are here very late and on short notice. *Thank you.* I apologize if I do not seem very friendly it's just...um. Big night, you know? Big. Bad. All the things." A wave of her hand. A wave toward Gray and his two helpers. A wave that did not include Kane. "But thank you. And, sorry we're back early. But we were thrown out of the bar." With that, she turned and kept striding for her destination.

Kane shut the back door. He watched her walk away. Such a phenomenal ass.

She disappeared from sight.

He let out the whistle he'd been holding inside. Not a wolf-whistle, though, yeah, Ana had a great ass. The whistle was more a happy-as-can-be whistle.

"You got thrown out of a bar?" Gray inquired.

"I might have grabbed a guy by the throat. Almost might have thrown him into a table. And punched him."

Gray squeezed the bridge of his nose even as the security team with him went back to their installation. "*Why* would you do that?" Gray asked. "Why, why, why? You were just supposed to keep her busy for a bit. Get an eye for the locals. Start cementing your cover story with her."

Kane smiled. Couldn't help it. "I did cement the cover story." Another little whistle as he headed across the kitchen. "Forget the friend ruse. That was never gonna work."

Another squeeze—no, a pinch of Gray's fingers along the bridge of his nose. "Do not leave me in suspense. What *is* going to work as the cover story?"

"Her boyfriend is back in town."

Gray's hand fell.

"Not the psycho ex-boyfriend," Kane clarified, "though we are certainly all waiting for his appearance, aren't we?"

Gray grunted.

"I'm here to reclaim the love of my life," Kane said, deliberately keeping his voice light.

Gray's jaw hardened.

"I couldn't get her out of my head, so I have to fight for her. Couldn't let her go off with some other creep who didn't know how to treat her." The bastard had *hurt* her at the bar. So Kane had wanted to hurt him back. As far as he was concerned, no one would ever hurt Ana and walk away unscathed. Just not going to happen. "She officially ditched the local she had only *casually* been dating. Not fucking, just so we're clear. She did not fuck that Turner Mitchell bastard." Kane knew the two men installing the security system were Feds, so he didn't hold back in front of them. If Gray hadn't trusted them completely, they never would have been in Ana's house.

"OhmyGod." Gray looked heavenward. Or maybe he was looking up at the second floor of the house—the floor with Ana's bedroom. "This is not information you need to share with the group."

Probably not, but it was information that made him stupid happy. "Everyone at the bar knows that she left with me tonight. I'll be staying here. In her home. With her. Consider my cover story cemented."

A sigh heaved from Gray. "Thank...you?" A definite question.

But Kane nodded. "You can always count on me for a job well done."

Chapter Six

THE SHARKS SWAM SLOWLY THROUGH THE WATER, their gazes directed forward. No emotion. Just savage beauty. Intensity. Drive.

Sharks never showed fear. They didn't hesitate. They just kept swimming. And biting.

"That was an amazing session, Ana." Zuri Harris curled an arm around Ana's shoulders. "You have no idea what my week has been like." She gave her a little squeeze. "I needed this so much. Thank you."

Forcing a smile, Ana turned toward Zuri. The other woman had been the first friend that Ana made after moving to Gulfport. All of five feet nothing, Zuri was a powerhouse who managed what was truly *the* best restaurant in the city. A landmark of delicious taste—as Zuri had proudly boasted on more than one occasion.

Zuri's warm brown eyes gleamed as she smiled at Ana. Her dark hair had been pulled back into a bun, and small, gold hoop earrings hung from her lobes. "My boss was a real pain in the ass for the last few days," Zuri revealed.

Ana laughed as the rest of the class packed up their yoga mats. "You *are* the boss."

Zuri winked. "And I was a total, demanding pain." She rolled back her shoulders and stretched. "The week was a bitch."

Agree. One hundred percent. But Ana bit those words back.

"Some of us might grab some wine in a bit." Zuri wiggled her eyebrows. "Feel like getting a drink?"

"I can't. Sorry." Because Kane would be picking her up and taking her home. The denial was also because she didn't want to put a bull's-eye on her friends in case Logan was lurking nearby. "Rain check?"

"Of course. There will always be more wine nights. Always. Bye, Dracula," Zuri called as she tossed a wave toward the enormous aquarium tank. The centerpiece of the entire building, the big tank was a three-story habitat called the *Oceans Explorer Zone*. Inside the tank, Dracula was one of the two sandbar sharks who called the aquarium home. As if on cue, Dracula did a sharp turn and dove in front of the glass.

Laughing, Zuri grabbed her bag. "See you next time, Ana!"

Right. Next time. Ana chatted a bit with some of the other students who'd showed up for the late-night yoga session. A De-Stress Evening By the Deep, as she billed it in her promos. Not that they were *actually* deep, but...

People liked coming to the aquarium for the night yoga sessions. It was a great way to unwind after a long day or a long week. And while she did teach a full yoga class, plenty of her attendees also just liked to curl up on their mats and stare at the huge tank right in front of them.

Because the yoga sessions were held after normal

aquarium hours, the yoga students were able to roll out their mats right in front of the glass. They could stretch and bend and watch the zebra sharks, the sandbar sharks, the bonnetheads, the sea turtles, the rays, the beautiful rainbow of different fish...and even the eel. An eel affectionately known as Mr. Rogers because he would occasionally pop his head out to welcome everyone to his neighborhood.

Normally, Ana found the yoga sessions at the aquarium just as relaxing as her students did. But, unfortunately, this was not a normal night.

Nothing in her life was normal.

Kane had moved into her home. All intense and broody and sexy and just...*there.* His presence was so strong that she could feel him in every inch of the house. She'd been sharing meals with him. He'd even done a grocery run for her, and damn if the man hadn't remembered all of her favorite things without her having to remind him of a single item.

Two years had passed, and he remembered every detail? Seriously? How? Did he truly recall everything about her preferences?

Or had he just gotten some really invasive, personal report from Grayson that listed all of the foods she liked to eat?

Kane was sleeping in the bedroom right next to hers. *Right next to hers.* And they were sharing a bathroom. The bathroom was a Jack-and-Jill bathroom that connected their two bedrooms, and she'd accidentally walked in just as he was getting out of the shower that morning. The man *could* have locked the bathroom door. It would not have killed him.

He had not locked the door.

She'd stumbled in just as he'd left the shower.

He'd only been wearing a towel. One wrapped around his hips. So many powerful muscles had been on grand display. Her fingers had itched to touch him. She'd visualized herself ripping his towel away. Pouncing on him.

Instead...

She'd retreated. Closed the bathroom door without a word. And pretty much fallen into a puddle.

Two days. Two days had passed since he'd roared back into her life, and she was already having sex dreams about him. Because, sure, why not? Why not have sex dreams? Of course, tonight's dream would probably be even more intense on account of the little shower peep show she'd gotten earlier.

"Bye, Ana!"

She jerked and waved and pasted on a bright smile.

The last of her students vanished. Her breath expelled. Soft, soothing music still played on the speakers. She'd hooked up the music using her phone, and she headed to the left so that she could turn off the sound system. A few swipes, and the music stopped.

The sharks kept swimming. The rays floated by. When the rays displayed their underbellies toward the glass, she could catch a glimpse of their faces. It always looked like they were smiling at her, even though Ana knew that was just a trick. Not a real smile but just the way their mouths and nostrils were centered on their faces. Still, it *looked* as if they were smiling at her. And their smiles usually made her feel better.

Slowly, Ana walked toward the massive glass. She didn't touch it. Didn't poke at it. Just stared as the fish swam by. Because she was a frequent visitor, some of those fish even started to swim closer—

The fish suddenly cut away. Darted off in a fast and furious exit. That was odd.

"Ana."

She gasped and spun around.

Turner stood there, dressed in black pants and a black shirt. His hands were loose at his sides.

"Ana, we need to talk."

Her heart slammed into her chest. "The aquarium is closed right now." Only her students would have been given admission by the security guards to enter. They would have shown their tickets and been granted entry. But the yoga session was over, and her students had all left. The security guards would still be patrolling, though—they would have checked out each student and then secured the exterior doors.

So what is Turner doing here?

"He's staying in your house, Ana."

She backed up. Almost bumped the glass.

"I worked so hard to get close to you." Turner took an aggressive step toward her. "And now he's in your house? You won't even *talk* to me when I call or text you!"

"There's really not a lot to say." She still had her phone in her hand. She'd grabbed it when she turned off the sound system. Her bag was near her feet. Her bag and her mat.

A muscle flexed along Turner's clenched jaw. "I had to wait until I could get you alone. Two fucking days."

She swallowed. A guard could come along on a patrol any moment. Any old moment would do. "How did you get inside?"

"One of the guards is a student at my dojo. Green belt. When I told him that I wanted to surprise my girlfriend, George let me enter."

Her stomach knotted. "I'm not your girlfriend,

Turner. This should not come as a shock given what happened the last time we spoke, but we are not working out."

That muscle along his jaw flexed again. "If you had just come with me to the concert, everything would have already been over by now."

Uh, no. The knot in her gut got tighter. "Over how?" Husky. She wet her lips.

His head tilted to the right. "I kinda liked you. Didn't expect to do that. I was paying back a debt. Waiting until I got the order."

No, no, no. This conversation was going from bad to worse with every second that passed. "The order?" she squeaked. Fear made her squeak.

"I was supposed to get close to you. Then I was supposed to eliminate you."

So he hadn't just been blown away by her looks and charm. Lovely. Fake relationship for the win. From the corner of her eye, she saw one of the sharks swim away.

"Don't worry," Turner continued, and his voice was pitched all low and sympathetic. "By the time I put you in the water with the sharks, you'll already be dead."

She could not breathe. Fear choked her.

He pulled out a knife. "And by the time anyone finds your remains," he added after a long sigh, "there won't be enough left to figure out that it was a knife that killed you, and not the teeth of a shark."

* * *

HE'D PARKED his motorcycle near the aquarium's main entrance. Kane watched as the people who'd attended the after-hours yoga session filed out. His arms crossed over his chest as he leaned against the bike and waited for one particular individual to appear.

Ana.

Beautiful, maddening, sexy-as-hell Ana.

He'd offered to go in the class with her. Not to participate because he'd tried before, and he could not do yoga for shit. But he would have been more than happy to watch her switch in and out of positions and get into the flow.

She'd denied his request. Immediately. With a sniff.

So now he waited.

The class attendees had filed out already. A few of the ladies were talking over to the side. He heard them chatting about going out for wine.

And...

No Ana. Was she still packing up?

The security guard began to pull the door closed.

Kane bounded forward. He threw out a hand before that door could close fully. "Hey, my girlfriend is inside!" Oh, yes, those words felt fantastic to say.

The guard frowned at him. "No, she's not."

Uh, yes, she was. "Does the yoga instructor go out the back door or something?" That didn't make sense. Ana had specifically told him that she'd meet him out front. He'd dropped her off, and he'd intended to be there to pick her up in the same spot.

He liked it when she rode behind him on the motorcycle. Loved it when her arms and legs curled around him. He would love it all the more if he was fucking her on the bike, but that was a story for another day. Correction, a fantasy for another day.

"I'm not about to tell you where the instructor goes." Hard, tight words from the guard. "Now let go of the door."

He let go of the door, but he didn't back up. "She's my *girlfriend*," he stressed. "Ana is my girlfriend. I'm supposed to wait out here and pick her up."

"No, she's not your girlfriend. She's dating Turner." The guard threw a thumb over his shoulder.

Why had he just thrown that thumb over his shoulder? As if he'd been pointing back inside the aquarium?

"Now, I don't know who the hell you are or why you want to harass Ana, but you need to get out of here. Go! Before I call the cops." The now red-faced guard began to slam the door yet again.

But Kane caught the door once more and stopped it from closing. He also inserted his very large foot over the threshold because that door would not be shutting anytime soon. His hand tightened around the hard edge of the door. "For the record," Kane said, making sure his voice remained flat, "Ana and Turner broke up. She's with me now."

The man's eyes widened. "He...didn't mention a breakup."

Oh, that was not good. *Turner had been talking to this guard?* Kane deliberately pushed the door inward. Slowly, steadily. "Also, for the record, I'm damn well not leaving here without her."

The guard's jaw locked. He almost moved his hand toward the taser clipped to his waist.

"I would not recommend it," Kane warned. "It won't take me down, but it will piss me off."

The guard swallowed. His Adam's apple bobbed. "You're not getting inside."

"Don't bet on it."

"*Hey!*" A sharp yell from behind Kane. A feminine yell. "What are you doing to George?"

George swallowed again. "This fellow is trying to pull

some B&E shit, Zuri. You stay back. I don't want you getting hurt."

"I'll call the cops," she offered immediately.

Yeah, actually—still keeping his hold on the door because it was not shutting—Kane glanced over his shoulder. He found the petite woman glaring at him with dark eyes and a locked jaw. She also had a can of pepper spray in her hand, and it was aimed in Kane's direction. "Call the cops," he urged her.

She blinked at him.

"My girlfriend is inside, I think something may be wrong, and your buddy George won't let me check on Ana."

"Ana isn't your girlfriend," she denied.

"We just got back together after a separation," he said and, sure, maybe those words came through clenched teeth. "She ditched that idiot Turner and is back with me."

"Total lie," George blared.

The woman—Zuri—frowned. "If they're broken up, then why was Turner sneaking toward the main tank area when I left? I started to call out to him, but he put his finger over his mouth like he was gonna surprise Ana or something."

Shit. Kane whipped back around toward George. "Get out of the way."

"No." Sweat beaded George's brow. "Not happening." He whipped up his taser and fired it at Kane.

The volts hit, but, as promised, Kane didn't go down. "That really pisses me off." He shoved the door all the way open and bounded inside even as George screamed for backup.

Chapter Seven

"You don't need that knife." Her voice trembled. Her gaze seemed fixated on the blade.

"I'm afraid that I do. I have to make you bleed so that the sharks will be drawn in."

The sharks were swimming behind her, but Ana didn't fear them. She feared the man in front of her. The man who'd been ordered to kill her? Her tongue slid over her dry lips once more. "Let me make sure I have this all right in my head." A ragged exhale. "You never wanted to date me. You were ordered to get close to me, and now you've been ordered to kill me?"

He nodded. "Glad you're following along." He advanced toward her. She could see the dark bruise on his jaw. A bruise that had come courtesy of Kane's fist.

"The sharks are well fed!" A desperate cry. What kind of weapon did she have? What was handy? Her yoga mat would be of zero use. Maybe her water bottle? It was right beside her bag. The bottle was made of stainless steel. It would be better than nothing.

And nothing was pretty much what she had, with the exception of that bottle.

"What the hell does them being well fed have to do with anything?" Turner glowered.

"Didn't you hear that story out of New Orleans a few years ago? What happened at their aquarium?"

"I'm not from around here, remember?"

Right. Crap. That info should have made her way more nervous sooner. "You said you weren't from New York." She'd specifically *asked* where Turner originally hailed from when they first met. He'd told her that he was from Maryland. They'd laughed about being two fish out of water. Bonded a bit.

"I lied. I've got plenty of friends up there. The kind of people who you want owing you favors."

He meant the mob. Check. "Did Logan give you the order to kill me?"

He took another stalking step toward her.

"I thought Logan just got out!" This wasn't making sense to her. "You've been here for months!"

The knife was way too close. Another ragged breath escaped her. Ana knew she needed to keep him distracted. If he was distracted, then he might not be stabbing her. "In New Orleans, they had this tour group at their aquarium years ago. Back then, there was this catwalk-like thing that went right over their big shark tank. Something went wrong. People on a tour fell into the water—*with the sharks.* But no one got bitten. Everyone was safe. Know why? Probably because the sharks are so well fed! And humans aren't their preferred meal and—"

"Bet those people weren't bleeding from knife wounds when they went into the water."

No, they hadn't been. She didn't intend to be, either.

Ana took a step to the side, a step that would put her closer to the stainless steel water bottle. "We don't even have the big, aggressive sharks here. Do you *see* any great whites swimming behind me?" With her phone still gripped in her left hand, she gestured toward the tank.

As she'd hoped, Turner's gaze automatically darted to the tank, and she used that opportunity to lunge for her water bottle. Her fingers curled around it just as—

Screams.

Someone was screaming. Shouting. She could hear the cries as they carried through the aquarium. Not her screams.

Turner grabbed for her. Before he could use that knife, she slammed her water bottle into the side of his head. As hard as she could.

Swearing, he stumbled back. He weaved.

She hit him again. This time, right in the mouth with the bottom of the bottle. Blood flew from his busted lips, and the impact might have also cracked some of his teeth. Ana didn't exactly investigate the damage. While he howled in pain and tried to cover his mouth, she spun and ran. But because he was between her and the door that led to the entrance of the massive aquarium space, she turned to the left and hauled butt toward the additional exhibit space. The lights were already turned off, and the only illumination came from the displays—aquariums of various sizes filled with sea horses and jellyfish and strikingly colored, smaller fish that flashed to the left and the right and she—

Ran through the waiting, viewing tunnel. A tunnel surrounded by thick glass. The glass separated her from the sharks. The octopus. The glass covered all sides but the floor, and she hurried to get to the other side.

She didn't make it.

A hard hand curled around her shoulder. Turner hauled her back toward him.

She kneed him in the groin. "Help!" Ana screamed, and the scream seemed to echo in the tunnel around her. "*Help me!*"

He hit her. A blow that she mostly dodged, but, unfortunately, part of his fist grazed her jaw. She stumbled back, managed to stand on her feet, and then was running the rest of the way out of that tunnel. She made it to the other side. Shoved open the staff door because *maybe* some of the guards were back there. "Help!"

No one was there.

She raced up the steps. Up, up, up. When the steps finally ended, she shoved open the door before her and stumbled straight ahead. Ana heard the echo of footsteps as Turner ran behind her, and, dammit, this was bad. So bad. Because she'd just raced straight to—

His laughter stopped her.

His laughter and the fact that she'd reached the end of the line. Literally. Because the water was in front of her. She'd reached the top of the massive three-story tank habitat. With her heart thudding in her chest, Ana whirled to face Turner. She should have turned to the right when she entered the staff area. She'd never been in the staff area until that moment, so she hadn't known which way to flee.

She could see the glowing red letters of the EXIT sign. But those letters were behind Turner. To escape, she'd have to somehow make it past him.

And now she was trapped.

"Thanks for coming to my planned destination." He swiped a hand over his mouth, and blood smeared over his lips. "Bitch."

"I don't think name calling is necessary." One bonus for her—there were lots of weapon options in that area. She saw big nets. A scary-looking hook. If she could grab something, she'd attack and fight with all of her strength against him.

"I was gonna make sure you were dead before the sharks got to you." Turner advanced slowly. "But now, I don't give a shit. If I have to do it, I'll just hold your fucking head under the water while you fight. You can drown and get eaten by the sharks at the same damn time."

"Guards are coming!" Ana yelled. And to think, she'd once thought Turner was *nice*.

"Nah, they're not coming. I asked for time alone with you. George is gonna make sure we're not interrupted during our romantic interlude. He thinks I'll give him free lessons at the dojo as payback."

Her heart was about to jump out of her chest. "What is going to happen when my body is recovered? Don't you think George will admit you were here with me?"

Turner's eyes widened as he tried to look innocent. Hard to do with blood on his face. "I'll say I left. You insisted on staying here all alone. Doing more yoga. But when the cops push me, I'll say that I *thought* I saw someone suspicious lurking around. Wanna guess who that suspicious person will be?"

She did not want to guess. She wanted to scream for help over and over again. But Ana was afraid that if she screamed again, he'd attack.

"The new boyfriend. The one on steroids. I'll say I saw him."

She thought that she heard the creak of the stairs. Maybe the thud of rushing steps? "Kane isn't on steroids. He's just strong."

"Not strong enough. Don't see him here to help you—"

"Right fucking *here*," Kane snarled as he burst out of the stairwell and ran for Turner.

Turner spun toward Kane, and Ana used that distraction to race to the left. Her goal was to grab one of the big nets and use it in an attack. Her fingers had almost touched the long, wooden pole that connected to the net when—

Splash.

She whipped around.

Kane and Turner had gone into the water. Her mouth dropped. She grabbed the net and rushed back to the platform's edge, stopping to kneel right by the top of the water. "Kane! Kane!"

He swam beneath the surface. The sharks darted right by him. No, they darted *away* from him.

"What is happening here?" George's familiar voice shouted.

"Call the cops!" Ana yelled without looking at him. Her focus was completely on Kane. A Kane who needed to rise to the surface. *Come on. Come up. Come up.*

"Already did." Zuri's shaking response.

Wait, when had Zuri arrived? But her friend was suddenly crouching next to Ana and staring down into the water.

"Are they gonna get bitten?" Zuri asked.

Ana shook her head. "No." Hopefully not. "But Turner had a knife. He tried to stab me, and he could stab Kane!" If Kane didn't surface in the next five seconds, she was going in after him.

"So Kane *isn't* the bad guy?" Zuri wanted to know. Then, lower, "Probably want to call the cops back and update them on that situation."

Kane broke the surface. Water flew around him as he tossed back his head.

"Kane!" Relief broke in his name.

His eyes locked on her. "You're okay." A statement. Not a question. Kinda more like a...*You'd damn well better be okay*.

"I'm not the one swimming in a shark tank!" Ana shouted at him. "*Kane, get out.*"

He swam toward her and hauled a spitting and shaking Turner with him.

"One touched my foot!" Turner screamed. "It hit me! I felt it! It's going to bite—it's going to bite—*get me the fuck out!*"

Kane kept his hard grip on Turner.

"He was going to kill me," Ana heard herself say. "Cut me with his knife, and he wanted the sharks to finish me off." That had been Turner's first plan. Should she mention the more recent plan? "He also had the idea of just holding me under while the sharks attacked."

Kane's eyes narrowed right before he dropped his grip on Turner. The man immediately sank beneath the surface.

"Kane!" Ana cried. "Kane, he was ordered to do it! We have to make Turner talk—*and we can't just let him drown!*"

"I'm going in," George announced from beside her.

Only he did not, in fact, go in. He just kept crouching. Waiting. Sweating.

"Those sharks aren't gonna bite, right?" George wanted to know. "Aren't they like, really well fed?"

She ignored him. "Kane! Get out—and bring Turner with you!"

Kane huffed out a breath. "Fuck." Then he disappeared beneath the surface. A few moments later, he was back, and he practically threw a sobbing Turner onto the observation platform near the water before Kane hauled himself out and stood up.

Water poured from his body. His clothes clung tightly to every single muscle.

"Holy shit," Zuri breathed. "I want one of those."

Zuri and Ana and George were still crouched near the edge of the massive tank.

Kane glowered at Ana. "You never let me kill anyone. That is a major problem, sweetheart."

"OhmyGod." A quick breath from Zuri. "I take it back. I do not want one. I like to *look* at one. Especially when he's all wet and dripping. And super hot. But I don't want one. You keep him."

Ana leapt to her feet. *I want him. I would love to keep him.* She threw herself at Kane and wrapped her arms around him as tightly as she could. "Thank you," she whispered.

One powerful arm curled around her.

"You saved my life," she told him. Her head tilted back. She gazed up at him. Found his intense eyes blazing at her. Seeming to eat her up. A ragged sigh broke from Ana. "What took you so long?" A flippant question. One created by nerves and fear, and she didn't even know what else.

The faint lines on the sides of his mouth deepened. "Getting tased slowed me down a little. Won't happen again."

Getting tased?

Before she could question him more, his mouth took hers. A deep, hard, frantic kiss. One that she had not expected at all. Not with Turner sobbing near them. Not with Zuri whipping out her phone and calling the cops again. Not with George—well, George seemed to be busy trying to figure out what in the hell was going on.

She didn't expect the kiss.

Wrong place. Wrong time.

She didn't care. Adrenaline and fear poured through her veins. Her hands curled greedily around Kane's arms as she held on tightly, and Ana kissed Kane back with wild abandon and true desperation. She opened her lips wide. His tongue thrust into her mouth. He tasted, and he took, and she moaned low in her throat as arousal flooded through her.

Wrong time. Wrong time. Wrong time.

She didn't care. She kissed him as if her very life depended on the task. As if—

Someone yanked her back.

Ana's breath sawed in and out. Her gaze collided with Kane's.

Hunger. Possession. So much lust.

"The cops are coming!" Zuri informed her. "Stop making out with the hero and talk to me!" She tugged Ana toward her. "What is happening? Why did Turner attack you?"

Her heart still drummed. "Pretty sure..." Ana stopped and cleared her throat. "Pretty sure he got an order to kill me."

Zuri's eyes were huge. "*Why* would he get an order to kill you? Who would even give that order?"

She wasn't supposed to say, was she? Wasn't that the whole point of having a new ID? A new place to live, courtesy of the US government? Except, if Turner had been there for *months* waiting on the order to attack, then her cover had been blown for ages. Her location hadn't been leaked in a recent hack. Logan had known for a long time exactly where she'd been hiding.

If her cover had been blown so completely, then why bother with more lies?

Ana exhaled. "So, I have this ex who was a mob hitman."

Zuri's jaw sagged open.

"I'm pretty sure he's angry that I sent him to prison." Pretty sure? More like one hundred percent sure. "He's not going to rest until I'm in the ground."

Terror flashed on Zuri's face.

"But don't worry," Ana hurried to reassure her friend, "Kane's here."

"Kane," Zuri echoed as her attention shifted to him.

"He'll make sure I keep breathing," she said.

Zuri nodded. Weakly.

"Damn straight, I will," Kane agreed.

And then—finally—the rest of the guards at the aquarium swarmed in from wherever the heck they'd been. They swarmed with tasers and flashlights and yells.

And the regular cops weren't far behind them.

Kane kept dripping.

Ana's knees kept shaking.

And Turner immediately demanded a lawyer.

Chapter Eight

Ana wasn't dead.

Ana wasn't floating in some watery grave. She hadn't been stabbed. He hadn't found her cold, lifeless body.

He'd gotten to her in time.

But it had been a freaking near thing.

Kane's fingers were shaking. He stared at them, surprised by the break in his control. Normally, he was always rock steady. Didn't matter where or when or what was happening, Kane remained cool under fire. He'd had bombs detonating around him, and his fingers hadn't quivered. He'd had gunfire explode and hit inches from his face, and he hadn't trembled.

But Ana...

His Ana...

"So, the guy clammed up after I started questioning him. Demanded to speak to a lawyer. Even named the man. Kyle Sanchez. Surprise, surprise—a lawyer out of New York who works at the same firm that has represented Logan Catalano in the past."

At those words, Kane turned toward Gray. They were

back at Ana's house. The cops had taken Turner into custody at the aquarium, but Gray had rolled in with his agents and eventually ridden away in the patrol cruiser with the perp. Gray was always good at throwing his FBI weight around. That weight helped to get him an all-access pass into all sorts of confidential situations.

Kane and Ana had answered plenty of questions, they'd filled out the police report on the attack but...

"He *did* say one or two things before shutting down," Gray revealed.

"Like what?" Kane demanded.

"Like...the perp is alleging that Ana attacked him first. That he just went to the aquarium to talk with her, and the next thing he knew, she was slamming a water bottle into his face."

Ana curled her legs under her as she huddled on the couch. "He had a knife. He was telling me that he'd make me bleed. He was planning to dump my body into the tank, and he thought the sharks would cover up any evidence of his attack."

The sonofabitch.

Kane had ditched his wet clothes. Switched into a dry t-shirt and old jogging pants. His bare feet pressed hard into the wooden floor as he maintained his standing—and protective—position near Ana.

"I slammed my water bottle into his head first—the temple, I believe." Her voice was low as she recounted the events. "It was the only weapon I had handy. I didn't exactly want him killing me with his knife, so when he lunged at me, I attacked. Temple first, then a hit in the face. I think that's when I busted his lips and maybe cracked one or two teeth."

She was fucking amazing to him.

"I heard screaming then." She rubbed her forehead, as if trying to remember. She'd changed when they got back to the house, too. Soft shorts. A tank top. No shoes. She appeared small and so fragile curled on the couch.

But she'd fought off her attacker. Busted his face.

Hell, yes, she had.

"The screaming gave me a distraction."

Yeah, he should say something. Not just keep staring at her like the obsessed bastard he was. "The security guard at the front wouldn't let me inside."

"Uh, huh." From Gray as he lounged in a chair near the couch. "This would be the guy who tased you? And then you shoved him on his ass? George Taylor?"

"He's lucky I didn't knock him out cold. I warned him that the taser wouldn't stop me. That it would just piss me off." It had. Then he'd run as fast as he could into the aquarium. He'd been desperate to find Ana. "George was the one doing all the yelling and screaming." George had kept yelling for Kane to stop. He hadn't.

Then he'd heard *her* scream. Her desperate cry for help.

The blood had iced in his veins.

"Turner is maintaining that he was trying to calm down Ana. De-escalate the situation." Gray rubbed a hand along his jaw. "He says she wasn't handling their breakup well."

"Oh, for fuck's sake!" Kane erupted.

Ana rolled her eyes. "He's lying his butt off. He *told* me that he'd been getting close to me for the last few months because he was following orders." She grabbed one of the pillows on the couch. Ana pulled it toward her, hugging it tightly to her chest as if the soft pillow could be some kind of shield. "And exactly how does that fit with the timeline of Logan's escape? Because you acted as if Logan *just* found me, but what Turner said makes it seem like my current location and identity have been known for a long time."

Yes, absolutely, it did.

"Working on that," Gray muttered. He did not look pleased. "Not like this will be the first time a bad actor got intel at the Bureau. I'm getting real tired of this shit."

"I'm not exactly thrilled with it, either," she huffed.

Gray pointed at her. "You told your friend Zuri that your ex was a hitman. Just announced it right in front of her and the guard."

"Yes, well." She grimaced. "Apparently, all the bad guys know where I am, and I had just almost been murdered so I didn't see the need to lie to her right then and there. She's my friend. I don't like lying to friends." Ana kept clutching the pillow. "If Logan is coming after me—if he's sending people after me—why not just go back to being Anastasia Patrick once again? The fake name isn't doing much for me in terms of protection."

No, it wasn't.

Gray's sharp stare shifted to Kane. "You went swimming with the sharks, huh?"

He rolled one shoulder. "I had to get the creep away from Ana. When I tackled him, we were near the edge of the observation platform. We went over."

"You know the guy couldn't swim, right?"

He'd figured that out the minute the dude started thrashing left and right and sinking to the bottom of the massive tank. "He lives at the beach. He should really learn how to do that necessary task, don't you think? Especially, if he's gonna be threatening to toss people into tanks."

"Did you try to drown him?" Gray's question was mild.

"If I'd tried, he would be dead. The guy slipped out of

my grip." Another roll of one shoulder. "I got him out, didn't I?"

"He's saying you tried to drown him. That you're a jealous lover who was bent on killing him."

Killing him wouldn't be the worst plan.

"Kane," Gray snapped, as if reading his mind.

"He's got good stories, I'll give him that."

"Yeah, well, he's also gonna be a pain in my ass. Because I'm betting he'll be out on bond soon." A heaving sigh from Gray. "He's also spouting off about you assaulting him at a bar recently. I wondered why the guy didn't press charges at the time."

"He ran away as fast as he could from the bar." *From me.*

"I think he was making plans," Gray corrected. "Maybe laying ground work to set up you as a fall guy."

Ana sucked in a sharp breath. "He did say—Turner told me that after I was dead, he'd tell the cops he saw Kane hanging out around the building."

That sneaky sonofabitch. "I should have let him keep swimming with the sharks."

"He *can't* swim," Gray reminded him.

Kane just stared at Gray.

"Fuck," Gray muttered. "Fuck."

Uh, huh.

"There are security cameras in the aquarium." Ana's calm and determined voice. "Everything will be on tape. The video will back up the fact that Turner pulled a knife on me. That I had to run from him."

"So...no." A wince from Gray. "It turned out that Turner made a pitstop by the security room before he went to pay you a visit. All cameras were off."

"Oh, like that doesn't look suspicious," Kane snapped.

"He had a plan." Gray's tone showed his frustration. "He intended to execute that plan."

Ana hugged the pillow all the tighter. "What you mean is that he intended to execute me."

"Yes." Gray didn't bullshit with her.

"I thought we were trying to catch Logan. If Logan is just sending flunkies to hurt me, then this whole setup here..." One hand let go of the pillow so she could wave toward Kane. "It's just not going to work."

"It's going to work." Gray remained adamant. "We just may have to *pivot* a bit."

Kane shook his head. "You pivot. Keep that jackass Turner in jail."

"I can't control local judges!"

"Can't you?"

Gray scraped a hand over his jaw. "Look, he's gonna get out on bail, and that's not necessarily a bad thing."

Ana raised her hand. "Hi."

Gray frowned at her.

She fluttered her fingers. "Remember me? I'm the woman he wanted to kill. I consider it a bad thing for Turner to be wandering the streets and coming after me. Very bad, in fact. Horrible."

At least Gray had the grace to squirm a bit, Kane would give him that.

"What I meant," Gray amended quickly, "is that we can keep a team of agents on him. We can monitor his every move. Turner is getting orders from someone—we'll track down that someone. I want to destroy Logan's entire web."

"Thought I did that before," she muttered. "And what is up with Turner being some kind of—of sleeper agent, or something?"

Kane's brows rose. Sleeper agent?

"Logan *must* have known my location for a while. If he knew, why wait on the order to kill me? Why wait until now? Why not just tell Turner to kill me when we went on our first date? Turner had the opportunity back then. I was alone with him in his car. He could have yanked out his knife, stabbed me right then and there, and dumped my body some place. That would have been way easier than stalking me through the aquarium."

Kane growled. No one would be dumping her body anywhere. Over *his* dead body would that happen.

"She makes a good point." Gray hesitated. "And I actually think I know why, though I can't say that you're gonna like my reasoning."

She widened her eyes. Waited.

Gray didn't elaborate.

"Oh, for shit's sake!" Kane blew out a hard breath. "Keep talking, man!" Now was not the time for Gray to get all mysterious and secretive. Though, come to think of it, Gray was typically mysterious and secretive. Two of his more annoying traits.

"Fine. Fine!" Gray did some hard and angry exhaling of his own. "I've received more notes from the psychiatrist. She's coming to town, by the way. Insists on being front-line for this thing when she has zero field experience." His jaw hardened. "But she's getting shoved down my throat by the FBI Brass who still have more power than me."

"Someone has more power than you at the Bureau? That shit doesn't seem possible," Kane mocked.

"I know, right?" Gray wasn't mocking. Just annoyed. "They think she's some kind of magical protégé when it comes to the killers. Like *I* don't know killers? Like I can't profile in my sleep better than she will ever be able to do in a million freaking years?"

107

Ana looked at Kane. "What is happening right now?"

"Oh, you can't tell?" Kane returned, keeping his voice mild. A real effort considering how much rage and adrenaline still poured through his system. All he wanted to do was rush out of that house, get down to the jail, and beat the ever-loving shit out of Turner Mitchell. "Clearly, Gray is losing his mind."

"I am *not*," Gray denied at once.

"Then get back to the real focus," Kane snapped. "In case you missed it, Ana is the focus. Not some prick psychiatrist—"

"Emerson Marlowe is not a prick. She's just a pain in my ass." Gray rolled back his shoulders. "I'll deal with her." Then, softer as if to himself, "I'll deal with her."

"Uh, huh. Fabulous for you," Kane told him. His heart still pounded too fast. And he could too easily imagine shoving Turner back beneath the water with the swimming sharks. *Yeah, I have issues.* Because Kane had issues, he did not have time to deal with Gray's troubles, too. "Why didn't Turner attack Ana sooner?"

Gray blinked. "Because maybe her ex wanted an up close view. Maybe Turner was waiting until Logan could witness her murder."

Ana jumped to her feet. She tossed down the pillow she'd been holding as if it was suddenly red-hot. "*What?*" Her voice had risen several high-pitched notches.

Another grimace from Gray. "I don't have proof. Just suspicion. Two scenarios are tumbling around in my head, based on what I know about the perp."

Ana and Kane both stared at him.

"Okay, yeah, a full explanation. You want that, don't you?"

"No, we just want you to be mysterious and annoying for the rest of the night," Ana snapped.

Fuck, she was fun. The woman had just stolen the sarcastic words right out of Kane's mouth.

Gray rose to his feet. He rolled back his shoulders. "Logan is possessive when it comes to you."

She wrapped her arms around her waist. "Tell me something I don't know."

"At the trial, Logan could not take his gaze off you. He tracked every single move that you made. His lawyer asked him to stop, said that he was too intense, that it was disturbing the jury, but Logan didn't. I think because he couldn't stop."

Kane hadn't been at the trial. He'd wanted to be there with Ana, but Gray and the other Feds had ordered him away.

So I waited outside of the courtroom. I'd watch her go in and out. And—

"He was pissed at you for betraying him, but Logan still saw you as *his*," Gray noted.

"I'm not a possession or a toy. I'm not his," she fired right back.

"Understood." Gray nodded. "It's possible that, if he got your location a while back, Logan wanted eyes on you. He told Turner to get close. To monitor your life. To monitor you. Maybe Logan wanted to make sure that there were no new lovers in your life."

A faint line cut between her eyebrows. "Turner started *dating* me! Doesn't that completely destroy this whole theory? Or hypothesis? Whatever it is? If Logan wants me all for himself, then why send someone else to date me? That's just bizarre."

"Date you," Kane heard himself say because he was not convinced that Gray was wrong on this idea. "Not fuck you." Logan had definitely been obsessed when it came to Ana. When he learned that Ana was working with the Feds, Logan could have cut his losses. He could have tried to flee the country. Instead, he'd stalked Ana like a predator after prey.

Her lips clamped together.

"No man would date you and not want to fuck you. He wouldn't be around you and not want to take you." Kane's words held a savage edge. "But maybe Turner was ordered not to cross that line. Maybe his job was to keep others away from you."

"Uh, that's...wrong." She rocked forward onto the balls of her feet but kept right on hugging herself. "Not every man who comes into my life wants to fuck me, I can assure you of that. Not like someone gets next to me and just has this overwhelming urge to have sex with me."

I do. That's exactly the way I feel.

"I mean, what guy would actually feel that way?" Ana asked.

"Kane." Gray just dropped his name like a bombshell.

Her eyes got very big and very round.

Kane locked down his emotions. He made sure his expression didn't alter though he did wonder why in the hell his friend had just outed him that way. *Thanks one hell of a lot, buddy.* Was no confidence sacred these days?

"What I meant..." Gray rushed to say into the stark and uncomfortable silence, "Is that Kane came back in your life. He moved into your house. It probably looked to Turner—and to Logan, if he's close and watching—like the two of you were fucking. That might have enraged Logan enough that he gave the order to kill you."

She settled back down on her heels. "Sure. Right. I

totally misunderstood what you meant for a moment there. Got it. Not like Kane is dying to fuck me."

Oh, sweetheart, I am. He ached for her. He wanted to kick out Gray and take her right the hell then.

"That's one option," Gray said.

Kane blinked. Was the man a freaking mind reader? What—

"The option that Logan didn't want any other guys near you because he thinks of you as his. His possession. His to punish for your betrayals. That's an option for motivation. When you took up with Kane, he decided he'd get his puppet Turner to attack." Gray sucked in his right cheek. "And option two is that he just told Turner to keep an eye on you. To make sure you didn't flee and vanish before Logan could work his master escape plan."

"A done deed. He's escaped," Kane pointed out flatly.

"Yeah, he has." Gray shoved his hand through his hair. "And that's why I said...maybe Logan wanted an up close view. The aquarium is over 80,000 square feet. That means there were plenty of places where Logan could have been hiding. In all the confusion after the attack and the swim in the tank, if Logan was there, waiting, watching, it would have been easy enough for him to sneak out without anyone noticing."

Ana's gaze collided with Kane's. "I didn't see him."

Kane hadn't been looking for the bastard. He'd been too focused on her.

"But I was just trying to get you out of the water. I...I barely looked around," she admitted.

He'd been trying to keep her safe.

A shuddering breath escaped Ana. "So Logan could be right under our noses."

"Yes." Gray didn't even blink.

"Good to know." She took a step back.

"If Turner gets bail, and it's still *if* because the judge could surprise me, then I'll keep a team on the jerk," Gray promised. "Turner very well may lead us straight to Logan. For now, we need to continue with the cover as we have it. You two are reunited lovers. Because of the attack, Kane, you'll be extra protective when it comes to Ana. With her every moment."

"Damn straight," he agreed.

"And we *will* catch Logan. We will stop him."

Ana didn't speak.

Gray closed in on her. "I know this isn't ideal."

She raised one eyebrow.

"You have choices," Gray told her. "I am not going to make you stay here. You want to run? Fine. You can run. Kane will go with you, or I'll get a different guard to accompany you if you decide to flee Gulfport. You can be out of this city in an hour. Or you can stay here. We can continue with the current cover story and our operational plans. *You* decide. You choose what you want to do."

"I want—" Ana stopped. Exhaled. "I want to sleep on it."

Gray nodded.

"I am scared, and I'm shaking, and I just—" She finally stopped hugging herself. Her hands fell to her sides. "I'm sleeping on it. I'll tell you my decision when I wake up tomorrow, all right?"

"I'm a phone call away." His head turned. His sharp stare landed on Kane. "Buddy, a word before I leave?"

Great. Now he was probably going to get a lecture. One of those, *we-don't-drown-a-perp* talks that could be so irritating.

But Kane just nodded. and he followed Gray out of the

house. Not the front door. The back. And Kane lingered on the small porch. He wasn't about to go wandering too far away from Ana. He *did* pull the door shut behind him so she wouldn't overhear this chat.

"You good, man?" Gray wanted to know.

Kane took a moment to consider the question. "Don't know that I've ever been *good*."

"Okay, let's rephrase." Gray's hands rested on his hips. "Do you have a single shred of control left? Pretty sure you almost killed a man tonight—that's a fun bit of business that I had to finesse my way around with the local law enforcement officers, by the way."

"He was attacking Ana. I stopped him." End of story.

"There's a difference between stopping an attacker and then, after he's *been* stopped, shoving the guy back under the water one more time."

Kane shrugged. "You're getting caught up on unnecessary details."

Gray's teeth snapped together. "You look at Ana as if you could eat her alive," Gray gritted out. "I'm in there, talking about Logan's obsession with her, but I think the guy has nothing on you."

Kane surged forward. Stood toe to toe with his friend. About to be former friend? "I would *never* hurt her. Not in a million years."

"I know." Immediate. "Physically, you would never hurt her. But you are just as obsessed. I see it. She must see it, too. Or maybe she's just too scared right now, and she doesn't realize just how much that mask of yours has cracked. Maybe you don't realize it, either. That's why we're having this *word* out here. You look at her like you're starving, and you're about to make her your seven-course meal."

Kane didn't speak.

"Do you have any control left?" Lower. "Because I can stay here for the rest of the night. You can crash at a hotel and be back at first light. I will protect Ana."

"You're not sleeping with her."

"Whoa! Definitely not. Not planning on doing that, so you don't need to think about wrapping those massive hands of yours around my throat. Ana is a friend to me. She's a good person. I want her safe. She's...look, if you do something with her when you're having a break in your control, you won't be able to take back your actions. There is no erase button in real life. I was there before, remember? Had a front row view. I saw her cry. I heard her when she said she loved you. And I—" He backed up. "Fuck. Pretty sure I was supposed to take that to the grave. Do me a major favor? Don't mention to Ana that I brought it up."

She didn't love me. She didn't.

But... "She told me that she was falling for me back then." That last fateful night. The reason he'd gone running. Because...

"Oh, well, then I'm not wrecking a confidence." Gray sounded relieved. "That was two years ago. I'm sure her feelings have changed in all that time. Yours have, too." Way less worried. More brisk.

My feelings have changed.

They'd deepened.

"So, you think you have control? That's great. You stay in your room. She'll stay in hers. I mean, it's already after one a.m. Not like there's a whole lot of night left, anyway. We'll regroup tomorrow and see what choice Ana has made. Done. No need to worry." Then, lower, "No need to worry." Like Gray was trying to convince himself of that fact.

Kane pulled in a deep gulp of the night air. It didn't cool

him down. The air felt heavy and hot, and the anger and adrenaline stirring in him were just as hot.

No, hotter.

Gray began to walk away.

Kane didn't move, not yet.

Gray was almost near his ride when he spun back to face Kane. "You *do* have your control, don't you? I can't seem to remember if you gave me an actual reply."

"No need to worry." Deliberately, he gave those words back to the Fed.

Gray laughed. But it wasn't a real laugh. Then he climbed into his SUV. Drove into the night.

"No need to worry," Kane repeated, just as Gray had done earlier. But then he added, "My control was ripped to shreds the moment I heard her scream." He turned and strode back into the house.

Chapter Nine

SHE SHOULD GO UPSTAIRS.

She should go to bed.

She should get in the bed, pull the covers up, close her eyes, and try to forget this nightmare of a day.

She should do all of those things and yet...

Ana just remained in the den. She kept pacing back and forth between the couch and the picture windows in front, windows that were currently covered by heavy drapes. Her stomach felt knotted, her heart raced too fast, and she knew that she rode a hard wave of adrenaline. Her fingers fluttered at her side, strumming a phantom harp.

Kane kissed me. He kissed me in the middle of that chaos.

They should talk about that kiss, shouldn't they? Or was she supposed to ignore it and act like the whole thing had never happened?

She heard the back door open. A moment later, it clicked closed. The faint beep of the alarm chirped as it was reset, then Ana caught the heavy and deliberate footsteps that she knew belonged to Kane. He was coming closer.

Closing in. Her fingers stopped strumming as her hands fisted. Twisted. Then she shoved them behind her back and straightened her spine because—not like she was going to confess to being in love with him again. *Been there, done that. Got the rejection memory to prove it.* No, this was different. This was—

"I want to fuck you," Kane announced.

She blinked.

"I want to fuck you until you come, screaming my name." He stopped about five feet from her. Tension seemed to swirl in the room around them. Between them. "I want to get so deep inside of you that you aren't sure where you end and I begin."

Um...

What was the appropriate response to those words? *Yes, please* probably wouldn't be it. Would it?

"I want you to come around my dick."

She swallowed.

"I want you to come against my mouth. I want you to ride my face."

Was this conversation actually happening? Carefully, with her hands still behind her back, Ana pinched herself. She felt the small sting, so, yes, real. Actually happening.

"I want to make you come at least three times. That's the *first* time I take you. Three orgasms the first time."

Ana swiped her tongue over her lower lip. His gaze immediately dropped to her mouth and that stare of his just went molten.

"Ana." He breathed her name like a prayer. "What am I going to do with you?"

From the sound of things, he'd had a couple of very good possibilities that he'd raised. But they'd done this dance before.

She lifted her chin. She also stopped twisting her hands behind her back and let them fall to her sides. Deliberately, she kept her steps slow and certain as she eliminated the distance between them. With every step Ana took, the heat in his eyes seemed to intensify. She was pretty surprised that he didn't burn her simply from his scorching gaze.

Ana stopped right in front of him. "You saved my life tonight."

"I'll save your life any night."

"Well, hopefully, that won't always be necessary. Hopefully, every night won't end with me being in mortal jeopardy." She raised her hand and placed it on his chest, right over his racing heart.

Fast. Hard.

"You saved me, then you kissed me."

His gaze was still on her mouth.

"Now you talk about f-fucking me." Dammit, she'd stuttered. When she'd been trying so hard to be all blasé about things. "Is this going to be one of those situations where you change your mind in five minutes? Where you tell me that it's adrenaline and fear or fury, and that we're not thinking clearly?"

"Ana." A shake of his head. "It is adrenaline. And fear. And fury."

Disappointment knifed through her.

"I feel all of those things. But I feel them plenty, given my line of work. And I don't typically want to fuck like crazy when they crash through my system."

Oh?

"As far as the next five minutes are concerned, I plan to be balls deep in you within five minutes. I plan for you to be coming around my cock in the next five minutes."

Say something, Ana! "I thought there were lines you

didn't want to cross. Rules to follow. You're protecting me. Doesn't that mean you can't fuck me?"

His hands flew out and curled around her waist. She felt that touch burn through her and seem to brand her skin.

"I played by the rules before. All that got me was blue balls and two years of aching for you."

Wait—*what?*

His hold tightened on her. "If you don't want this, if you don't want me, then go up the stairs." And he just let her go. After the big "two years of aching" bombshell, the man just dropped those hot hands of his. He even took a step back. "Go up the stairs, shut the door, and I'll keep my hands to myself."

She mulled over his words. Nodded. And turned for the stairs.

Ana heard his sharp inhalation of air behind her.

She climbed the first step. The second. The third. The fourth—Ana spun toward him, her hand gripping the wooden banister. "What if I want your hands all over me?"

He bounded toward her. Stopped at the foot of the stairs.

She stared into his blazing eyes. "What if I want you to fuck me? What if I've wanted it for a very long time?"

"*Ana.*"

"I've always liked the way you say my name." She smiled at him, but then lost the smile in the next breath because his expression was just so savage. "I haven't been with anyone since Logan." There. Done. Said.

"*Bastard.*"

Yes, her ex was, indeed, a bastard.

"Just telling you so that you'll understand that I might be a bit rusty at things."

He grabbed the banister and leaned toward her. "You will be fucking perfect."

"Three times, huh?" Ana leaned forward and pressed her hands to his jaw. His beard teased her fingers. That soft, sexy beard. "I'd settle for one really good orgasm. You do not have to be an overachiever with me."

"You'll get three. For starters." His head turned. He nipped her fingers. Licked them. "I am going to fuck you until you scream."

A strange burst of euphoria seemed to fill her. Maybe from the adrenaline. Maybe from the whole nearly-being-murdered experience. Or maybe just from the sheer joy of getting what she finally wanted. "Promises, promises."

His pupils flared. "You should run."

She would rather jump on him.

"If you don't get up to the bedroom, right now, I will be fucking you here."

"On the stairs? Hardly seems comfortable." But she did turn away. And she did hurry up the stairs. Didn't run, though, because her knees were shaking, and she'd rather not fall and break her neck before the promised round of great sex. With every step, he was right behind her. Chasing her up the steps and she—

Was being lifted up.

Very carefully placed—uh, tossed?—over his shoulder. "Kane?"

He carried her the rest of the way up those stairs. "You won't get away from me. Not ever again."

Sounded fabulous to her.

He shoved open the door to her bedroom. They crossed the threshold, and he didn't lower her down until they were right beside her antique, brass bed.

"It will be a tight fit, but we'll make it work."

Her lips parted in a big O. Was he talking about—

"The bed, Ana. We need a king-size, but this will work."

She glanced over her shoulder. Looked at the bed. Then looked at Kane.

"I don't hurt you." His voice was flat. "I do *not,* understand?"

She frowned at him.

"Anything I do that makes you feel uncomfortable, anything gives you a moment's pain, you stop me. Immediately. Got it? I know I'm fucking huge, and you're small and delicate, but *I will not hurt you.* One of the reasons you will come three times. I will make sure you're ready when I thrust into you."

It was sweet that he was worried, but pain was the last thing on her mind. So she smiled at him right before her hands went to his waist. She shoved his jogging pants down and out of her way. She leaned down toward him—that bobbing cock of his was definitely on the massive scale, just like the rest of him, and she gave his dick a light lick, right before opening her mouth and taking in that gorgeous head. Sucking. Swirling her tongue over him and, in a blink, she was on the bed. Flat on her back. Legs spread. *Fast.*

Ana blinked. "Uh, Kane?"

"I'm not exploding in that sweet mouth, not the first time." He yanked his jogging pants back into position. Then he yanked *off* her shorts. And the scrap of panties that she'd been wearing. So she was on the bed, naked from the waist down, and his voracious gaze was eating her up.

One of her hands flew down to cover her sex.

"Nope." He caught her fingers. Lifted them away. Put her hand back on the mattress and then his strong fingers were pushing her legs wider apart. He hauled her closer to the edge of the bed as he leaned over her. His breath blew lightly over her exposed core.

Ana sucked in a breath. Uncertainty pulsed through her. "Kane?"

He kissed her. With her legs spread. With her body totally open. His mouth pressed to her with sensual possession. He licked her. Kissed. Tongued her clit again and again, and then his tongue dipped into her.

She fisted the bedding around her.

He didn't relent. At first, he was careful. Teasing.

But the teasing changed. The licks of his tongue became more possessive. More demanding. His fingers joined his mouth and tongue. He thrust one finger into her. Worked a second inside even as his mouth kept worshipping her clit. Mercilessly. Relentlessly. Kissing her with wild skill. Wicked intent. Utter possession.

Two fingers thrust into her, but his left hand rose, and he curled that hand around her breast. He stroked her tight nipple. Pinched her lightly. Kept tasting her and taking, and she was utterly and completely lost. Too much sensation. Too much pleasure.

Her hips slammed up against his mouth. Her hands stopped gripping the bedding, and they flew down to grip him. To sink into the thickness of his hair.

When he swiped his tongue over her again, when she felt him suck on her clit, she ignited. An orgasm raced through her body, shaking every single part of her, and Ana didn't try to bite back her cry of release. She happily screamed for him. And kept screaming as the orgasm seemed to wreck her and delight her and leave her utterly satiated and boneless on the bed with his face still buried between her thighs.

Her breath shuddered out even as the thundering beat

of her heart seemed to echo in her ears. *Boom. Boom. Boom.* "Wow." She wet dry lips. "That was..."

Oh, whoops. Her fingers were still in his hair.

She hurriedly let go.

He looked up at her, and the shuddering breaths she'd taken just froze. There was only one word to describe Kane's expression.

Feral.

"You are delicious." More growl than anything else. "Do not fucking move."

She had not planned to move. Not like her legs could hold her. Not with the way they were currently shaking.

But he moved. He shot to his feet, turned, and hurried out of the bedroom.

Woman, get it together. So what if that was just the best orgasm of your life? It was the—

Kane was back.

He stalked toward the bed.

She scrambled up. Back. Onto her knees. Tried to pull her shirt down over her body a wee bit more. Though why she bothered, Ana had no clue. Maybe because he was eating her up with his eyes?

Oh, come on, you know you love it when he eats you up.

Kane put a box of condoms onto her nightstand. A whole box. Her gaze flew to the box. He'd brought clothes in to the house before, when he first moved in with her. Grayson had also delivered a few bags for him. Had Grayson brought the condoms? Had Kane gone out and purchased them? Had he been so certain they'd have sex? Why was she obsessing over this point right then?

"Got them yesterday," he said, as if reading her mind. "If you decided you wanted me, nothing was going to stand in our way this time."

Her gaze whipped back toward him.

"It's been over two years," Kane began. His voice was rough and deep and rolled over her in all the right ways.

"Two years since I've had sex," she agreed. Yes, she'd told him this before.

"Two years since *I've* had sex," Kane corrected.

She had no response. Well, she did. *"What?"*

"If I couldn't have you, I didn't want anyone else."

Hello, bombshell.

Chapter Ten

IF I COULDN'T HAVE YOU, I DIDN'T WANT ANYONE ELSE.

Ana shook her head. She must have imagined those words. She did have a pretty phenomenal imagination, after all. She'd imagined all sorts of sexy scenarios that involved Kane over the last twenty-four months. Only, this wasn't her imagination. Was it? "Say that again?"

But he didn't. He reached down, and he yanked off his shirt. He dropped it to the floor behind him. "Normally, control isn't an issue for me."

He was talking. She should be listening. Instead, she was staring at his chest. His abs. Those insane muscles.

"But it's been a long time, and it's you." His hands went to the waistband of his sweats. "The way I feel about you? The way I want you? It's dangerous."

"You're not dangerous to me." She would not believe that. Time and time again, he just saved her. Twice, he'd literally saved her life. That wasn't dangerous.

That was protective.

Amazing.

Hot.

"I won't last long with you. Not the first time. My control is far too tenuous." A guttural warning. "That's why it's so important that you be ready for me. I'm big and you're small, and, sweetheart, you *have* to be ready for me. Are you ready? Do you want me, Ana?"

She had to stop looking at the way his dick tented the sweats. She also should stop thinking about the way his dick had felt in her mouth. "I want to taste you again."

"*Ana*. If your mouth gets around my dick right now, I am done."

"Would you come in my mouth? I've—I've never had someone do that before. I honestly don't have a lot of experience at, uh, going down on someone." She could feel her cheeks burn. "But I loved putting my mouth on you. When can I do it again?"

A snarl was his answer. A growl. Then he was in the bed with her. She reached for him. Their mouths met in a tangle of need and desire. Her hands flew over him. She stroked him. Loved his muscles. Loved the heat of his skin and the power of his body.

She loved—

No, Ana stopped the thought. Immediately. This wasn't about emotions. This was just pleasure. Sex. Only sex. She tore her mouth from his and began kissing a path down his chest. Licking lightly.

But he drew back. He caught her shirt. Yanked it over her head and sent it flying. His gaze dropped to her chest. "You are perfect."

She was small. Had always wanted bigger boobs. But he made her feel so sexy. Feminine.

He bent his head. Put his mouth on her nipple. Sucked her. Licked her. Her eyes basically did a roll because his mouth felt so insanely good on her. He was kissing and caressing, and Ana was just lost. Her hands wrapped around him, and a gasp left her when he lifted her, twisted her, and she found him.

Ana's hands flew down to press against his chest.

"You're going to take me in," he told her.

She slid down a little, maneuvering until she was spread over Kane's big, thick dick. Ana began to rock her hips, riding over the soft cotton of his sweats. Riding the surging cock that she felt just beneath those sweat pants.

She angled her hips. Made sure that—even through the soft fabric—he rubbed against her clit. A moan broke from her.

"Ana. Take me in." An order.

She rode him again. Dry humping? Whatever. It felt wonderful.

"Ana." A distinct growl.

With her breath heaving, she looked up at him.

"Get a condom. Put it on me. *Take. Me. In.*"

She practically jumped off him as she grabbed for the nightstand and a condom. Ana ripped open the package, and he ditched the sweats. She climbed back onto the bed. Onto him. With fingers that trembled, she rolled the condom onto his dick.

Massive form. Not unexpected, of course. Not given his other dimensions.

"Take. Me. In."

She straddled him again. This time, his hands locked around her waist. He lifted her up and began to ease her down onto him. At first, he slid in just fine. The head of his cock pushed into her.

Ana gasped.

So good.

Then he pushed in deeper. Deeper. Another inch.

Pain threatened.

It *had* been two years, and Logan had not exactly been built along the same lines as Kane. He'd tried to warn her. She'd just been so excited about having sex with him that she hadn't exactly heeded that warning.

She bit her lower lip.

"Ana."

She pushed down more.

"No." A snarl from him. Kane lifted her up. Off him.

"Kane, no!"

"Kane, *yes.*" He rolled her beneath him. "No pain, remember?" He loomed over her.

Ana's hands clamped onto his shoulders. "I don't care if it hurts for a minute! I want you! I want you inside me." Who cared about a flash of pain?

"There's nowhere else I'd rather be, trust me," he assured her. "But you will not hurt. We'll just give you orgasm number two right the hell now."

He'd give her the second one? Now? Sure. Why not?

He thrust her legs apart. His skilled fingers went to work on her. Rubbing her clit. Stroking her. Dipping inside of her. Out of her. His mouth clamped onto her nipple, and he sucked and licked, and he didn't put any weight on her body. He held himself off her while he explored and took.

His fingers plucked her clit. Pinched. Rubbed.

He licked her nipple. Sucked until she was chanting his name. His attention shifted to her other nipple. He bit her lightly.

She went off hotter than any rocket. *"Kane!"*

Then he was pushing his cock at the entrance to her body. Even as she came for him—the second time—he drove into her. There was no pain. There was no hesitation. She was slick and eager and still pulsing from her release when he sank into her.

All the way in.

Her nails dug into his shoulders.

She'd never been so full in her life.

He filled every inch. Stretched. Dominated.

He was lodged so deeply inside of her that, yes, he'd been right. She could not tell where he ended.

And she began.

She *loved* it. "Kane!"

He moved in a flash. Moved *them*. He shot upward on the bed, kept his hands locked around her hips so that she flew up with him. Her legs wrapped around his waist as he knelt in the middle of the bedding, and he pounded into her with a wild, untamed desperation.

She held on for the fabulous ride.

He shifted his body. Went flat on his back on the mattress. Her knees hit down on either side of him. He lifted her up and down with his grip. Up. Down. Over and over. His long, hard dick slid in and out, and she felt every single inch of him within her sensitive inner core.

She clamped her muscles around him. Greedy for everything he had to give her.

"So tight," he bit out. "So perfect."

He thrust into her. Lifted her up off the bed with that powerful thrust, and she gasped out his name.

There was no holding back. No stopping. Not that stopping was what she wanted. He was everywhere. She breathed and tasted him. His heat and power surrounded her. They were wrecking the bed. She heard it squeaking and groaning, and Ana did not care. Nothing would have stopped her in that moment. She was too focused on release. Far too focused on how wonderful she felt with Kane.

Far too focused.

He exploded within her, and she came with him. At the same time? A breath after? Ana didn't know. Didn't care. Her core seemed to contract around him, and her mouth opened in a scream, but no sound emerged. She was too far gone for any sound. A silent scream. Pleasure that lashed and lashed and was too good. Too consuming.

His hold remained fierce on her even as she collapsed against him. With her head on his chest, she could hear the hard thuds of his heartbeat. So strong.

Her breath whispered out. Her eyes closed.

She had always known sex with Kane would be good. No, correction, great.

She just hadn't realized it might ruin her for everyone else.

Lesson learned.

* * *

HE WAS ALREADY GETTING HARD INSIDE of Ana again.

Fuck. He'd have to ditch the condom. Get another one.

Or go bare in Ana. Be skin to skin. Feel every inch of her hot, tight sex around me.

His jaw locked. She'd cuddled up against him, kinda like a sweet kitten. He didn't want to move her. He did want to fuck her again. His growing cock posed one hell of a dilemma.

Dammit, he had to ditch the condom. "Ana?"

She murmured something. Her words were sleepy and slurred, and Kane found himself smiling.

She cuddled closer.

His dick was nearly at a full salute. Yeah, problematic. "Sweetheart, I have to ditch the condom."

She was limp on him.

Carefully, he lifted her up. She opened her eyes, blinked a bit blearily, and told him, "That was fantastic."

Yes.

"Three times?" Sleepy. Satiated. "You are a man of your word."

With her, always.

She sent him a slow, wide smile. "You were worth the wait."

You were worth it, Ana. But he would never wait again. He'd had her. He'd have her again and again, and, this time, he would not give her up. He'd keep her. Kane pressed a soft kiss to her lips. "Be right back." He eased her into a more comfortable position on the bed, nestling a pillow under her head and moving back to pull up the covers. But Kane paused. Frowned.

She stretched a little. Yawned. The stretch had made her gorgeous breasts move in the best possible way.

"What's wrong?" Ana asked.

Holding the covers in his left hand, he reached out and touched the red marks he'd left on her inner thighs. Then rose to skim his fingertips over the redness on her breasts. "I marked you." He *hated* that.

Ana laughed sleepily. "I think it's a little beard burn. Hazard of the situation." She snuggled against the mattress. "No worries."

But he had worries. He didn't want to ever hurt her. "I'll shave." Right away. He carefully placed the covers over her and turned for the bathroom.

She threw out a hand and caught his wrist. "Don't you *dare.*" Not so sleepy.

He blinked.

"Your beard is sexy as hell. And there are barely any marks on me. Forget it."

He would forget nothing when it came to her.

Her gaze dropped and lingered on his cock. "You, um, you...weren't satisfied?"

"Baby, I was definitely satisfied. I just want to go again." He eased away from her and pulled off the condom. "And again and again."

She bit her lower lip. "We weren't just a one-time deal? A tonight-only situation?"

Now his jaw locked. Hell, no, they weren't a one-time deal.

"Adrenaline. Fear. Fury. Danger." She seemed to be clicking off a list. "When it all passes, we'll go back to our normal lives."

He didn't know what normal was. "I'll be right back." Kane spun on his heel. Made it to the bathroom. Ditched the condom. He spared a glare for his reflection in the mirror. Oh, that beard would be leaving soon. He wasn't going to give Ana a burn anywhere again.

Kane headed back to the bedroom. The lamp's light still glowed. When he'd first entered the bedroom with Ana, the bedside lamp had already been turned on, and he'd appreciated the light. It had allowed him to perfectly see Ana's gorgeous breasts. The sensual temptation between her beautiful legs.

As he approached the bed, he drank her in. She'd turned away from him, and his gaze lingered on her right shoulder. And the small, black, musical tattoo on that shoulder. A tattoo he hadn't noticed until that moment. He reached out, and his fingers brushed over the dark mark. "This is new."

She tensed at his touch, then rolled toward him. Ana

held the covers over her breasts. Her eyes blinked at him. "Zuri and I got tattoos about six months ago. Music is in my blood. Only made sense that it should be on my body, too."

You're in my blood, Ana. I need you on my body. She had been, moments before, riding his cock like his hottest wet dream come to life. Hell, what would she do if he got her name tattooed on him? Probably freak the hell out. He should slow down. Not start trying to figure out where to get tatted for her.

"Music is a part of me. I wanted it to *always* be a part of me." She darted her gaze over him. "You, um, going back to your room?"

"I hadn't planned to do that." But he bent to snag his discarded sweats and haul them on. As much as he wanted to drive deep into her and spend the rest of the night fucking her into oblivion, he was gonna try and be a gentleman.

Yeah, right. Too late for that bullshit.

"What do you plan to do?" Ana inquired, voice very polite.

"Share the bed with you."

"Why?" Blank. Perhaps a bit confused.

"Because I want to sleep with you. Because..." An exhale. "Because you almost died tonight, and I want to make sure I'm close. I don't want to be next door. I want to be where I can reach out and touch you and make absolutely certain that you're safe."

She scooted over. Patted the bed. "Turn out the light, will you?"

When she scooted over, the covers shifted, and he caught a glimpse of the scar on her side. The small line that had come from Logan's knife.

Rage seethed inside of Kane, but he didn't say a word.

He turned out the light. Slid into the bed. Promptly took up all the space.

"This might not work," she said, poking at his side. "To paraphrase your favorite movie, we're gonna need a bigger bed."

A surprised rumble of laughter burst from him. Deep and warm and Kane couldn't actually remember the last time that he'd laughed that way.

"You have a really nice laugh," Ana murmured.

No one had ever told him that before. He rolled toward her, and yeah, they did need a bigger bed. Stat. "You remembered how much I liked *Jaws*."

"You were always turning on horror movies for us to watch. I shouldn't have enjoyed them so much, seeing as how my life was a horror show back then." A soft sigh. "But you did it to distract me, didn't you? The movies, bringing me the snacks I liked to eat for the viewing sessions. You were always trying to help me." Memories teased in her voice. "And you used to tell me random facts about each movie. Like, in *Jaws*, we didn't see the shark until much later in the movie because the mechanical shark that was being used kept breaking down. So we got the POV of the shark when he was attacking early on and that actually wound up making things even scarier." A pause. "Not knowing what is going to happen next, not being able to see the threat coming for you—that is scary."

They weren't talking about a fake shark. He got that. "I'm going to stop Logan."

"And everyone else he sends after me? You just going to fight every threat that comes? You're big, Kane, but you're not a one-man army."

"That's just insulting." He tugged her closer. Wrapped an arm around her. Tried to ignore how insanely right she felt against him. As if he'd been searching for her his entire life and he'd finally found the person who fit. "I am definitely a one-man army. Anyone who says otherwise is a dirty liar."

She put a hand over his chest. "I was scared when you went in the water."

"I was scared when I heard you scream."

Silence.

Then, just when he thought that she'd gone to sleep, Ana whispered, "You want me, but you're not trying to have sex with me again."

"I'll always want you." A basic truth for him.

"Why aren't you trying to have sex with me again?"

He was tenting his sweats and the covers, and he was sure her eyes had adjusted to the darkness so she could see that fact. "Trying something new," he told her. "Being a gentleman."

"You've always been a gentleman with me."

No, he'd been a dangerous bastard with her. At his core, that was exactly what he still was. "You hadn't had sex in two years. It hurt you when I first went inside. I'm trying not to make you too sore." His turn to pause. "Because I have plans for you."

"You hadn't had sex in two years, either."

Ah, he'd wondered when she'd get to that fun trivia bit. Kane grunted.

"Why not?" Ana asked him.

"Why didn't you have sex?" He turned the question back on her.

"Because my last lover turned out to be a killer. I have major trust issues."

Yeah, fair enough.

"What about you?" Ana pushed.

"Told you, sweetheart, if I couldn't have you, I wasn't interested."

"That's—that's not true."

It was. She just might not be ready to handle his truth. "I tried to warn you before. You should have listened to me." Now, it was too late. Did she even remember the words he'd given her on that long ago day? Kane did. He'd been dead serious.

I'm not a safe harbor. I'm a nightmare. One that you won't be able to escape, not if you give yourself to me.

But she'd done it. She'd given herself to him.

When the time comes for me to step back, for you to move on to a new life, I won't let go. I won't step back.

She didn't speak again. Neither did he. Her hand remained over his heart, and his arm remained locked around her.

Chapter Eleven

GRAYSON "GRAY" STONE DIDN'T LIKE TO MAKE mistakes. Mistakes annoyed him. Miscalculations pissed him off.

Ana should not have been in jeopardy that night. She shouldn't have been running for her life, and Kane shouldn't have barely gotten to her in time to keep Ana alive.

She'd wanted to run.

Gray had stopped her.

But maybe that was a mistake.

And mistakes just fucking annoyed him.

He'd gone back to the police station even though it was nearing one thirty in the morning. Gray had fired off some FBI bullshit and waved his ID around and gotten one of the greener officers on the skeletal, late-night staff to give him access to holding and to Turner Mitchell. When Gray walked into the holding area, the SOB was sleeping in his bunk. Sleeping hard and deep, like the prick didn't have a care in the world.

Gray grabbed a nearby tray that had been left out after

the dinner shift, and he ran that tray along the bars, creating a loud, grating clatter.

"*Hey!*" A shout from Turner as he shot upright in the bottom bunk. "*Hey!*"

"Wakey, wakey," Gray chimed.

From another cell down the hallway, someone yelled, "Asshole, shut the hell up!"

Gray tossed aside the tray and glared through the bars as Turner swiped the sleep from his eyes. "You are a problem," Gray informed the man.

"*I'm not talking to you!*"

"Fabulous. Don't talk to me. Listen instead. Because I'm trying to give you lifesaving tips." Probably wasting his time but, whatever. "You made a powerful enemy tonight." Groundwork had to be laid. A cover story amended.

"What?" Turner swung his legs to the side of the bunk.

"Kane doesn't forget, and he doesn't forgive. When you get out of here, you'll have a target on your back."

Laughter. The prick rose from the bunk and sauntered toward Gray. Cockiness oozed from his pores. "Do I look scared?"

You look like you got the hell beaten out of you. Turner's lips were swollen and busted. At least one tooth appeared cracked. "Pretty sure I heard you were shaking and begging by the time you were hauled out of the shark tank. Can't swim, huh? Bad mistake considering all the water around here." Gray thought he heard the faintest tread of a footstep. Sounded like it came from the entrance to the holding area. Was one of the cops eavesdropping? Maybe even the green officer who'd let him in? Gray didn't bother to look over his shoulder. As long as he wasn't interrupted, the cop could listen his heart out. Maybe he'd even learn a thing or two.

"Are you *threatening* me?" Turner demanded. "That's police harassment!"

"I'm warning you. Trying to keep you alive. That's called being helpful. A good person." Gray stared through the bars. "Tip one, learn to swim."

"I'm not afraid!"

"You should be afraid of me. Of Kane. You should also be very worried about what will happen when you meet up with Logan Catalano. I mean, he's right here in Gulfport, so once you get out, a meeting will be imminent."

Turner's chin notched up. He blinked. A little too fast. "Who told you that?"

You did, dumbass. Right now. "When you get out, I'm sure Logan will let you know how very displeased he is with you. You had one job, and you screwed it up. Way to go, Ace."

Turner swallowed. "Don't know what you're talking about."

"Of course, not. After all, you don't have any useful intel that you want to trade to me, do you? Intel that might have brought you a deal. Perhaps even protection." Gray paused a moment and let those words sink in. "Sweet dreams, Turner. Sleep tight. Don't let the sharks bite." With that, he turned and sauntered back down the hallway that led out of holding.

"That shit supposed to be funny?" Turner called after him.

"*Shut up, assholes!*" The same annoyed voice from earlier blasted that order. "Some of us want to sleep!"

Gray whistled.

"It's not funny!" Turner yelled. "It's not!"

"I think I'm fucking hilarious," Gray argued and then he turned the corner.

139

Cynthia Eden

He came to a dead stop.

A woman leaned against the wall near the door that would take him out of holding. A woman wearing a black dress, one that skimmed her knees, scooped at her neck, and left her shoulders and arms bare. Red pumps covered her heels, and her black hair skimmed her shoulders in a sleek bob. Her eyes—the brightest, boldest blue he'd ever seen in his life—locked right on him.

She'd crossed her arms over her chest and pressed her shoulders back against the wall. She looked casual. Gorgeous. Drop-dead sexy.

She also looked like the bane of his existence. Which she was.

"Hello, FBI Special Agent Stone." Her voice held no accent, just a touch of husky, sensual temptation. She quirked a dark brow. "Having fun with the prisoner, are we?"

Gray flashed her a broad smile. He knew her face, though he had to admit that Emerson Marlowe was even more gorgeous in person. When he'd first been told that the psychiatrist working with Logan Catalano would be coming to join him for this takedown case—a Dr. Emerson Marlowe—Gray had been less than thrilled. Then he'd done some basic research on the shrink. Found out that Emerson was not the pencil-pushing academic bastard he'd originally suspected, not some Ivory-tower professor who wanted to dip a toe into the world of criminal investigation.

Oh, no. First, Emerson wasn't a *bastard* at all. She was delicate. She was feminine. She was witchily beautiful— yeah, the woman had a witchy vibe, especially with her black dress, and the vibe totally worked for her.

Sue me. I always liked the Wicked Witch. To me,

140

Dorothy was the pain in the ass. Always whining about wanting to go home and dragging that poor dog all over Oz.

Emerson had a fistful of degrees, and while she'd spent plenty of time working at Vanderbilt, she'd also partnered with both local and federal law enforcement personnel on at least a dozen cases.

Plus, her mother was a senator. So, yes, the woman had pull. Enough pull to get Emerson moved into the FBI when Emerson had never trained at Quantico like a typical agent. Instead, she was a "consultant" who was there to utterly fuck with Gray's life.

"Emerson Marlowe." He paused. "*Dr.* Emerson Marlowe, I mean." He sauntered toward her. "You arrived sooner than I expected."

She didn't change position. Just stayed, seemingly relaxed, against the wall. "Is that why you snuck in and had a private chat with the suspect? Because you didn't expect my arrival yet?"

Her skin was a warm honey. Her lips were unpainted. Lush. And those thick eyelashes of hers could not be real. "I just wanted to check in with the man. I was worried about him. Doing my due diligence and all."

"You were baiting him." A moment of consideration. "And trying to terrify him into making a mistake."

He could deny it, but why bother? "Guilty."

"You...or him?"

"Oh, that bastard is dead guilty. He tried to kill Ana tonight. Stalked her through the local aquarium, threatened to stab her and feed her to the sharks. A lovely human being, don't you think?"

"No, I don't think so."

"He's guilty and so am I." Of so many things. Things most would never, ever know about him. "He slipped up.

141

Logan Catalano—your former patient and current escaped pain in the ass—is already in town. By the way, did I ever mention to you—in those ever-so-entertaining email and text exchanges that we've shared—that I thought the idea of interviewing mob hitmen and enforcers in order to create some sort of new handbook on homicidal and narcissistic behavior was an absolute shitter of an idea?"

Her lush lips pulled down. "Please, tell me what you really think."

He stepped closer. Her scent—summer nights, jasmine, innocence—teased him. Gray shook his head because...what in the hell had just happened? And how the hell did anyone smell like innocence?

Clearly, he'd been working too long. A vacation to some tropical paradise should be in his future. Once he had Logan back in custody.

"I think," he began, trying to stay somewhat careful with his language, "that you are a civilian who should not be playing with fire." Another step toward her. "And if you didn't have mommy's political power behind you, the fire would never have been started." Okay, so maybe he hadn't been quite so careful with his words. Sue him.

Her eyes narrowed. "I'm here because of my own qualifications. My mother has nothing to do with it."

"Really? Because I got a personal phone call from her—and my boss did, too, by the way—saying that we had to play nicely with you or we'd find ourselves being called in for a full accounting in the senator's office."

A furrow appeared between her eyebrows. "What?"

"See, that's a fun little tell." He reached up and touched her between the brows. A light, quick touch.

Electricity surged through his whole body.

Gray snatched his hand back as if he'd just been

burned. Because he had been. "Shouldn't have touched you," he said instantly. He meant those words with every fiber of his being. "My mistake. It will not happen again." He backed up.

"What? What just happened?"

"Won't be touching without permission," he rasped.

Her head tilted. Her hair spilled against her shoulder. "And what happens if I give you permission?"

"FBI Agent! FBI Agent!" A bellow that echoed from holding.

"Will you assholes shut the hell up?" The other prisoner in holding, still just as annoyed.

Gray didn't move. His gaze never left Emerson. "You didn't know your mother was pulling strings. The surprise showed in that cute—" No, shit, he was tired and being sloppy. "The surprise showed in the scrunch between your brows. Watch the tell." And he needed to watch himself. No more slip-ups where he referred to anything about her as *cute*.

"FBI Agent!" Turner bellowed again.

"He really wants your attention," Emerson told him.

"The longer he waits, the more desperate he'll be. Free pro tip for you."

"Thanks so much," she gushed, widening her eyes. "That is a real gem of knowledge you've bestowed upon me."

He did not miss the sarcasm. Her *thanks so much* sounded an awful lot like *fuck you and the horse you rode in on*.

Gray bit his lower lip.

"Something amusing you?" Emerson inquired. Very polite. Very cool.

"Nope." He cleared his throat.

"How did your suspect slip up?"

"He had a tell, too. His watery eyes got too blinky."

She straightened from the wall. "You're assuming Logan Catalano is in town because your suspect *blinked?* Blinked too much?"

"Yes."

"That's ridiculous."

"That's field experience," he corrected. "That is having spent years facing the worst criminals in the world and not just helping on a handful of cases."

"You're exceedingly arrogant."

"Thanks for noticing."

"FBI Special Agent!"

"I think he doesn't know your actual name," Emerson murmured.

"I think you're right." Gray checked his watch. "I'd like to get into bed, so how about we get this show moving?" He peered back up at her. "You want to question him?"

"No, you go right ahead. I'll just watch and admire your skills."

"Suit yourself." He turned and strolled back toward Turner Mitchell's cell.

"Oh, fuck, pretty lady..." This came from the other prisoner—the one who'd been yelling for silence so long and calling everyone assholes. "You come to tuck me in for the night?"

"Say another word to her," Gray told him, voice flat, but he shifted his body so that he was between the cell and Emerson, "and you won't see daylight."

Another word was not said.

"You seem grumpy," Emerson noted. "Are you, by any chance, playing bad cop?"

He grunted. "No, as a rule, I'm just a general dick." He kept moving.

Turner stood in his cell, gripping the bars. As soon as he saw Gray, he blurted, "My lawyer works for Logan."

He'd walked all the way back for that? "Tell me something I don't know."

"*Logan is in town.*"

He waited. There was nothing else. Sighing, Gray directed yet again, "*Tell me something I don't know.*"

Turner's knuckles whitened as his grip tightened around the bars. "I'm not the only one in town who was told to watch Ana."

Gray felt tension settle along the nape of his neck. "Who else?"

Turner's stare darted to Emerson, then flew back to Gray. Blinking, once, twice, three times, he promised, "I'll tell you *after* you get me a deal. I want out of this cell, I want out of this city, and I want protection! Someone else is waiting to swoop in and kill Ana, and if you want that ID, then you cooperate with me, got it?" Two more blinks. Then, slowly, a smirk.

Gray stared back at him. Unblinking. "Do I look like the type to enjoy fairytales?"

The smirk froze.

"Do I look like I want to be told about some princess being kissed by some creep and waking up from some death-like sleep? Like I want to hear about some chick with blond hair eating a bear's soup?"

"What are you talking about?" Turner demanded. Spittle flew from his mouth. "Are you fucking crazy?"

Quite possibly. "I don't like fairytales," Gray enunciated slowly. Flatly. "You were the attacker, the sleeper here in town. There is only you. Don't insult my intelligence with fake claims. Besides, if Logan is here—and we both know he is—there is no need for someone else to be watching Ana. Logan can take over the job himself. So don't waste my time. Don't bullshit me."

"I'm not!"

Gray turned away. Slanted a glance at Emerson. "Let's call it a night."

She nodded. "I am feeling sleepy. Long drive, you know?"

Without looking over at Turner, Gray tossed back at the perp, "When you feel like giving me an actual location, when you feel like telling me specifically where I can find Logan—and when you stop spinning fairytales—*then* we will make a deal. Until that point, you're on your own."

"He will kill me!"

"Yeah, that's kinda the point."

Turner was still shouting even when Gray signed out of holding. Emerson didn't say a word. Her heels just click-clicked as they made their way through the station and then exited via the main doors. As soon as they were outside, the humid night air hit them.

He hurried down the steps.

Click, click, click. "You like playing with criminals, don't you? Are mind fucks fun for you?" Again, her voice was polite. Cool. Only mildly curious.

He stopped at the edge of the sidewalk. His car waited just a few yards away. Holding tightly to his patience, he turned toward her. "I don't need lies. I need facts."

She was under a streetlamp. They both wore. So he saw her eyes widen.

Oh, what? Did he sound like a hard ass? Too bad. "I need—"

Emerson leapt at him. Shoved her whole body at him—

hard—and they both slammed into the sidewalk. Right as he felt the snap of a bone breaking in his wrist. Even as he opened his mouth for an epic swearing session, Gray heard—

Rapapapapap. Fast and furious gunfire. He could even smell the blasts in the air.

A moment later, tires squealed, rubber burned, and the shooter roared away.

Emerson heaved herself up. Her breath shuddered out. "Saw the shooter," she said as she shoved her hair back from her face and peered down at him. "I just saved your life."

His eyes narrowed. "You just broke my fucking wrist."

"Oh. Well, that, too."

Sonofabitch.

Chapter Twelve

ONE BED.

Two people.

Three orgasms.

Ana opened her eyes and stared at the shadowy form right in front of her. Beside her. Around her? Because Kane's warm, strong arm was still over her hip. She was on her side, cuddled close to him, and it honestly felt like the most natural position in the world.

Like that didn't terrify her to the soles of her feet.

She'd fallen asleep in his arms. After those truly epic orgasms. The man should come with a warning label. *May give orgasms so intense that you'll never want to use your vibrator again.*

Now what was she gonna do? Before, she'd just had fantasies about Kane. After giving herself to him, she knew just how intense the pleasure between them would be. Except...she had a fake life, and she didn't think he intended to stick around once the case was closed and Logan went back to prison.

I didn't talk about love. Kane didn't talk about love. This isn't about love. It was sex. Really good sex, and nothing was wrong with that.

Carefully, she eased from beneath his arm and out of the bed. Ana grabbed a robe—soft terry cloth, bright blue—and slid into it before she tip-toed out of the bedroom. Insomnia wasn't new for her. In fact, since discovering that her ex was a killer and having her whole life upended, Ana didn't think she'd actually had one full night's sleep.

She pulled the door shut behind her. Crept down the stairs. Normally when she couldn't sleep, she'd head downstairs. She'd play the harp. The music soothed her. Settled her. Typically the routine let her unwind enough to go back to bed.

So when she stepped off the staircase, Ana turned on the downstairs lights, and she went straight to the harp. But she didn't pluck the strings. Just stared at it. Same time. *Two a.m.* She always came down right around two a.m. That was her middle-of-the-night wake-up time. Maybe because...

Once upon a time, I was with Logan. I woke up, and he wasn't there. I slipped down the hallway. I went looking for him. Found him in the basement. I was just about to call his name.

Then she'd realized he wasn't alone.

And by the time she'd realized that fact, he'd just cut the throat of the man who'd been in the basement with him.

Too late. Too late. Too. Late.

So now she woke up at two a.m. Always trying to stop a murder that had happened long ago.

Her fingers hovered over the harp strings. She wouldn't play tonight. Kane needed his rest, and, even with the bedroom door shut upstairs, he might hear the music and wake up. Her shoulders sagged a little bit as she turned away from the harp. Instead of touching the strings, her fingers reached out and tugged open the drapes in front of the nearby window. One of the big, floor-to-ceiling windows that sat in the front of her house and gave her such a beautiful view of the beach. On full moon nights, she'd leave her drapes open while she played. She'd look out and see the reflection of the moon on the water, and peace would settle in to chase out the fear that she felt.

"Are you going to play something?"

Ana jumped. She whirled around, with her hand flying to cover her heart.

Kane stepped off the staircase. "Sorry." Gruff. "Didn't mean to scare you."

How could someone so big move so soundlessly? It should have been impossible for him to sneak up on her.

"I was worried when you left the bed. Wanted to make sure you were all right." He advanced slowly, inexorably toward her. "You still wake up every night around two, huh?"

Of course, he would remember that. Ana's hand fell away from her heart. "I'm sure I'll stop. Eventually."

"Will you?" Soft.

"I had a shrink who offered to prescribe medicine so that I could sleep through the night."

"But you didn't take the pills." He kept advancing.

"But I didn't take the pills." He was nearly right in front of her. Wearing his sweats again. They hung low on his hips, and his bare chest was close enough to reach out and touch. They'd had sex, insanely wonderful sex, but *that* felt like a dream. Embarrassed, shy, unsettled, she eased away and sat down on the stool that she used when playing her harp. Her fingers stretched out and strummed lightly over the strings.

"Why didn't you take the pills? They could have helped you."

"They would have knocked me out completely. If someone came inside when I was taking them, I might not be able to wake up." More soft strumming. Music drifted in the air. Beautiful, but sad. She hadn't intended to play anything sad. Her fingers stilled. "If I can't wake up, then I'm too easy of a target."

"Do you still dream of the dead man?"

The victim she'd seen. With the knife shoved into his throat and the blood pouring down his shirtfront as he tried to scream. A sound that would never break from him. "I dream that I arrive too late, as always. The knife is in him, the blood is everywhere, and the man I'd been sleeping with is the one who is the monster."

Kane crouched beside her. "It's not your fault that man is dead. He was involved with the mob, too. He'd stolen from the wrong people. Gotten on Logan's hit list as a result. The man could have gone to the Feds. He could have turned on the power players. He could have gotten a new life."

"Like me?"

He reached out. Tucked a lock of hair behind her ear. "You're not like him."

Because she wasn't dead. Didn't have a knife shoved into her throat. Check. But she had turned on Logan and his associates. She'd worn a wire. Done the undercover bit. Sent Logan to prison.

Got a new life as payment.

A muscle flexed along Kane's jaw as he crouched before her. "Does it help you to play?" Careful words. A careful touch of his fingers against her cheek. "When you tiptoe down here in the middle of the night and you go to your harp, does it help?"

"Music therapy." A wan smile tipped at her lips. "It can soothe the soul. I play and the demons leave me and the fear goes away, and, after a while, I can go back upstairs and close my eyes again." That was her long-winded way of saying...yes. Yes, it helped. More than anything else ever had.

"Music is supposed to soothe the savage beast, isn't it?" Kane lingered before her. "Pretty sure that's an old saying."

"It's, um, a little wrong."

He lifted a brow.

She licked her lips and quoted, "*Music hath charms to soothe a savage breast, to soften rocks, or bend a knotted oak.*"

He blinked.

"Breast, not beast." She smiled at him. A real smile. "It's something we all get wrong. It came from a really old play, one called *The Mourning Bride*. I always figured it was talking about how music can soothe anyone, even those with too much pain and rage in their hearts."

A nod. Considering. "I always thought I was the beast in our story."

She sucked in a surprised breath. "Our story?"

"Yeah. Yours and mine. You're the beauty. You have all the grace. The delicacy."

Ana shook her head. He was so wrong.

Kane pulled back his hand. Stared at it. Curled his powerful hand into a fist and turned it over. "I was always bigger than everyone else. Always rougher. I'll break every damn thing in a store if I'm not careful. I'll break everything in my life."

Her hand flew out and curled around his fist. "You're

not a beast, Kane." He should never see himself that way. It was certainly not how she saw him.

"Sure I am, sweetheart. I'm the beast who would rip apart the world to protect you."

He was still crouched before her, one knee on the floor. She wanted to throw her arms around him. To hold tight.

"That's the job, isn't it?" Kane rumbled.

Her heart seemed to shrivel.

"Protecting you. Destroying anyone who comes after you. It's the reason Gray wanted me in the first place. He's always appreciated the way I fight dirty."

Of course. She let go of his hand. He was protecting her because Gray had called Kane back into service. Because she was the current job. Kane wasn't doing the protecting and defending bit because he was hung up on her.

Fucking and loving were two different things.

And that was fine. She didn't *still* love him. She'd gotten over that roller coaster of emotion long ago.

"Ana?"

Her head turned away from him. Blindly, she stared at the harp strings. Then she scooted closer to the harp, nestling her shoulder beneath it. "It's a lever harp. Thirty-six strings. Fifty-four inches tall." A slow release of her breath. "You've probably felt the calluses on my fingertips from the harp strings. But, then again, I had calluses from my violin, too." That was just part of the price to be paid in order to play. She'd had calluses on her fingers for as long as she could remember.

"Ana, did I say something wrong?"

No, he'd just said the truth. Instead of answering, she began to play. Slowly. Softly. Then hitting deeper notes. Going faster.

He rose. Moved to stand behind her. Between her and

the drapes that she'd left open just a bit. She could feel his eyes on her. Watching her every move. Her fingers moved faster, the movements automatic for her as she closed her eyes and sank into the music. She didn't usually have anyone watching her when she played the harp. Just her and the music.

But this time, it was different. The song was different.

She poured all of her emotions into the music. Pain and fear.

I almost died in that aquarium. The attacks just won't stop.

Anger and betrayal.

Logan said he loved me, but he was a killer. Hiding his evil behind a smile.

Sorrow and...hope.

I wanted more. Wanted more from Kane. Wanted a real life and someone who would love me.

Love.

Something real. Something deep. Not just sex. Not fleeting. But for always. For—

A roar of an engine reached her, growling over the notes of the harp.

Her fingers stumbled. The music clanged.

She glanced toward Kane, but he'd spun to face the window. Alarm flared, threatening to choke her. "Kane?"

She should relax. It was probably just some kids, driving hard and loud late at night or maybe someone with a souped up truck.

"Down!" Kane roared.

Only Ana didn't have time to get down. He was already launching at her. Kane flew toward her. Their bodies collided even as she heard the fast explosion of gunfire. Blasting again and again.

Ana screamed.

Her window shattered. First one window, then another as gunfire slammed into the front of her house. The glass flew inward.

She was already on the floor, with Kane on top of her. The glass rained down around them even as the screech of tires shrieked in the night, and the vehicle squealed away.

She couldn't move. Couldn't breathe. Kane crushed her. Covered her completely. And he...

Her hand rose to press against his arm. "Kane?" Barely a breath of sound.

She knew she'd screamed his name before.

Her fingers slid down his arm. "I think they're gone."

Her fingers were wet. Ana's heart raced even faster.

Her fingers were definitely wet. Wet and red. Red covered her fingertips. Red coming from Kane. Blood.

No, no, no. *"Kane?"*

His head lifted. His hands pressed into the floor on either side of her body as he levered himself up. "You are not hurt." A statement, not a question.

She grabbed for him.

"You are not hurt," he said again. Sharper. Harder. More determined.

"No, dammit, I'm not!" Because she'd had a giant bodyguard fling himself on top of her. Ana held up her blood-covered fingers. "But you are!"

Chapter Thirteen

"THIS IS BULLSHIT." KANE GLOWERED AT THE DOCTOR and the nurse who seemed intent on trying to admit him to the hospital. For cuts that were not nearly as bad as the ones he got while shaving. "I have scratches. I am not littered with bullet wounds. I don't need to be kept in the exam room any longer, and there is *no freaking way* you are keeping me in this place for observation! Thanks, but no thanks. I am leaving in the next five minutes."

Ana stomped in front of the doctor and nurse. "The hell you are," she said flatly. Her little hands balled on her hips. "If they want you to stay, you are staying."

At least she was wearing clothes again. When the first responders had rolled onto the scene, Ana had been wearing that sexy, little blue robe. One that had a tendency to gape and show too much of her pert breasts. He'd insisted she change before he would agree to get in the ambulance.

The ambulance. Kane snorted. Talk about another colossal waste of his time. He'd only gone on that ride because he'd wanted the EMTs to make absolutely certain that Ana hadn't been hurt by the flying glass and damn bullets. If she'd had so much as a cut on her delicate skin, he probably would have lost his mind.

Luckily, Ana had been unharmed, and he'd been able to keep breathing.

"You have stitches," the doctor stated from behind Ana. The woman sniffed. "Glass had lodged pretty deeply into your shoulder."

He was aware. They'd been painstaking about the removal of the glass. If someone had just given him tweezers and a mirror, he would have ripped the shit out himself. Only no one had obliged when he'd made the request. Then they had taken their sweet time stitching him up.

"We needed stitches to close the largest wound," the doctor added. And she sniffed again.

Bullshit. He hadn't needed stitches. He'd had way worse wounds over the years. What he needed was to get out of that hospital. To get to Gray. To find out who the hell had littered Ana's house with bullets.

As if he didn't already know, though.

Logan Catalano.

"If you don't listen to our orders," the nurse announced with a definite arctic bite in his voice, "then you will just break open the stitches."

Yeah, that was probably gonna happen. It had happened before with other injuries. It would happen again. He'd survive.

Ana kept her gaze on Kane. "You are a terrible patient."

He crooked his right index finger at her.

Her gaze sharpened.

He crooked the finger again.

Kane sat on the exam table, with his legs sprawled in front of him. He wore the same sweats as before, though now they had blood on them, so he'd have to be ditching them soon. Tennis shoes. Socks. No t-shirt because the EMT had been poking and prodding at his wounds and hadn't let Kane put one on.

Ana crept closer to Kane. Her hands remained on her hips.

"Damn straight, I am," he admitted when she was grabbing close, and, oh, but he wanted to grab her. Grab her, haul her against him, and kiss the hell out of the woman.

They tried to shoot her. If she'd been in that room, playing the harp without me there, the bullets could have slammed into her.

Shit, shit, shit.

"I want time alone with my girlfriend," he snapped to the doctor and nurse even as he refused to take his gaze off Ana. "Now."

"Kane!" Ana shook her head. "We are in a *hospital*."

He knew where they were. The antiseptic smell and the exam equipment were dead giveaways.

"You don't get to order the nurse and the doctor around!"

Fine. He angled his head toward their audience and finally took his eyes off Ana. If she wanted him to play nicely, he'd try. For her. "May I *please* have time alone with my girlfriend?"

"*Kane!*" Again, from Ana. Still sounding annoyed. "It's a hospital, not a hotel! We don't get a private room for fun."

Had the doctor just snorted? Sounded like it.

"We have paperwork to complete," the doctor announced. "Not like we want to just hang out with you all night."

He almost smiled at that bit of bite. Maybe he could like the doc.

"You're stitched up," she noted. Dr. Asha Quinn. She'd introduced herself immediately after entering the exam area. The nurse was Sean Hill. The doctor pursed her lips and continued, "I am going to advise you to follow all release protocols that you will be given in your departure paperwork. I'm trying to help you heal with a minimum of scarring."

Nice of her, but he didn't care about the scars. He just cared about getting the hell out of there and getting Ana into a new safe house.

She is not going back to her house. She can't. The house he'd wanted to be a home for her. The bastard with the gun had shattered that home as surely as he'd shattered the windows.

"Good luck," the doctor said. Those words seemed to be —very pointedly—for Ana.

"Yes, thanks," Ana responded. "I'll need it."

The doctor laughed. But she did fire one more firm look Kane's way. "Don't rip open those stitches."

He would make no promises.

The doc and the nurse exited.

"That was rude," Ana told him as soon as they were alone. "You were rude."

Right, fuck, he had been. "I'll send an apology note."

"Don't you dare mock me."

He wasn't mocking her. He was dead serious. Probably not the time to tell her that his mom had been a stickler for manners. Thank you notes had been required for any and all gifts and if he fucked someone up—like the time he broke that jackass Bryan Kendall's nose in the sixth grade—she'd made him send an apology note.

Dear Bryan,

I am sorry that you are an ass. You shouldn't pick on

people smaller than you. If I see you doing it again, I'll just have to break your nose a second time.

Your (never-gonna-be) friend,

Kane

His mom had insisted he write the notes, but she'd never actually read them. Or if she had read them...for some reason, she'd still let him mail the suckers.

She'd done her best with him. He'd *loved* his mom. And then, one day, she'd just been gone. An aneurysm. No warning. No stopping it. Just—*gone.*

Sometimes, you didn't realize what a giant, gaping hole someone would leave in your life, not until the person was gone.

After Ana had left, there'd been another hole in his life. One so big that it threatened to swallow him alive.

He'd written a letter to Ana at the time. A note apologizing for the way he'd left her. A note spilling out his guts. Only, he'd never given her the note.

Dear Ana,

I'm sorry that I am not there with you right now. But at my core, I'm a cold-blooded bastard, and you need more than me in your life. I'll drag you into the dark, and you belong in the light. Hell, you are the light. At least, you are to me.

You told me that you were falling in love with me. When you said those words, all I wanted to do was grab onto you and never, ever let go—

Ana started to back away. Kane couldn't have that, so his hands flew out and curled around her waist. He pulled her toward him.

"Kane!"

He jumped off the exam table. Spun around and put her on it. Then he began to carefully inspect every single inch of her. Just in case he'd missed something before. Kane believed in being thorough. Particularly where she was concerned.

Ana batted at his hands. "What are you doing?"

"Looking for cuts." He tried to lift up her t-shirt.

She shoved it right back down. "I told the EMT on scene, I told you like four times already—I am *fine!*"

"Yeah, but you could have been lying. All those times." He tried to lift the shirt again.

She shoved it down once more even as she gasped, "How dare you accuse me of lying!"

"Oh, come on, sweetheart, you could probably have lost a limb and you wouldn't complain. Do you remember how you were after the attack at that lame-ass, no-tell motel? I had to force you into the ambulance even when you had blood streaming down your side." A memory that would be forever burned into his mind.

Luckily, though, he didn't see any blood on her body.

This time.

"You were the one cut by flying glass," Ana reminded him. "Not me. How could I possibly be cut? I had my own personal human shield covering every inch of me."

He checked her neck. Lifted her hair. Damn straight, he was her shield.

"I do not have any cuts," Ana enunciated clearly and slowly. "You do. Thus, the stitches."

He let her hair fall. "I think you should strip."

Her hand slammed into his chest. "I think you should get your sanity back. I am not cut. I am not shot. I might have a bruise on my ass from hitting the floor when you tackled me, but otherwise, I assure you, I am perfectly fine."

The door squeaked open behind him.

He ignored the squeaking door. "Let me see your ass."

"*No!*" Ana blasted. "You are not seeing my ass right now! I am not stripping for you!"

"Whoa, whoa, whoa!" Gray's quick exclamation. "Big time-out here, people. Big. No ass showing, and that's an order."

Kane's teeth snapped together. "I'm trying to make sure Ana isn't hurt!" He spun around and frowned when he saw Gray. "What in the hell happened to you?"

Gray lifted—partially lifted, anyway—his left wrist. A brace covered his wrist and snaked up his forearm. "You mean this lovely new accessory? It was a gift from the ER doc who recently treated me. No worries. I get to follow up with an orthopedic specialist, ASAP. Joy. Should be fun. Maybe if I'm lucky, I'll even get surgery." Faint lines bracketed his mouth. "What can I say? It's been a busy night for us all."

Ana tried to jump off the exam table and approach Gray.

Kane wrapped an arm around her and put her right back on the table.

"Kane!" Ana snarled.

He kept a hand on her waist. "How the hell did you break your wrist?" he asked Gray.

"Oh, the usual way." Gray lowered his wrist.

"What is the usual way?" Did it look as if Kane had endless patience? His friend could spit out the details at any moment.

Before Gray could respond, there was a soft knock on the exam room door.

"Don't come in!" Gray yelled.

The door opened anyway.

"I knew she'd come in," Gray muttered. "That's what

happened to my wrist, by the way. I mean, *she's* what happened."

A woman crossed the threshold. A woman wearing a black dress and one broken high heel. Technically, she wore two heels. One was broken. One wasn't. So she had a lurching walk as she advanced. "Good news," she announced. "The nurse at the check-in desk wears the same size shoes that I do. She has an extra pair of sneakers in her locker that I can buy from her." She smiled at Kane. Then Ana. "Hello."

"Who the hell are you?" Kane asked her.

"Emerson Marlowe." She approached with an outstretched hand. Her dark hair slid against her shoulders. "Nice to meet you."

He took her hand. Swallowed it and immediately let go.

She offered her hand to Ana. "I have been dying to meet you, Ana," Emerson told her.

Like those words didn't give Kane a bad feeling in his gut.

"*Dr.* Emerson Marlowe," Gray clarified for the group. "As in, remember the shrink I told you about? The one who'd been having sessions with Logan Catalano? It's Emerson."

Ana had just been shaking Emerson's hand, but at that news, she hurriedly pulled her hand back. "Why were you talking with Logan?"

"Because someone had to do the job." Emerson squared her shoulders. "I think there is a great deal that we can learn from the criminal mind. Once we understand how some can commit acts of heinous violence so easily, then perhaps we can find a way to eliminate those acts and prevent future victims."

Ana remained on the exam table. If anything, she

inched her body a bit closer to Kane. "What did you want? To figure out how to—how to change Logan? How to stop him from being a monster?"

"I wanted to know when he became a monster. Because the guy went from being a church choir boy in his youth to one of the most feared mob enforcers on the East Coast by the time he was an adult. Sure, everyone changes in life, but that was quite the brutal one-eighty, don't you agree?"

Kane looked over at Gray. His buddy was frowning at his wrist brace.

"Logan was good at pretending." No emotion entered Ana's voice. "Maybe he pretended to be a good choir boy just like he pretended to be a good boyfriend. A good human being. But the truth is that he was always evil at his core."

Gray looked up. His gaze collided with Kane's. Kane forced his back teeth to unclench. "There was a drive-by at Ana's place. That's two attacks in one night."

"Three," Emerson corrected as she headed toward Gray's side. One heel clicked. The other just sort of slid across the floor. "Three attacks. The attack at the aquarium, the attack at the police station, and the attack at Ana's house."

Kane took a step forward. "What happened at the police station?"

Gray waved his wrist brace.

"I saved Grayson's life," Emerson confessed. "I saw the truck's window rolling down as the vehicle advanced. I saw the tip of the gun, and I knew what was going to happen even before the engine roared and the driver barreled fast toward his target." A pause. "A target that was Grayson. I leapt into action. Tackled him. Saved him."

"Broke my wrist," Gray groused. "And, yes, she saved my life. I don't think she will ever let me live that down."

"I will not," Emerson assured him as she lifted her chin just slightly. "But at least you get to keep living, so there's that bonus."

"Wait!" Ana jumped off the exam table.

Dammit, he'd put her—

"Do not *dare* try it again, Kane," she ordered in a chilling tone. "I get that you're worried about me, but you don't need to be. You were the one standing in front of the picture window. You were literally between me and danger. I didn't get hit." Her eyes were big and deep and so very golden. "You were the one dripping blood. I was afraid that you'd been shot. When I found out that it was just glass that had cut you..." An exhale. "I was relieved. Still scared because there was a lot of blood, but at least you didn't have bullets in you." She reached for his hand. Squeezed it. Her voice warmed and softened as she told him, "Take a breath. Stop worrying so much about me. I am okay."

He would always worry about her. His hand twisted so that he could cradle her fingers in his. When he finally looked up and around again, he found Emerson's eyes on him.

Curious. Considering.

Then she caught his stare. Blinked. And he could read nothing about her expression.

"I talked to the cops on scene at Ana's place." Gray began to pace around the small room. He always paced when he was delivering bad news. "We got footage of the vehicle thanks to the doorbell camera. Same truck was involved in both shootings. It looks like there were two individuals in the truck. The driver and the shooter. First it went to the station, where I got the spray of bullets, and then the truck drove over to Ana's place." He frowned at a blood pressure cuff that had been left on a rolling tray. "Lots of her neighbors came out to watch the circus when the cops swarmed and the crime scene teams went to work. Mrs. Shirley Hosier— Mrs. Shirley's grandson had given her a doorbell camera for Christmas. He didn't like for his grandma to go to the door without knowing who might be waiting outside. She gave links to view the footage to the cops, and they discovered that the truck idled near Shirley's place for a good five minutes before taking off and shooting. It was like the perps in the truck were waiting for something." He stopped frowning at the cuff and turned his frown on Ana. "Almost like they were expecting a signal to attack."

Ana shook her head. "There was no signal. I was playing the harp. Kane was listening, standing near me, and then, in the next moment, he was yelling for me to get down and launching his body to cover mine."

He hadn't been sure that he would get to her in time. When Kane swallowed, he tasted the fear that lingered. It was like bitter ash. He'd seen the truck, seen the gun—the tip, just as Emerson had described—and he'd known that the attack was seconds away. He'd leapt for Ana, only wanting to protect her.

It was his job, after all. Gray had deposited a big-ass check from the federal government in Kane's bank account. Another freelance gig.

I'll put that money into the same savings account that I've used for all of Ana's rent payments. I won't touch a dime of it. Because he didn't need to be paid for watching Ana.

"Why on earth were you playing the harp in the middle of the night?" Emerson asked. Her head tilted to the right.

"Uh, Emerson." Gray shook his head. "Not really the

point. The point is the bullets that were flying. The point is that there were two attacks from the perps in that truck. One at the station. One at her place. There is an APB out for the truck now, FYI, everyone. We will find that vehicle. We are also pulling all traffic cams from the area. Maybe we'll get a pic of the driver or the passenger—the shooter. Unfortunately, we already know the ride was reported stolen, so the driver isn't the guy who owns it. The real owner is a farmer up in Hattiesburg who doesn't know how his truck got all the way down here."

Emerson moved to stand in front of Ana. Click. Slide. Click. Slide.

Kane frowned at her feet. "I'd probably just trash them."

"They were really expensive shoes. Hoping I can get them repaired." She focused on Ana. "Why were you playing the harp? At two a.m.?"

Ana glanced at Kane.

"Oh." Emerson cleared her throat. "Had you two been, uh, were you busy, um—"

"They have a cover story of being involved," Gray cut in to say. "They aren't lovers. Cover story, Emerson. Not reality. They aren't involved."

Yeah, buddy, we are. Not that he intended to broadcast his business. Kane had never been the type to kiss and tell.

"Jeez, Emerson," Gray grumbled, "get your mind out of the gutter."

Your mind is dead-on-track, Emerson.

"I have trouble sleeping," Ana suddenly disclosed.

Kane's attention shifted right back to her. Her cheeks had definitely reddened.

"I tend to wake up at the same time each night. I wake up at two. I go downstairs. I play the harp to calm down.

To soothe myself. After a while, I'm able to go back to bed."

"Logan loved hearing your music," Emerson murmured.

Kane stiffened. *That bastard took her music away from Ana. She should still be on a stage, still performing with the New York Philharmonic, but instead, she had to run. She didn't feel safe. She had to give up her whole life because of that piece of crap."*

Emerson wet her lips. "He told me that he fell in love with Anastasia—"

Kane growled.

"He fell in love with her when he first saw her perform. She had a solo, and it was the most beautiful performance he'd ever heard. Her face was completely focused, lost to the music, and Logan knew then and there that she was meant to be his."

"Ana is not and will never be his." Guttural. "Never."

Ana squeezed his hand. "I'm okay, Kane."

He took a deep breath. His head turned toward her. He drank her in even as he promised, "I won't let him get close. He will not hurt you. I don't care if I have to take a bullet or if I have to shoot into the bastard until he stops moving—*he will not have you. He will not hurt you.* I swear it."

Another knock at the door. *What. The. Hell?* Who was it this time?

The nurse popped his head inside. Frowned at all the people. "So, what, this is some kind of group meeting in my exam room? Why don't you take that meeting outside to the parking lot?"

Gray flashed his ID. "FBI. I'm interviewing the vics, and I need privacy."

The nurse vanished.

Gray huffed out a breath. Stalked closer to Ana and Kane.

"Logan is very focused on revenge," Emerson told them.

"Tell me something I haven't figured out already," Kane muttered. He wanted to sweep Ana out of there. Take her far, far away from any and every threat. "We can't go back to Ana's house now. The front windows are broken to hell and back. She's not safe at that location."

"You're going to the Royal Suite." Gray rattled off the name of the swankiest hotel-slash-casino in the area. One not in Gulfport, but down the way a bit in Biloxi, Mississippi. "Top-notch security. The only suite on the whole floor. You have to use a special keycard just to access that level. I've already booked the place. You'll be spending the rest of the night there."

Not like there was a lot of night left.

"Logan kept talking about 'eye for an eye' justice in our sessions." Emerson's voice was mild. "He told me that he always took back what had been taken from him. It was the rule he'd lived by his whole life." She backed up a step. Another. *Click. Slide.* "The gun at the police station was aimed at you, Grayson." Emerson motioned toward him.

"Gray," he muttered. "Just call me Gray."

"You shouldn't have been at the station. It was so late. You *wouldn't* have been there, if you hadn't been trying to cut me out of the investigation."

That sounded like Gray.

But he denied the charge, saying, "I was trying to get Turner to reveal Logan's location. The guy is in the city. We all know that. I want the perp located and locked up."

"Yes, absolutely." Emerson nodded. "I believe Logan is here. One hundred percent. There is no way he would not come in and get up close with Ana. I actually believe he was the shooter. He told me that he began his career with drive-bys. He liked the feel of the gun in his hand. The blast echoing in his ears. Liked seeing people fall in front of him like toy soldiers."

Everyone focused on Emerson.

"The sonofabitch got awful chatty with you," Gray allowed. An odd note had entered his voice. One that Kane couldn't fully define.

"He liked bragging to me." Her hands remained loose at her sides. "He wanted revenge. But it wasn't just Ana who had wronged him. In our sessions, he routinely mentioned two other individuals. Rage always entered his voice whenever Logan spoke of them." She swallowed. "FBI Agent Grayson Stone. The agent who Logan said turned Anastasia against him. The man who forced her to wear a wire and collect evidence and testify against the man she loved."

"I didn't love him," Ana denied. "You can't love a lie."

Gray's gaze whipped toward her.

"And Anastasia's protector," Emerson continued without missing a beat. As if she wasn't at all surprised that Ana had never loved her ex. "Logan didn't know your full name, Kane. It is Kane, isn't it? Kane Harte. When we shook hands, you didn't identify yourself, but I've done enough digging into Grayson—uh, Gray's life that I know who his best friend is. I even know that your nickname is 'Heartless' Kane Harte."

Kane stiffened.

She slanted a glance at Gray. "You would pull in your best friend on Ana's case. It stood to reason you'd do that because you wanted someone you could trust completely. Especially with the recent spate of leaks at the Bureau." She pointed toward Kane. Then Gray. "You two served in the military together, didn't you? *Semper Fi.*"

"Holy fuck," Gray breathed. He seemed both impressed and horrified. "You've profiled me."

"It's what I do." Modest.

"I don't know if I should be offended or flattered." Gray tapped his chin. "Gonna go with flattered. Just because I'm way too tired to be offended."

"Get to the point," Kane urged. They were all freaking tired.

But Ana frowned up at him. "Semper Fi? Isn't that the motto for Marine Corps?"

He inclined his head.

"You were a Marine." A considering pause from her. "That fits."

"Once a Marine, always a Marine." Emerson had turned brisk. "Always faithful. That *is* the translation for Semper Fi, um, Semper Fidelis, isn't it? Always faithful. And Kane, you have been a very faithful friend to Grayson —Gray. Someone who he trusts above all others. Someone who he knew would come rushing back to help when he needed assistance with an old case."

Ana wasn't an old case. *She's everything.* "I think you were supposed to be getting to the point, Dr. Marlowe."

"That would be really great," Ana agreed. "If you could just speed things along and stop being dramatically suspenseful."

"Sorry." A grimace. "Logan was angry at Grayson. He blamed Grayson for Ana's betrayal."

"Gray," Gray muttered. "Told you to call me *Gray.*"

"I didn't betray the man," Ana fired back at Emerson. "He was a *killer.* I saw what Logan did. You want to know why I wake up at two a.m. every single night and can't go back to sleep? Why I go downstairs and play that harp every night at that time? I've done that routine since I bought the harp. Before that, I would just go downstairs and stare out at the darkness. Now I play music. It soothes me. It helps me to deal with the memory of waking up, going down to the basement, and discovering that Logan had just shoved a knife deep into a man's throat."

Kane wanted to haul her into his arms. Hug her. "We are done here. Gray, you say that room is ready?"

"Oh, yeah. It's ready and waiting for you."

Good. Ana needed sleep. She had to be dead on her feet. *Dead.* No, no, Ana wasn't dead. He guided her toward the door.

Emerson stepped into their path. "Logan didn't know your identity, Kane. All he knew was that you were the man who put a gun to his head. A man who wanted to pull the trigger. A man who *would* have pulled the trigger, if Ana hadn't stopped you."

Gray cursed. "Fuck, but he sure got chatty with you, didn't he, Emerson?"

She ignored Gray's words and told Kane, "You were a mystery to Logan. He only knew your first name. *Kane.* No last name. No identifying background information. Hard to find a ghost when all you have is a first name. But, when Logan got out and Gray thought Ana was in danger, Gray called you in. You came running." Her gaze darted to Gray, then back to Kane. "You both came running, and now he has all three of you together. He has you all in his sights."

And Kane realized why there had been three attacks that night.

He realized why Turner hadn't been ordered to kill Ana sooner. Gray had been wrong when he thought it was because Logan was possessive, that the man saw Ana as his.

Gray had been wrong when he thought that Logan wanted to personally handle the attack—or at least, he'd been partially wrong.

The truth was...

If Emerson was right...

Dammit.

"He waited until we were all here and as soon as Turner told him that I'd made an appearance in town, Logan moved to attack," Kane said. It would have been easy enough for Logan to give Turner a description of Kane. Kane knew that he tended to stand out in a crowd, and as soon as Turner confirmed to Logan that Kane was in the area, sticking close to Ana...

You moved in to eliminate me, didn't you, you bastard?

"That's what I believe." Emerson's face showed no emotion. "I believe that Logan set a trap. He waited because he had three targets that he needed to pull together. And the attacks tonight were him executing his plans for revenge. First, he launched the attack on Ana. He sent in Turner to get close and kill her. Then, the bullets flew toward Grayson. And, finally, he came after you, Kane. I believe *you* were the intended target at the drive-by that occurred at Ana's house. After all, Ana just said that *you* were the one in front of the window. If the lights were on inside, I bet your outline was quite visible from the street."

Kane was sure he had been visible because the lights had been on and the curtains had even been partially open. Amateur mistake. He'd still been dazed from fucking Ana and not thinking clearly. *Or I was still just thinking with my dick.* He should have been more aware.

"If Turner had been watching her closely—and my gut says he had been very, very watchful—then he would have known exactly when Ana awakened each night. He would have seen the lights turn on downstairs. Maybe even caught the sound of the harp drifting in the air. He would have fed that information to Logan, and Logan would've had a timeline to use. Two a.m. He just had to wait for his target to move into position. Then, bam. He attacked."

"Fuck," Gray rasped.

Every muscle in Kane's body had locked down as killing fury pulsed through him. He exhaled slowly and then told Gray, "Buddy, I think she's just as good at mind games as you are." A pause. "Maybe even better."

"Fuck," Gray said once more.

Yeah, they were fucked.

No, we aren't. Because I'm going to kill Logan Catalano long before he ever touches Ana again.

Chapter Fourteen

DING.

The elevator doors opened. Ana didn't rush out. She was far too tired to rush anywhere. Besides, Kane had a fierce grip on her wrist, and even though the top floor at the swanky hotel was supposed to be secure, he exited first. His gaze swept the hallway, apparently saw no threat, and only then did he tug her out after him.

The hotel was connected to a casino on the bottom three floors. But at this time, nearing five a.m., no one had been inside the casino. The hotel itself had been like a graveyard. Grayson had sent two plain clothes Feds to provide extra protection for Ana and Kane, and the Feds stepped out of the elevator after her exit. But they didn't actually follow Ana and Kane. More like, the Feds lingered in the hallway.

She looked back at them, frowning.

"Ana." Kane's voice. Low and determined.

Blinking, she turned her head back toward him.

"They're going to stay in the hallway. Extra protection for a while. Gray isn't taking risks." He had opened the door that led to the Royal Suite. One hand was still around her wrist, and the other one had shoved open the door. She didn't even know what he'd done with the keycard. Probably tucked it in a pocket.

He'd changed clothes before they left the hospital. The change of clothing had come courtesy of Grayson. Grayson had given Kane a new shirt, jeans, socks, and boots. Grayson had assured them that they'd find anything else they needed waiting in the suite, including Ana's go bag.

"Come on, baby. Let's get you to bed."

Baby. The endearment was so casual and easy. Not like it meant anything. Kane had to be just as exhausted as she was. But as Ana crossed the threshold and Kane shut and locked the door—setting the *three* locks on it—she realized that she wasn't just exhausted. Jittery. Maybe that was a better description. Her fingers held a faint tremble, her heart seemed to race a bit too fast, and a nervous tension held her in its grip even as weariness pulled at her.

I will never forget the sound of those shots firing. The glass shattering. I will never forget touching the blood on Kane and fearing that he would die right before my eyes.

Ana exhaled. She pulled her wrist from his grip.

His jaw hardened. "You're going to be safe here."

Sure. She believed that. Safe for as long as she was hiding in the swankiest suite in town. One that had two Feds guarding its exterior hallway. "Are the Feds really going to just stand out there all day?" Because as far as she was concerned, night was long gone. Five a.m. equaled day time.

"They'll stay as long as they are needed." He scraped a hand over his jaw. "They are following Gray's orders."

Grayson is on Logan's hit list, too.

Grayson and Kane.

"Logan wants to kill you," she blurted, and Ana wrapped her arms around her waist. It had been bad enough when she was the one being targeted, but to know that Kane was in the line of fire? Because he'd tried to help her? Talk about a nightmare.

Kane shrugged. "I think the bedroom is this way." He turned away. Moved to a door on the right. Threw it open. "Fuck." His jaw immediately clenched. A hard beat of time passed before Kane cleared his throat. "Yeah, yeah, the bedroom is in here. You take it."

She looked around the huge suite. It had a pool table. An actual pool table. Why? She didn't think that was super necessary. But it did have one. A pool table. A gorgeous, white couch. White end tables. Gleaming, white, marble counters in the small kitchen area. A tall, wooden table with four stools.

Even a baby grand piano waited to the right.

And then there was the bedroom. The one that had made Kane's jaw clench. "What's wrong with the bedroom?" Suspicion filled her.

"Not a thing."

"Is the bed too small for us?" She closed in on him. When she headed for the bedroom, her body brushed past his.

Ana didn't even pretend not to feel the powerful surge of awareness at that brief touch.

"You offering to let me in the bed with you?" he rasped.

She'd just caught sight of the bed. "Fuck," she said, repeating his curse.

The bed was huge. It was also heart-shaped. With black covers. Satin? And red rose petals were sprinkled on top of the black spread. Champagne chilled on the side of the bed, nestled in an ice bucket. Two long-stemmed champagne glasses had been placed right next to the bucket.

"I think Gray must have told the hotel manager that he had a high-rolling couple who needed a place to stay. We both know how Gray loves his cover stories." The words seemed gritted out from between Kane's clenched teeth. "Guess we got the romance package, courtesy of the concierge."

"Oh, God." She looked at the scene, aghast. "Are we in the honeymoon suite?"

From the corner of her eye, Ana caught his wince.

As if she'd needed her answer confirmed. Okay, so, for future reference, the *Royal Suite* was the *honeymoon suite.* And it came with a big, heart-shaped bed. A bed that was, indeed, big enough for Kane's large size.

"We're in the honeymoon suite." Now her words weren't a question. "Got it. The cover is quick and probably necessary." Her head turned. She'd needed to get her eyes off that bed. She found herself staring right up at Kane.

He stared back at her.

Honeymoon suite.

"I'm sorry Logan wants to kill you," she whispered.

"He's not killing me. I'm killing him." Cold words. Brutal words. And, in the next breath, he'd leaned down and scooped her into his arms.

"Kane!"

He stalked across the room. Deposited her right in the middle of the bed. Rose petals drifted in the air. The sweet scent of the flowers teased her.

"I should have killed him long ago. The day the bastard put a knife to you and made you bleed." Kane eased back.

Her hand flew out and caught his. "You're not a killer, Kane."

"Yeah, baby, I am."

"No, you're *not*. You're a hero. We're going to catch Logan. We are going to stop him. No one is going to die!"

A shrill ringing followed her words. A ringing that was coming from the back pocket of Kane's jeans. "Hold the thought," he told her.

Her hand fell back to the bed. A rose petal had fluttered over her thigh. She shoved it aside.

When Kane had picked her up and carried her toward the bed, she'd thought he was being all alpha and dominating and that he would kiss her. Rip her clothes off. Take her right then and there.

But, no, he'd just dropped her among the rose petals. And told her that he was going to kill her ex.

Still alpha and dominating and...

Scary.

Because Kane wasn't a killer.

He was not.

Right?

Kane pulled his phone from his pocket. "Gray," he said, when he saw the screen. His fingers swiped over the screen as he put the call on speaker. "Gray, are you missing me already?" he mocked.

Ana shoved another rose petal out of her way as she leaned forward.

"We found the truck." Flat. No amusement from Grayson. "And the driver."

Relief had her shaking. "That's great news!" Ana chimed. The driver would lead them to Logan.

"You have me on speaker?" A sigh. "Dammit, warn a guy, would you?"

"Like you *warned* me that Ana and I would be in the

honeymoon suite? With freaking champagne and rose petals waiting on us?"

"You're welcome," Grayson snapped. "Listen, how about you take me *off* speaker phone?"

"Don't you dare," Ana warned Kane. She got that Grayson thought he was cutting her out of the conversation. Not happening. Her life was on the line, too.

Kane rolled back his shoulders. "Whatever you've got to say, just spit it out."

"Fine." Grayson cleared his throat. "We found the truck. We found the driver."

Ana crouched on her knees in the middle of the bed. "Get the driver to take you to Logan. This is the break we need."

"Yeah...no."

Her eyes narrowed. "What does that mean?"

"It means the dead can't lead you anywhere, Ana." Softer. "I'm sorry. The driver has five bullets in his chest. Close-range shots. He isn't leading us anywhere. The guy was dead behind the steering wheel."

She fell back on her ass. The rose petals fluttered.

"I've ordered the locals to keep their hands off the vehicle. I want a crime scene team from the FBI going over that ride. We *will* find proof that Logan was inside."

"Logan killed that man." Ana's cheeks felt too hot. Then too cold. "And now Logan has vanished."

"*You've* vanished, too," Grayson reminded her. "You're hidden, Ana. You are safe. He's not going to look for you in that suite. Stay out of sight. Rest. Order room service. Do not leave that location. Do you hear me? Do not leave. Get some rest. Eat. Sleep. Repeat. When I know more, I'll come to you."

Her cheeks seemed to be turning numb. "I thought the plan was to use me as bait."

"You were the bait, Ana." Stark. "Logan's bait. He used you in order to lure both Kane and me to him."

She couldn't control her flinch.

"It's ending," Grayson told her. "We will stop him."

Or he will stop us. He will keep coming.

"Keep eyes on her, Kane," Grayson ordered. "Stay with her. Do whatever is necessary, got it?"

Kane's eyes *were* on her. Drilling into her. "Got it," he growled. "Watch your ass, buddy," Kane told his friend.

"Already calling in backup," Grayson assured him. "Someone we both trust. The cavalry will be here by lunch. And if he has to whisk her away, it will be done. Get prepared for that."

Hold up. He was talking about whisking *her* away? "I have a say in what happens to me—"

"I got a body to transport to the morgue," Grayson cut through her words with his brutal announcement. "I'd rather not have to transport you, too, Ana. That would fucking suck." He hung up.

Her breath shuddered. "Yep, a trip to the morgue sure would suck for me."

Kane slowly lowered the phone. He put it on the nightstand, right between the two champagne flutes. "You're not going to the morgue. Over *my* fucking dead body."

She shot back up to her knees. Her hands flew out and fisted in his shirt. "Exactly!"

His eyes were chips of burning intensity. Heated enough to nearly singe her with just a glance. "What?"

"The bullets were flying. I was screaming. Your blood was on me!" Okay. Way too loud. Clearly, her control was

gone. Completely frayed. The news that Logan had killed the driver of the truck...*It could have been Kane. Kane could be dead with bullet wounds in his body.* "You got lucky. The bullets missed you. You could have been dead. You could have been on top of me, protecting me while you were bleeding out, and then you would have been *gone*."

His hazel eyes glittered. "My job is to protect you!"

"Forget the job! *You* aren't supposed to die! You aren't supposed to be a target!" Her fingers fisted, and she jerked the material of his shirt. She'd intended to jerk him toward her. Maybe get him to tumble onto the bed with her and then Ana had thought she'd kiss him because kissing Kane suddenly seemed incredibly necessary.

Kissing him.

Holding him.

Making sure that Kane wasn't going to die. Doing whatever was necessary to make sure that Kane *would not die.*

But Kane was an immovable object. Her yanking on his shirtfront had zero impact. He didn't budge so much as an inch.

His eyes kept right on glittering as he glowered at her. She crouched in the bed, with rose petals around her, and Kane wasn't even touching her. She was touching him.

"My job is to protect you," he said again, lower. Raspier.

"Your job isn't to die for me." They needed to be clear on that point. "I don't want bullets flying and you getting hit because you're near me." No, it was more than that. So much more. "You're a target because you're protecting me." She snatched her hands back. "You're fired."

He blinked.

"You're fired, Kane!" Ana pointed to the door. Was she being way too dramatic? Hell, yes. But was she still firing him? Hell, yes. Because a man was dead. And Kane needed someone to protect *him*. She'd be that someone. "Go out, get on that Harley you rode in on, and drive the hell back to wherever you came from."

He did not move. Hardly shocking.

"You're fired," she said again. Had he missed that part? How many times did she need to say the words?

His eyes narrowed. His jaw hardened. And he shook his head. No.

"Yes," Ana whispered.

His hand rose. His fingers curled under her jaw. Cupped her carefully. "Sweetheart, you can't fire me."

Right. Because she wasn't the one paying the bills. "I'll call Grayson back. He can tell you that you're fired. I'll get another guard." Another guard would work better. Logan wouldn't want to kill the other guard. He wanted to kill Kane because of a personal vendetta.

Kane had put a gun to Logan's head. He'd wanted to pull the trigger.

She'd stopped him.

"I'm not leaving you, Ana. You *can't* fire me. Not now. Not ever." Kane leaned toward her. The faintest rumble of what could have been fury vibrated in his words. "Nice fucking try, though." And then...

Then his mouth crashed down on hers.

* * *

DEAD BODIES WERE SUCH a pain in the ass.

Gray had been so close to getting to his hotel room. Crashing. And then the stolen truck had been found.

The truck *and* the body, and now he was peering inside

the open driver's door of the vehicle and glaring at the dead man.

Dead men couldn't talk. They couldn't lead him to the killer he was after.

"That's a lot of blood," a husky, feminine voice pointed out.

Of course, she'd followed him to the scene. Emerson and her sexy dress. Though she'd ditched the broken heels and now wore the sneakers she'd bought from a nurse at the hospital.

Her voice seemed a bit off, though.

He glanced back at her. The light from a nearby streetlamp fell on Emerson's face. Maybe it was his imagination, but she seemed to look a bit green. Now, wasn't that interesting? Gray backed away from the vehicle, making damn sure not to touch anything. His head cocked as he studied her.

Her gaze darted to the blood-stained windows of the truck. She swallowed quickly. Repeatedly. Then her gaze averted. Fast.

Definitely interesting.

He closed in on her. "There tends to be a lot of blood when someone is shot five times." He'd counted each entry wound. "At close range." Gray stopped right in front of her. "Can't handle the blood, can you?"

She hissed out a breath. "I can handle it just fine."

Nope, she could not, in fact, handle it. "That why you're swaying on your feet? Because you handle things just fine?"

She sent him an icy smile. Her body also swayed again.

He caught her elbow. To help steady the sway and to guide her away from his crime scene. "If you can't handle blood and gore," he said, keeping his voice low and ignoring the incredible softness of her skin beneath his touch, "then why in the hell are you playing around with maniacs like Logan Catalano?"

"Maniac?" she repeated. "That a clinical term?"

"He just shot a man five times. You want me to call him an upstanding member of society? Because I don't think that description fits the situation."

"We don't know that Logan fired those shots."

He rolled his eyes. "I am too tired to deal with your delusions." He deliberately stepped to the side. "You've been interviewing the killer for months. Maybe you had fun playing games with him, but this is reality. And, in reality, Logan Catalano is a twisted freak of a killer. He came after me. He came after my friends. He also just left a dead body for us to find, so, yes, there's that." He moved closer to her. When he'd been peering into the truck's interior, the scent of blood, death, and excrement had flooded his nostrils because when the poor bastard driving had died, his bowels had emptied.

Death wasn't pretty. Death wasn't kind. It was brutal and sick, and twisted pricks out there like Logan Catalano were maniacs. They were brutal beasts. He wasn't going to sugar coat for the pretty psychiatrist.

But as he stepped closer to her, Emerson's scent washed away all others. A sweet scent. Light. Fresh. *Innocent.* That stupid thought again. What. The. Fuck?

"I don't have delusions," she told him.

He thought he'd heard a hitch in her voice.

Now his attention was utterly fixated on her. "Logan Catalano was a mob enforcer. A hitman. The real fucking deal." He shook his head. "You had to see photos of the crimes linked to him. What is this, your first time to see a kill up close and personally?"

185

"Yes." She swallowed hard. "It is my first time. To be, uh, up close and personal." Then her hand flew over her mouth. "And if you will excuse me..." Words muffled by her fingers even as her horrified gaze held his. "I'm about to be very, very sick."

And, dammit, she was. Emerson went careening away from the truck. He knew she was going to vomit.

Hell.

He rushed after her, and as she doubled over, he swept back her hair just in time.

Then she vomited right near his shoes.

Dammit. *On* his shoes.

He *hated* working with partners.

Chapter Fifteen

No, NO, FUCKING, *NO*.

Kane jerked away from Ana. He stumbled back. Got the hell away from the bed because he was not going to push her. He was not going to take her. He was not doing this *now*.

Ana's eyes opened. Her cheeks were flushed. Her lips swollen from his kiss. All he wanted in the entire world was to go back to her. To pull her against him. To kiss her again. To take her until they both drove into the hardest orgasms of their lives.

But she was wrong about him.

"I am a killer." A low growl. Ana needed to ditch the rose-colored glasses where he was concerned. If she wouldn't ditch them, then he would have to smash them for her. "It's what I'm good at. Baby…" He looked at his hands. The hands that had touched her. The hands that he always tried so hard to be careful with—especially when he was around Ana.

His hands had killed.

"You can pretend I'm something else." Everything seemed pretend these days. Maybe because Gray was always tossing out cover stories left and right. When you played enough roles, sometimes, it got hard to remember who you really were. *What* you really were. "But when you strip everything else away, I'm the man who was trained to kill. I'm the man who has eliminated threats that should not be walking this earth." An exhale. "I have killed people, Ana." No sugar-coating. Just a blunt and brutal truth. "I went on missions. I did the jobs. I knew the risks. Once, I...I was in a place that was as close to hell as you could get. The world was on fire around me. It was kill or be killed, and I beat a man with my hands until he stopped fighting back."

Her eyes widened. Her lips hung open in shock. Surprise.

Horror?

"I could tell you that he was evil. That he'd bombed a hospital. That he'd killed innocents. That he was planning to kill more, and if he'd gotten out, if he'd detonated one final explosion, more than a dozen lives would have ended that day." A swallow. "I could tell you that he'd sliced me with his knife. Shot me in the back. That we were down to hand-to-hand combat and that every second counted. Life or death. I could tell you all of that, and it would be true, but here is something that is true, too." A ragged exhale. "I didn't hesitate. I killed him with my bare hands. I survived. I did whatever was necessary, and it's not the first time I've had to kill. Not the last, either. My government sent me on missions because sometimes, you do work off the books in order to protect the greater good. Sometimes, you take a fucking sledgehammer, and you send him out because that is what has to be done. You see, that's what I am. Brute force in its most savage and basic form."

"Kane..."

"You really think I'm going to let Logan Catalano go back in a cage?" The question that he shouldn't have asked, but they had to stop pretending. The longer they pretended, the more stupid hope he had. But there shouldn't be hope, not for him. Because she would not want forever with him. She'd had enough of monsters. "Do you really think that I'll ever risk him getting out and coming after you again?"

He shouldn't touch her. He shouldn't.

But he did.

He crept back toward the bed. His hand extended. And he touched her on her side. Through the soft shirt. His hand hovered over the scar that would always mark her. "He should have been dead that night. I let him live because of you."

"I asked you to stop."

No, she'd *begged* him to stop. "You said I wasn't a killer."

Her hand covered his as it pressed to her side. "You're not. Fighting in self-defense doesn't make you a killer. Fighting so that you can stay alive doesn't make you a monster."

"I stopped that night with Logan not because you begged me, but because I didn't want you to see the truth of what I was. I liked it too much when you looked at me and you said you were falling in love with me. I knew you didn't love me, of course. Not really."

She blinked. After a beat, her hand fell away from his. "Of course." Her voice had gone wooden.

"But I liked it. I liked the way I felt when I stared into your eyes. You looked at me, and...no one had ever quite looked at me the way you did." *You're still not telling her the full truth. You're not telling her...*

You stopped because you hoped that, deep down, she might really love you one day. That it might be possible. That it might be real.

But if she'd seen him kill, that hope would have died.

The hope *was* dying because... "I'm not going to stop, Ana. Logan has to be eliminated. He's coming after me. He's coming after Gray. He's coming after you." *Can't happen.* "I will kill him, and, when I do, you will see me for exactly what I am."

"Saving someone doesn't make you a monster!"

Ah, but she hadn't seen him kill yet, had she?

"I knew I shouldn't have fucked you," Kane said. All along, he'd known it would be better to never cross that final line. But he'd wanted her too badly. A bit of heaven to hold close all the days when he would be in hell.

Ana flinched. "Fucked." A nod. "That's what it was. Fucking." Another nod.

The best fucking of my life. "Sometimes, you want something so much that your control breaks. Then you damn the consequences and take what you want." He was still touching her. His fingers lightly caressing the scar that he hated.

He backed away. Again. "My control is close to breaking with you." Barely holding on by a weak thread.

"Kane..."

"It's *dangerous,* don't you see that?" Didn't she understand? "To give a man what he wants so much, but to make him know that he can't ever really have—" Kane stopped. "You'll see me for what I am. Because I *will* kill Logan. Those shots fired in the house could have gone through me. They could have hit you. Even as I shoved you to the floor, all I could think was that I was moving too slowly. That I was too late. You were going to die, and if you'd died in my arms..." His hands fisted. "Do you think I would have made his death quick? Or do you think I would have taken my time beating the hell out of him until every bone in his body was broken?"

A faint squeak emerged from Ana.

Nothing else. Just the breathless, squeaky sound of shock. Kane knew he'd stunned her. Hadn't that been the point? To make Ana afraid...of him. To make her realize that she had to pull back. That she needed to stay the hell away from him.

Fucking rose petals were all around her. Was that some dumbass joke from Gray?

Honeymoon suite, Kane's ass. He'd never have a honeymoon with Ana. Never have a life with her. Never have the closely kept secret dream of a family with her.

But I will love her until I die.

The deepest, darkest secret that he carried. He'd loved her for over two years. He'd love her until he died.

"You need to get some sleep, Ana." Stilted. Gruff. "I'll bunk on the couch."

"You'll be way too big for the couch." She remained on the bed.

"Then I'll sprawl on the floor. I've slept in far worse places than the Royal Suite." *Honeymoon suite.* He exhaled. "You'll be safe in here. You have to be exhausted."

"So do you."

"To get to you, any attacker will have to come through me." He turned away from her. Marched for the bedroom door. "An attacker would have to get past me and past the two FBI agents in the hallway. You are safe."

"Kane."

His shoulders tensed.

"I know what you are."

No, she had this romantic image of him. The bodyguard. The protector. "Even killers can do an occasional good deed."

"And even heroes can get pulled into the darkness sometimes."

Now he did glance back at her, stunned.

"I used to have a thing for bad boys. *Boys*." She shook her head, as if mocking the term. "Seems silly now. When I much prefer strong men."

He would not go to her. Even though every cell in his body yearned for Ana.

"I know exactly what you are, Kane Harte. I just wish you knew, too. Do me a major favor? Stop seeing yourself as the villain. Villains don't protect the way you do. If you were as twisted as you're trying to claim, you would never be here with me."

Oh, she still didn't get it. A smile pulled at his lips, and he knew it was savage. "Oh, Ana, you don't understand me at all."

A faint line appeared between her eyes. "Then make me understand."

"I'm here because you're my obsession." *No, she was so much more.* "And no one hurts what belongs to me."

Then he left the room. Had to leave because if he'd stayed there even five seconds more, he would have gone back to that bed. Kissed her. Taken her.

You are my obsession.

Screw that lie. She was his whole world.

* * *

192

THE BEDROOM DOOR CLOSED.

Ana remained crouched on the bed. The rose petals stuck to her clothing. She batted them away even as Kane's words rang in her head.

You are my obsession.

She didn't want to be an obsession. Not for Kane.

She was Logan's obsession. Hadn't Emerson said those same words? Logan viewed her as a possession. Something that he would not let go. He'd even kill to punish her.

But Kane...

Kane will kill to keep me safe.

And, honestly, she was really over Kane's bullshit. Two years over it.

Eyes narrowing, Ana climbed from the bed. She ignored the rose petals that fluttered around her. She ditched her shoes. Her jeans. Her shirt. Clad in only her bra and panties, Ana squared her shoulders.

Kane had been positively adorable with his dramatic exit. All intense and dark and dangerous.

Did he not get how hot she found that to be? How hot she thought he was?

Didn't he understand her at all?

Maybe it was time to make the man understand. She'd put her pride on the line two years before. Why the hell not go for round two? Especially when the reward was so high.

She crossed the room. Opened the door. Kept her chin up and ignored the chill and the goosebumps that chased over her body. When you were walking around in just your underwear, you had to be prepared for a bit of a chill.

Her bare feet made no sound as she trekked out of the bedroom. The lush carpeting quieted her steps. She went into the den. At least, Ana figured the massive room was a den. Her gaze darted first to the white couch.

No Kane.

Her gaze leapt up, and she searched the room. She saw Kane. His back was to her as he stood in front of the pool table. He leaned over the table, with his hands gripping the sides.

She took a quick step toward him.

"Ana, stop." He didn't look back.

How had he known she was there?

"You need to go back to the bedroom. This isn't a good idea."

Maybe not. But she didn't care.

"You don't get how weak my control is."

Another step toward him. "What are you assuming?" Ana wanted to know. Her voice was breathless. Maybe a little scared. Fair enough, she was a little scared. "That I came rushing out here to seduce you?"

His powerful shoulders tensed. He gripped the pool table harder.

"Maybe I just wanted a glass of water. Something to quench my thirst." Another step. "Quite arrogant of you to think that I came running in here because I wanted to make that control of yours snap into a million pieces."

"I'll get the water. I'll bring it to you." Kane whirled. "You should just—*Ana.*"

"Yeah, I don't want water." Her hands remained at her sides. Her fingers fluttered. Strummed. "I came running in here because I wanted to make that control of yours snap into a million pieces."

He backed up—tried to, but there was nowhere to go, not with the pool table right behind him. "Ana, you aren't wearing clothes."

"I am, Captain Obvious. I'm wearing a bra and panties." She took her time closing in on him. His eyes were on her body, drinking her in. But it wasn't the grand *rush-at-me-and-kiss-me-like-your-life-depends-on-the-act* response she'd wanted.

Fair enough, she'd just have to work harder.

Ana stopped right in front of him.

"Ana." A warning. A delicious growl.

She took one of his hands and put it on the edge of the pool table. Then she caught the other hand. She raised it to her mouth, and she parted her lips. She took his index finger inside. Licked. Sucked it. A long, slow suck.

His pupils flared. *"Ana."*

She put that hand on the pool table's edge, too. "Hold on, would you? No touching me."

"What the fuck are you doing?"

"Oh, I think you know." She reached for the snap of his jeans. Undid the snap, eased down the zipper.

"Ana, I am trying to be good."

"I got that. What you missed, though? Being good is totally unnecessary." She shoved the jeans and boxers he'd worn out of her way so that she could curl her fingers around the long, thick, and very, very erect length of his dick. "I'm going to suck you until you come, Kane." Her knees touched down in front of him. "Be a sweetheart and keep holding that pool table, will you? I don't want to be interrupted."

Then she took him inside. Took that broad, thick head of his cock into her mouth. She pulled him in, her cheeks hollowing as she sucked. Then she eased back. Licking. Kissing.

She took him in again. A little deeper this time. Her fingers curled around him—around as much of him as she could, and she dipped her head toward him. Her nipples were tight. Her sex yearning. Every lick and every suck that she gave him just seemed to turn her on more and more.

She wanted him to come in her mouth. Wanted his control to break so much that he just let go.

He was heavily aroused, and Ana loved the feel of his dick in her mouth. She parted her lips wider. Sucked and he thrust against her. Pushed that dick deeper and she gasped because—

His hands flew out and locked around her shoulders.

Ana immediately pulled back. Breath heaving, she stared up at him. "You just broke the rules."

"Fuck the rules."

"But I want you in my mouth!"

"And I tried to warn you."

He scooped her up. Spun. Put her on the edge of the pool table. She still wore her panties and her bra, but in a flash, he'd ripped her panties away. The torn scrap floated to the floor.

"You think I was playing?" Brutal lust blazed in his eyes and on his face. "*I can't let go. I can't keep fucking you and let you go. I can't.*"

"Good. Because I love you."

He hadn't lost control when he saw her in her underwear. Fine, maybe she'd been hoping too much on that score. Not like the sight of her partially clad body would send the man quaking.

He hadn't lost control when she went to her knees before him. Not when she'd taken his dick into her mouth.

But right then, as soon as those words tumbled out—

I love you.

She saw the change on his face. His eyes widened. Ferocious hunger, need, blazing desire and longing all flooded his expression. The faint lines on his face seemed to deepen. He shoved her legs apart, and she fell back, her shoulders hitting the green cloth on the pool table as he leaned over her and just *devoured* her core. His mouth pushed between her legs. He licked. Sucked. Worked her with his fingers and his tongue, and she thrashed against the top of the pool table.

An orgasm built within her. Surging and growing and—

"Getting in you, *now*." Guttural.

She shoved up on her elbows. Ignored her racing heart. Pool balls rolled around her, and she pushed them aside. "You were supposed to come in my mouth."

He hauled her toward him. Plunged his dick into her.

All the way inside.

He'd gotten her ready to take him with his fingers and lips and tongue. It was still a tight, thick fit, but she wanted him so much that there was no pain. Her breath shuddered out. She could feel him, so strong and warm inside of her.

Skin to skin.

Her eyes widened. "Kane?"

He pulled her up against him, perched her on the edge of the pool table. He withdrew, only to slam back inside. One hand went to her clit as he pounded into her. Again and again and again, and she screamed because the orgasm couldn't—wouldn't—be held back. It was too powerful and consuming. She thrashed against him. Her legs curled around his hips as she pounded her body into his.

Skin to skin.

She clamped tightly around his dick even as he kept driving into her. He wasn't wearing a condom. She knew that. She knew— "Kane!" The orgasm wouldn't stop. Or was she having another one? Pleasure poured through her. "Kane!"

But he stilled. "No...condom."

Had he just realized that fact?

She forced her gaze to lift. Ana stared into his burning, too bright eyes. She'd never seen the hazel look that way before.

He didn't even seem to be breathing. Meanwhile, her breath shuddered in and out. Kane just stared at her as if he wanted to eat her alive.

"I'm on birth control," she told him. The words trembled because she was shaking with the after-effects of her orgasm. "And I've had a health ch-check." Speaking was way too difficult. Especially with him lodged so deep in her. "I—"

"I'm clean, Ana. Haven't fucked anyone in two years." Deep and dark and hot. Words that she *felt* roll through her. "I want you bare."

Her legs tightened around his hips. "I want you that way, too."

That was it. He erupted. Thrust deep and hard. Fast and wild. She grabbed for his shoulders, held on as tightly as she could. Her hips tried to meet his thrusts, but there was no restraint. There was nothing but the wild, hot ride.

He still had his fingers on her clit. Rubbing. Pinching. Another climax poured through her body, and she opened her mouth to scream.

But he kissed her, muffling the sound. Probably a good thing, with the Feds outside.

Still kissing her, Kane dragged her off the pool table and fully into his arms as he kept pumping into her. A few steps, and she felt a wall at her back. He pinned her there. Held her with one hand while he rammed into her over and over, and it was amazing. Fantastic. His mouth moved down her neck. Licking. Sucking. Biting lightly.

The pleasure would not stop. It just kept going, and she was shaking and shuddering and utterly *his* in that moment.

Every breath...his.

Every thrust...his.

She was consumed. She was taken. She was...

"I love you," Ana whispered.

He erupted inside of her.

She was his.

Chapter Sixteen

He had Ana pinned against the wall. He was buried balls deep in her. Bare. Fucking *bare*. And his eager dick was already swelling again.

His mouth pressed to her throat. He could feel her racing pulse beneath his lips. He'd bitten her at the end. Marked her.

He needed to pull the hell out of her.

Pinned against the wall.

He needed to make sure she was all right. That he hadn't hurt her. And he would if he could just withdraw from the hot heaven of her body.

I love you.

Those words wouldn't stop playing in his head. Over and over again. A dream that could not be real.

His dick was lodged inside of her. Fully erect. Yeah, that had been fast. Fully erect again, already.

Her legs were still locked around him.

I still have her pinned to the wall.

He should withdraw. He began to slide out of her.

Ana gave a little gasp. Sexy as hell.

She doesn't love me. She can't. His head rose. He looked down at her.

Her lips were swollen from his kisses. Her long, dark lashes lifted, and she stared at him—she stared at him as if...

This is my dream.

This is my Ana.

She stared at him as if she really did love him.

He drove right back into her. She gasped, and her legs tightened around him. Her nails bit into his shoulders. Her head tipped back, and she moaned and then asked, voice sliding over him in the best possible way, "How can I still want you this much?"

He eased out. Drove in.

Kane couldn't speak. That function was way beyond him. He was ravenous for her. Too lost. Too intent. Too focused on her and on the way her hot, tight pussy sucked in his dick. She was wet and warm and utterly perfect around him.

He slammed one hand on the wall. The other remained curled around her waist. He eased back, just enough to look down at their bodies. To watch as his dick sank into her.

So. Fucking. Good.

The wild drumming of his heartbeat filled his ears. Every breath he took, it tasted of Ana. Her scent surrounded him. *She* surrounded him. That hot, tight core sucking him in.

He withdrew, nearly pulled out.

Then plunged all the way inside.

She gasped for him. Arched her hips. Slammed up to meet him.

He thrust into her. Again and again. The curtains were open. Sunlight spilled into the suite. No one could see them, though. This was the highest floor in the hotel. The highest one in the whole freaking city. The glistening water and the beach waited beyond the window.

A killer view that he didn't give two shits about because he was fucking his obsession. His Ana.

In and out.

Shoving inch after inch into her. And Ana began to tremble. To buck harder against him. He felt her inner muscles clamping around him, and he knew that she was coming for him *again*. His heart pounded harder. He thrust *harder*. Drove into her endlessly and felt those inner contractions of hers stroke along his eager cock. There was no stopping his own release. It poured from him as he clenched his teeth to hold back a guttural shout. He emptied into her and he wished—fucking *wished*—that he could make Ana pregnant.

Because then maybe she'll begin a new life with me.

Yeah, he was a selfish prick. When it came to Ana...

I want her. Every bit of her.

And...

I will have her.

Her legs slid off him. He withdrew, slowly, hating to slide out of her because she felt so incredibly good. He could fuck her forever and never get enough of Ana.

He eased her to her feet. But when she swayed, his hands instantly steadied her. "Ana?" Shit, had he hurt her?

A sleepy smile. "I think I still have on my bra."

Yeah, hell, she did. A waste, because he loved to see those sweet breasts of hers.

He also still had on his shoes. How the hell had that happened? He kicked them away. Tossed his socks. And ditched the jeans and boxers that were half-down his legs. He also discarded the shirt. Not like he needed it.

"Oh, no!" Her horror was real. "Kane!" Ana reached for him. "Your stitches! Did I hurt you?"

He blinked at her. Then laughed. A deep, booming laugh burst from him.

She frowned. "Kane? Are your stitches okay?"

He bent and pressed a kiss to her soft lips. "I have no clue if the stitches are okay or not." They'd been the last thing he thought about. "I just know fucking you is like sinking into paradise, and having you is worth any pain in the world. Sure as hell worth a few popped stitches." Then he scooped her up against him.

Her right arm curled around his neck. "This is *not* the way to stop stitches from tearing!"

Yeah, but who cared? It was the way to carry her. And carry her, he did. Back to the bedroom. Back to the big bed. He lowered her carefully into the middle of the mattress, nestled her there among the rose petals. Then he frowned. "Stay right here."

She blinked. Frowned.

Oh, shit. That had sounded growly. He amended, "Please?"

She quirked a brow. "Am I staying *alone* in the bed?"

"Just for a second." Like he could leave her alone for longer than that.

"Fine, but the bra is coming off."

Sweet hell. He double-timed it to the bathroom. He half-expected to find a heart-shaped tub waiting. But, no. Just a shower that filled up three-fourths of the bathroom space. He yanked on the water, had steam pouring out, then he rushed back to collect Ana.

The bra was, indeed, a thing of the past. He staggered to a stop and stared at those pretty, tight nipples. Nipples that he needed to feel in his mouth. Against his tongue. That he was dying to taste and suck and she was so sensitive when he sucked her nipples.

Could he make her come from nipple play alone? Oh, he would love to know.

"Kane?"

Right. He shook himself out of his stupor and scooped her up again.

Her mouth brushed against his ear as she chided, "You are going to pop a stitch."

His head turned toward her. He brushed her mouth with his. "I don't give a shit."

Soft laughter from Ana. Then, "You'll care when you have to get stitched up again."

Nah. He wouldn't. He took her into the bathroom and eased her under the warm water. Not too warm. He didn't want it too hot for her. He followed her inside, lathering up his hands.

"Kane!" Real alarm now. "*Stitches!* How many times do I have to tell you to be careful?"

He kissed her and put his slick fingers between her legs. He cleaned her completely and made her come at the same time. There wasn't any other talk about stitches, but he *did* try to avoid letting the pounding water hit that particular area of his body. An easy enough task because he wasn't trying to get clean.

He was enjoying the hell out of stroking her. When Ana came around his fingers, when she squeezed him so tightly and he could feel the quake and shudder of her orgasm, he intended to just keep working her core. He intended to hold back on his own pleasure and glory in hers.

He'd just fucked her.

But...

But her lashes lifted.

Steam drifted around them.

Water droplets slid down her cheeks. "I want more than your fingers, Kane."

Hell, yes.

So he did take her again. Even as she'd finished one orgasm, he was lifting her up against the tiled shower wall. He was lodging his dick at the tight entrance to her body, and he was pushing it in. Squeezing it inside her tight heat and loving the way she felt around him.

Losing his mind because the pleasure was so intense. Because she gripped him so well.

Because he was fucking his dream.

His Ana.

When she came, she gasped, "I love you!"

He greedily drank up the words. He held her caged against the shower wall, and he pounded into her, and he erupted on a blasting wave of release. His teeth snapped together. A snarl escaped him as he poured into Ana.

The orgasm surged through him. Lasted and lasted. Left him utterly wrung out and soul satisfied.

Her head sagged against the shower. Her eyes drifted closed. "If you pulled stitches, it's your own fault."

He smiled. She didn't see the smile.

Ana yawned. "Gonna need you to carry me back to bed." Sleepy. Slurred. *Gonnaneedyoutocarry...*

He withdrew. Let the water wash over them again. Then he took her out of the shower. Dried her carefully. Yanked a towel over himself. And had her back in the bed even as she was nodding off against him.

He shoved away rose petals. Eased her beneath the covers. Hesitated. "Do you want me to stay?"

Before, she'd—

"Yes." Another yawn. Eyes closed.

He slid beneath the covers with her. Tucked her against his side. Felt peace settle over him. Then Kane slipped instantly into sleep.

* * *

He was in hell. Explosions were going off all around him. Blasts of fire. Screams filled the air. The rat-tat-tat of gunfire.

Women were hurt. Children were crying. And the demented bastard in front of him was going to kill *more*. Kane launched at him. He flew through the smoke and the fire, and he tackled the SOB even as he felt the cut of the knife across his skin. He ignored the pain. He pounded with his fists. Drove them at the bastard over and over again.

He couldn't stop.

He wouldn't stop.

Except...

The bastard before him—his face changed. Even as Kane's fist drew back, the figure shifted. It was no longer the terrorist who'd planted all the bombs in that long ago hospital. It was...

Logan Catalano.

Smiling. Smiling with a busted lip and a broken nose. And he was saying..."*You can't save her. She's mine, and I'll kill her before you can save her.*"

Kane's fist drove down, but he just hit the floor.

Logan was gone.

The smoke and the fire and the screams—gone.

He was...

In a house.

Ana's house.

He could hear the faint strain of a harp playing. He

whirled around, and Kane saw Ana. She was sitting at her stool, and her fingers fluttered over the strings of her harp. Her hair blew around her face. Why? Why was her hair blowing?

The drapes behind her were blowing, too. Blowing inward because the glass was broken.

He rushed toward Ana, then staggered to a stop.

Her fingers stilled on the harp.

"There's...there's something on your shirt, Ana." His voice felt distorted. *He* felt distorted.

"It's blood." Her head tilted back. "Where were you?"

Kane shook his head. "What?"

"You didn't save me." She began to play again, and blood seemed to drip from her fingers, turning the strings red. "And now I'm dead."

No. No. No. No. *No!*

He leapt for Ana. Grabbed her hands and pulled her up from the stool, but there were bullet holes in Ana's body. Blood covered her.

"You weren't here," Ana said softly. "Not when I needed you. Where were you, Kane?"

He pressed his hands to her wounds. The blood just soaked through his fingers.

"Where were you?" Ana asked again.

"I'm here, Ana." He pressed down harder. The blood soaked him. "I'm here. I'm here. I'll protect you, Ana. *Ana!*"

* * *

KANE THRASHED IN THE BED. Ana grabbed him. "Kane!"

He shot upright. *"Ana!"* A bellow.

A *loud* bellow. Jeez, had the Feds heard him outside? Were they about to break down the door?

207

"I'm okay." Her hand flew over his arm. His shoulder. "I think you were having a nightmare."

His head whipped toward her. He blinked. Seemed to be trying to see her in the shadows. Light trickled through the blinds, but it was a faint glow. His hand flew out, and he turned on the lamp. His gaze locked on her fingers. "You're bleeding." Horror whispered in his rough voice.

"No, you are." She turned her hand over. Showed him the blood on her fingertips. "Those stitches. They definitely tore. I warned you about that."

He hauled her against him. Held her in a crushing grip. "Kane?"

He tightened his hold. Seemed as if he would never, ever let go. "I'll protect you."

"What?" She tapped him lightly. "You've got to ease up so I can breathe." A squeak.

He eased up, barely. Then he shuddered and let her go a bit more. Enough so that he could stare down at her. "I will always protect you. I will stand between you and any threat."

"Kane?" A shiver skated down her spine. "You were thrashing around in the bed."

He blinked.

"Did you have a bad dream about me?"

Another blink. His expression shut down.

"What happened to me in the dream?" Ana pushed.

Kane swallowed. "We should go back to sleep."

"*Kane.*"

She heard pounding in the distance. Had to be at the suite's main door. Someone needed to go reassure the Feds before they broke down that door.

"I wasn't there, Ana. The bullets hit you." He exhaled

on a ragged breath. "I will protect you." A vow. "If Logan wants to hurt you, he truly will have to go through *me*."

But...

But if that happened...

Then you could be the one who dies, Kane.

And she couldn't let that happen.

The pounding came again.

"Let's go tell the Feds there is nothing to worry about," Ana murmured. But she had plenty to worry about. Too much.

Because there was no way she'd let Kane take a bullet for her. When you loved someone, you protected the person, no matter what. There was no one in this world that she loved more than Kane.

So she would do whatever it took in order to keep him safe.

Chapter Seventeen

Someone was pounding at the door. Again. Jeez.

Ana cracked open one eye. She discovered a very close-up view of a powerful chest. Mostly because she was sprawled across said chest.

The pounding came again. *Was it the Feds? The agents in the hallway?*

"What in the actual hell?" Kane rumbled. A rumble Ana felt against her ear.

She scooted up, away, and took the sheet with her because she was completely naked. "We have company. Probably our friendly Feds." A squint toward the bedside clock. "Unless it's a delivery. Maybe room service? Breakfast?" The digits on the clock had come into focus for her. "Lunch?" It was later than she'd realized.

The pounding continued. Even more demanding.

"Didn't order room service." Kane jumped from the bed. He stalked, naked, out of the bedroom.

She blinked. His ass was fantastic, but where was he going, totally naked? Ana scrambled out of the bed, but she wrapped the sheet around her. "Kane!" He was moving fast. "Kane!" She followed in his wake.

He stopped near the suite's main door and peered through the peephole. Somewhere between the bed and the door, the man had managed to pick up a gun. No clothing, but he had a gun.

"Bastard," he snarled as he stared through the door.

"Don't open it when you are naked!" He'd at least put on a robe when he reassured the agents outside that all was well before—when he'd woken up bellowing from his nightmare. No way could he go confronting them *naked* now. She rushed across the room and tossed him the jeans that he'd ditched earlier. "Put these on."

He cursed, but Kane put on the jeans. He let go of his gun long enough to haul on the jeans—and to zip and button them—and then the gun was in his hand again, and he was hauling open the door.

"Hello, sleeping beauty," a deep, amused male voice drawled. "Took you long enough. Despite these two Feds out here assuring me that no one had entered your suite, I was starting to think I might have to break down the door just to do a welfare check."

Something about that voice seemed vaguely familiar. Ana crept forward.

"I don't like to tell other people their business," the voice continued, "but, Kane, my friend, you have a rose petal in your hair."

Kane's free hand rose and shoved through his hair. The rose petal fluttered to the floor. Correction, two rose petals fluttered to the floor.

"Rose petals in your hair, and a gun in your grip." Laughter from the man. "Good morning to you. Or, afternoon, considering it's past noon."

"Get inside," Kane ordered. He backed up.

The man entered. Tall and muscled. Dark hair. Steely blue eyes. A face that could have been carved from granite. His eyes swept the room and immediately fell on her. He smiled. "Hi, Ana. Nice to see you again."

See you again.

She sucked in a deep breath.

Kane whirled toward her. His eyes widened. "Ana, shit!" He slapped the gun down on an end table and bounded to her side. No, he bounded in front of her, making his body into a wall that he positioned between her and the new arrival. "You aren't dressed!"

"Very true," Ana agreed. She should dress. "But at least I have a sheet wrapped around me. Until five seconds ago, when I tossed those jeans to you, you were the one answering the door in the raw."

The man who'd entered their suite said, "Oh, jeez. Thanks for saving me from that fate, Ana. A million deep, heart-felt thanks."

Kane grabbed the shirt on the floor—his shirt. The one he'd stripped off previously, and he tugged it over her head. Over her head and over the sheet that she wore.

What. Was. He. Doing?

His shirt swallowed her. And her sheet.

"Covered." Kane nodded. He folded his arms over his chest. "How the hell does Tyler know you?"

Tyler. Tyler Barrett. Because as soon as she'd seen his face and those steely blue eyes, she'd known their visitor's identity.

"Fuck me," Kane breathed. Then he whirled to confront Tyler. "It was *you.*"

Tyler held up his hands. "I feel like there is some

animosity in the room. Shall we take things down a notch or two?"

Kane's hands fell to his sides as he stalked toward Tyler. "*You* took Ana away!"

"Well, if you mean...*I was the US Marshal who escorted her to safety and gave her a new ID.* Then, yes, guilty as charged." Tyler dropped his hands. His gaze raked the room. The floor. He stalked around a glowering Kane and bent to scoop up—wait, what was he scooping up?

Horror rolled through her. Ana felt her cheeks burn.

"I gave her a new identity," Tyler disclosed, "but how was I to know that you were fucking her?" Panties dangled from his fingertips. Torn panties.

Her panties.

The silence in the suite cut like a knife.

"I wasn't fucking her *then,*" Kane growled.

Ana stalked to Tyler. She snatched her panties. "We are fucking *now,*" she clarified with as much dignity as she could muster. Not a lot considering she was wearing a sheet, Kane's shirt, and holding her ripped panties. "You know what?" She pasted a bright smile on her face. "I'm going to shower and get dressed. Maybe one of you could order lunch? I'm starving. And we'll just have our big talk over the meal." Because if Tyler was there, a big talk had to be imminent.

In fact, the US Marshal's presence could only mean one thing.

Gray wants me to leave town. He wants to move me again. He wants to give me a new identity. And if that was the case...

This might be the last day that I see Kane.

She left the room with her shoulders squared, her chin

up, the sheet dragging behind her, and her panties fisted in her hand.

* * *

THE BEDROOM DOOR CLICKED CLOSED. Kane exhaled on a low, hard breath. He also forced his hands to unclench as he confronted his friend. "You embarrassed Ana." A pause. "I should kick the shit out of you for that."

Tyler arched one eyebrow, not appearing even mildly concerned by the threat of an attack. "You can try. But I'm pretty sure I can take you."

Kane shook his head. "You can't."

"Are you certain about that? You're a little bigger, granted, but I fight dirtier."

"Don't count on it." Every instinct he possessed told him to chase after Ana. To throw open that bedroom door and—

Tell her that I love her. Tell her that I will always fight for her. Don't care how dirty I have to fight, I will always protect her.

"Where did the rose petals come from, if you don't mind me asking?"

"Gray is a dick."

"Commonly understood. But where did the rose petals come from?"

"He checked us into the honeymoon suite. The rose petals were here when we arrived. I'm sure that was his doing. Like he hasn't pulled similar BS before with cover stories."

Tyler rocked back on his heels. "The man does believe in authenticity." He cleared his throat. "But I'm thinking

Gray isn't responsible for the clothes I see scattered about or the panties that were ripped nearly in two."

Enough of this shit. Kane moved to stand toe to toe with his friend. He liked Tyler. Screw it. He loved the man like a brother. They'd been Marines, serving in nightmare situations. Tyler had saved his ass more times than Kane could count, just as he'd saved Tyler. They didn't have a blood bond, but some connections went far deeper than blood.

He'd take a bullet for Tyler. Had, in fact. And he knew Tyler would do the same for him any day of the week.

However, there were some things that Kane would not allow. Time for those rules to be established. "Never touch her panties again."

Now both of Tyler's brows shot up.

"Never make her feel uncomfortable. Never say any shit that makes her flee a room again, understand me? What is happening between me and Ana has nothing to do with you."

"Uh, yeah, it does, actually." A wince. "Gray called me in specifically because of what is happening with Ana."

Kane could have sworn the breath froze in his lungs. "You are not taking her away from me." Not again. He could not lose Ana again.

"She can't stay holed up in the honeymoon suite forever."

Kane *knew* that, dammit.

"Gray feels the threat level is too high in this area for her. "

"You are not taking her away from me."

"Big guy, settle down."

Oh, the hell he would *settle down.*

"Gray says as long as you are close to her, you're in danger too."

Screw that. "I don't care about danger."

"Understood. Tell me something I don't know." Tyler pointed toward the hallway. "But you care about her, don't you?"

Hell, yes. *But I didn't tell her. I fucked her again last night. I took her, got lost in her, fed my obsession for her, and even when Ana told me that she loved me...*

He hadn't given her the words back.

Because he—

"You care about her so you get that it will be easier for her to vanish without you right now, yes? I'll take her out of here. I can have her on a plane in forty-five minutes. I can make her vanish. Then you and Gray can take care of the mess here in Mississippi." His hand fell. "Apparently, you both have targets on you just as big as the bull's-eye on your lady. So with her gone, you can know she's safe. You can take out the threat without being distracted. You can march up and down the streets and draw out your enemy. All without worrying about Ana being hurt."

"So that's Gray's new plan? For me to be bait? For him to be bait?" Kane nodded. He much preferred that plan to Ana being at risk. What he didn't prefer...*Losing Ana.* "Where will you take her?" *Tell me. I can go and get her as soon as the danger has passed.*

Tyler's lashes flickered. "I'm not at liberty to tell you that."

"Are you serious right now?"

"Dead serious. What happens if you are compromised? If you know her location, you might reveal it."

"That's not funny, Ty. You know I would *never* betray, Ana. I've never betrayed anyone." He could take torture. He

216

could take hours and hours of pain. He could not take jeopardizing anyone he cared about in this world.

"You wouldn't betray her..." Tyler took a step to the side. His head cocked as he studied Kane. "Because you love her?"

"Love has nothing to do with this!" An angry snarl. And...

Sonofabitch, Ana was in the hallway. How had he not heard the bedroom door open? Yet there she stood. Wet hair. White robe.

Had she taken the fastest shower on record or what? And would he ever forget the stark, hurt look in her eyes? "*Ana.*"

"I was going to ask for a club sandwich for lunch." Brittle. "Could you make that happen, please? And thank you." With that, she turned on her heel. Went back in the bedroom.

He definitely heard the click of the door shutting.

"Oh, yeah," Tyler drawled as he curled his hand around Kane's shoulder. "Love has nothing to do with this. Why don't you try telling that to your *face?* Because, my friend, you look like hell right now."

"Move the hand, Ty."

Tyler moved the hand. "How about I order everyone sandwiches? And you can go get dressed yourself. Not like you can leave the hotel in just your jeans." He looked at his watch. "By the way, Gray wanted me departing in an hour with your Ana. So, time is ticking."

One hour?

One freaking hour?

Without another word, Kane stalked for the bedroom. He didn't knock. He just threw the door open.

Chapter Eighteen

LOVE HAS NOTHING TO DO WITH THIS!

Well, sure, he could have just ripped her heart right out of her chest. Or Kane could have practically yelled those devastating words—which he'd done. Both had the same effect.

He shattered me. Because, for her, love had everything to do with her relationship with Kane.

Ana unbelted her robe. Blinked rapidly and tried to act as if her very soul didn't ache.

The bedroom door flew open and banged against the wall. "We have to talk."

Kane. Sure, he would have followed her. Right. Check. She turned away from him and finished stripping. Bonus, her hands only trembled a bit as she took her clothes from her go bag.

She pulled on new panties. A bra. Hauled on her jeans and a flowing, tunic-style shirt. Then her feet slid into a pair of ballet flats.

Done.

Her hair was still wet. She wore zero makeup. She

should go find a blow dryer, and she should finish getting herself ready for the day. After all, who knew what exciting delights waited for her? Maybe another attempted murder? Or two?

"Ana." Kane touched her shoulder.

She jumped. "You are way too big to move so soundlessly. Don't make me put a bell on you." She spun toward him. "Let me get the blow dryer out of the bathroom." It was probably in there, somewhere. The blow dryers were always hidden in hotel bathrooms. "And then you can shower."

"*Ana.*" A muscle flexed along his jaw. "Let me explain."

"Explain what?" Too bright. Too fake.

"What you *heard.*"

"Oh, you mean when you said love had nothing to do with us? That bit?" She waved the words away. "Not like it's anything I didn't know already. I am quite aware that you don't love me." She'd been quite aware when she gave him the words as they'd been making love, and he hadn't said anything back.

It was making love to me.

It was fucking to him.

"I have no regrets." Ana stared straight into his eyes as she delivered this news. "Zero. I knew what I was doing, and I expected nothing in return from you." Having no regrets didn't mean that she felt no pain. She felt plenty of pain.

"Ana?" His hand lifted, as if he'd touch her, but he didn't. His big hand sort of just hung in the air.

"You didn't love me two years ago. You've barely been back in my life for a few days, and I get that you didn't magically fall in love with me this fast. You want me. I want you. The sex is incredible between us. But I knew it wouldn't last. I knew there was going to be no future relationship between us. This—this moment in time, it's all we have." Because when the threat was over, he'd go back to his life. "I don't even know where you live," she suddenly blurted. The words were the absolute truth. "I don't know what you do when you aren't protecting me. What makes you happy. How you spend your days and your nights. *I don't know.*"

His eyes seemed to see straight through her. "You're right. You don't know."

Okay, that hurt even more. What was she, a glutton for punishment? "The bathroom is yours." Forget drying her hair. She'd go out and take her tattered pride with her.

"No, you're mine."

Uh, say again?

He stalked ever closer to her. The look in his eyes and on his face was just so predatory and possessive and dark that she found herself backing up. A quick retreat even though Ana knew that—physically—Kane would never hurt her. Emotionally? Oh, yes, he'd wreck her emotionally.

Been there, done that.

But you couldn't make someone love you so—

"You are mine," he said again.

Her back hit the wall.

His hands rose and caged her, palms pressing into the wall on either side of her. "And you don't know."

Uh, hadn't she covered that part already? She didn't know what his life was really like when he wasn't protecting her.

"You don't know that I have spent the last two years thinking about you."

Her eyes widened.

"How do I spend my nights? I spend them dreaming about you."

No, he had not said that to her. No way. This was an auditory hallucination. Must be.

"My days? I do protection gigs. I'm strictly freelance because I have a freaking ton of cash that I've amassed over the years. Cash I got from taking some of the most dangerous jobs out there. I only work by referrals now, and those referrals typically come from Gray or Tyler. You see, we all served together years ago. Semper Fi." A growl.

She wet her lips.

His gaze fell to her mouth. He sucked in a breath. Slowly, very, very slowly, his gaze rose to catch her stare once again. "Always faithful," he murmured.

Yes, yes, she knew what Semper Fi meant.

"That's what I've been since the first time I met you."

Ana shook her head, not understanding.

"I'm a damn liar, sweetheart."

She wanted to retreat more, but he'd trapped her. Maybe she could duck under one of his arms and run past him.

"I've lied to you before. And I just lied my ass off to Tyler two minutes ago. Because love has everything to do with the current situation. At least, where you are concerned."

There was no way Ana was hearing him correctly. No. Way. She went back to her auditory hallucination theory.

"I met you two years ago. You were scared and brave and funny and so vulnerable at the same time. I wanted to take you away. I wanted to eliminate every threat to you. But I knew it was the wrong time. You were living on nerves and terror, and the last thing you needed was me telling you that I'd live and die for you."

Ana blinked.

"But here's the truth." He leaned in closer. "I would live and die for you."

Ana could not breathe.

"My nights are spent dreaming of you. My days? When I'm not fighting, hunting, protecting and serving, and doing the whole life-or-death drama bit—hell, even when I *am* on missions and working cases, I still think of you. I wonder if you're happy. I wonder if you're playing music. I wonder if you're smiling. Because, you see, Ana, I've been faithful to you since we met. It's why I snuck around to see you. It's why I'm here right now, telling you...*You will always be safe.* Because you are my main mission in this world. Your safety is what matters most to me."

She had no words.

He stared into her eyes. Gazed at her with stark possession and need and savage hunger and...love? Was he staring at her with love? Had he *always* been doing it and she hadn't seen the truth?

"It's because you matter so much, sweetheart, that I have to say..." Kane shoved away from the wall. "Repack that go bag. Your sweet ass is leaving town with Tyler. You will not be threatened. I *will* put Logan Catalano in the ground for you." Then he turned, marched into the bathroom, and shut the door behind him.

Her mouth was still hanging open when she heard the thunder of the shower turning on.

* * *

"I THOUGHT YOU WERE STARVING." Tyler frowned at her. "You've barely poked at your club sandwich."

She'd poked. Taken some bites. Managed to choke them down. They felt like lead in her stomach.

Meanwhile, Tyler and Kane had both gobbled up three sandwiches already. Three. Each.

She was busy staring at Kane when she should have been eating.

Her hair was dry. She'd applied some makeup—makeup made her look less terrorized and sleep deprived and a little more in control. She'd repacked her go bag.

Except Ana didn't actually intend to go anywhere.

Tyler checked his watch. His wedding ring caught the light, and the gold band gleamed. "Why don't you try to eat a little more, Ana? Then you and I will go meet our ride." He sent her a reassuring smile. "Before the sun sets tonight, you are going to be safe."

Uh, huh. "Safe in a new life. With a new name. In a new place."

"It's a good place," he hurried to note.

Was it? How wonderful. She took a sip of her water and carefully put the glass back on the table. Her hands then dipped beneath the table. "I'm assuming that Kane is not accompanying me to this, ah, good place?"

"No." From Tyler.

"No." From Kane. Spoken in near perfect sync with Tyler. "I'm not even going to know where you're going."

Well, why the hell not? Her fingers fisted beneath the table. Enough of this bullshit. Her eyes narrowed as she glared at Kane. "So you basically tell me that you love me one moment. Then you tell me to get my sweet ass out of your life in the next second."

Tyler had raised his glass of water to his lips. At her words, he choked. Sputtered.

Kane reached out a hand and slapped him on the back.

"Thanks," a gasp from Tyler. "Went down the wrong way."

Ana didn't look at Tyler. Her focus remained on the man who seemed determined to drive her to the brink of sanity. "That's called giving mixed messages, Kane, and in case no one has ever told you before, it's extremely uncool."

His lips parted.

"You don't tell a woman you would live and die for her and then announce that she has to get lost. Super rude. Super confusing."

"This feels like a really personal conversation," Tyler mumbled.

"As personal as picking panties up off the floor?" Ana returned sweetly. "Sorry, Tyler, but you're part of the discussion. Especially seeing as how you're the man who is going to whisk me away."

"Yeah, that whisking is supposed to happen in the next five minutes." He cleared his throat. "Tick, tock."

Ana exhaled. "It's not happening."

Kane leapt to his feet. His hands gripped the table. They'd been sitting at the tall, square table in the suite. He gripped the edges and leaned toward her. "Oh, it is happening."

"I don't think that Tyler is the type to kidnap a woman. To tie her up, toss her over his shoulder, and make off with her in the middle of the day."

"Don't be so sure about that," Tyler retorted. "You have no idea how my wife tests me."

What? But Ana just waved him away, for now. "Kane, though? Badass Kane Harte who uses his motorcycle to block a fleeing woman? *He'd do it.*"

Tyler exhaled. "Oh, I'm sure he would. In a heartbeat. Totally seems like his style."

Kane leaned toward her even more.

She jumped to her feet. And leaned toward him. Since she was nowhere near his size, her lean wasn't nearly as intimidating as his.

"You were *fleeing*," Kane reminded her. "As in...leaving town. That was when I stopped you with my motorcycle. And, by the way, fleeing the area was your original plan. We are simply going back to it now. You don't get to argue when it was *your* plan!"

"I can argue anytime!" A huff. "And the plan has changed. Everything has changed since that day."

"Why? Don't you still want to protect your friends? Aren't you still worried that they will be threatened if you stay here?"

"I'm worried they will be threatened if I leave! I'm worried Logan will turn his attention on Zuri." She had to call Zuri and let her know that she was all right. Ana was sure the shooting at her house had made the news. Where in the hell even was her phone? It hadn't been in the go bag. Ana was highly suspicious that Gray had confiscated her phone. "I'm also worried Logan will come hard after you, Kane. He tried to kill you with that hail of gunfire, and he'll come at you again. Especially if you are the red flag that is just waved in front of him when I'm gone."

Kane eased back. The man shrugged.

She wanted to scream. "I happen to care if you live or die."

"Good." That was it. Just that grunt from Kane.

He was clearly trying to make her insane. "You aren't facing the threat alone!"

"Baby, I am used to handling threats. It's what I do. You're not used to them. You're used to playing music and teaching yoga and driving that cute-ass Jeep around town with your army of ducks near the front window. You don't need to face off with Logan. He will hurt you."

"The plan was to use me as bait! Gray's plan, remember?"

"Ahem." Tyler cleared his throat. Loudly.

She whipped her head toward him.

"I believe that was Gray's plan *before* you were nearly fed to sharks. And before Gray realized that he and Kane were targets, too. Now they are the bait, and you're the witness that I am about to relocate out of town." Tyler's lips pulled down. "Our five minutes are probably up. Let's take your sandwich to go."

"I am not going *anywhere*." How much clearer did she need to be? "I ran before. Logan escaped prison and came after me. I'm done running."

"Ana." Kane spoke her name softly. Almost sadly. He slowly exhaled. "You were right."

Her head turned back toward him.

"I would kidnap you." Said with zero remorse or regret. "I'd handcuff you. I'd throw that sweet ass over my shoulder, and I'd take you out of here. I'd put you in Tyler's vehicle, and I'd make sure that you got out of town and to a safe location. See, that's why I told you that you didn't really want to be with me. Because I'm an asshole. A bastard to the core. I would kidnap you and never have a single regret."

She marched around the table. Stabbed a finger into his powerful chest. "Oh, be sure, I would make you have regrets."

"You'd be alive, sweetheart, and that's the only thing that matters to me."

"Uh, excuse me," Tyler interrupted.

"*You* matter to me," Ana snapped at Kane as she

ignored Tyler. "Do you get that? Did you miss it when I told you that I loved you last night? You know, when you were giving me the nonstop orgasms and I was holding onto you for dear life?"

"I should not be here," Tyler said. "Should not be."

Kane's eyes glinted. "I didn't miss it. I never miss a damn thing about you. But I do get weak when you're near me."

She sucked in a breath. "What?"

"The only reason that prick Logan is still breathing? Because I didn't want you to see what a monster I can be. So I stopped. I didn't pull the trigger even though your blood was soaking your shirt." Rage vibrated in his words. He backed away. No, correction, moved away. Moved a good five feet from her.

Ana's hand fell back to her side as she stared at him.

His nostrils flared as Kane continued, "And when we were at your place and you were playing the harp, I was so caught up in you that I didn't see the warning signs. I should have heard that truck approaching sooner. I should have realized I was presenting a target. *We* were presenting one. I was slow, and you almost paid the price for my inattention."

"You were the one who got cut by the glass! And no one got shot."

"Not that time. But if you're close, I am weak."

That was just—that was—

"You have to leave so I can stay safe."

She bit her lower lip. Swallowed.

Silence.

Kane kept staring at her. "You leave. I do my job."

"And then what?" Ana asked. "You come and find me and we live happily ever after? That how it's all going to be in the end? I wait where it's safe. You take the risks. Then you come for me?"

"If you want me, I will always come to find you."

"Wanting you has never been a problem for me. It's the loving you that has hurt." She stiffened her spine. "Because in the end, it comes down to this—you don't trust me."

"What?" He blinked. Took one more step away from her.

"You don't trust me. You didn't trust me two years ago because you didn't think my feelings were real. And I suspect you feel the same way now—that if I see you do something that's too dark or dangerous, I'll turn away from you. That I won't love you anymore. Newsflash. That's not how real love works. With real love, you love the person completely. Dark spots and light."

"You didn't love Logan when you found out what he really was."

She sucked in a breath. "You're not Logan. You're not a demented killer who gets off on someone else's pain."

"I am a killer. I'm a liar. I'm a cold-blooded bastard. You deserve far better than someone like me."

"I happen to think you're a hero. A fighter. A good man who has needed to do bad things." Screw this. She advanced toward him.

"I should have waited in the hallway with the Feds," Tyler muttered. He reached for her mid-advance, trying to stop her before she reached Kane. "Ana, we have to go. Your transport is waiting outside the hotel."

Fine. Fine. *Right. Whatever. The transport. The big escape run. Yes, got it.* She shrugged off Tyler's hand and finished making her way to Kane. She tossed her hair over her shoulder and demanded, "Do you think—for one, single second—that Logan has ever protected anyone in this world?"

His lips remained firmly closed. That was an answer, wasn't it?

"Do you think—for one, single second—that Logan has ever fought to protect innocents? Do you think he's taken bullets for anyone? Do you think he's willingly stepped into hell in order for someone else to survive? Do you think he has ever made a sacrifice for someone else? Ever put someone else's safety over his own?"

Kane's lips pressed together. A bit harder. Tighter.

"He hasn't," Ana informed Kane. Her hand lifted. Pressed to the softness of his beard. She freaking loved that beard. *I freaking love him.* "But you have. Over and over, you have. You're doing it again, right now. Sending me away so that I'll be safe while you take all the risks."

"Told you." Gruff. "I can just fight better when you aren't near. You distract me."

"You distract me, too. Full disclosure, you also infuriate me." She pulled in another deep breath. He hadn't said the big words yet, not exactly. Not actually said, *I love you.* But he'd come close. He'd told her, *I'd live and die for you.* Those deep and dark words that had completely made the planets realign for her. Because when Kane said those words, she knew what he meant. So Ana threw caution to the winds, and she flatly announced, "You love me." There. Done. Bold as could be.

She waited for a denial. None came.

But his head did turn. His mouth brushed over her fingers.

A sensual charge poured through her entire body.

"You loved me two years ago," she whispered. "Yet you still sent me away."

His gaze held hers. So many emotions swirled in his hazel stare.

"You love me now," she realized with utter and complete certainty. "And you're still sending me away."

"Because you have to be safe. Sending you away is the best way to ensure your protection. If you're not safe, then I'm not sane."

Tyler cleared his throat. Poor guy. How many times had he cleared it already? He also heaved a sigh. "We have to go, Ana. My phone is blowing up with texts from Gray."

It was? She hadn't noticed. If there had been any telltale dings as the texts arrived, she'd missed them.

"Turner made bail," Tyler revealed. "Gray wants to tail him. He wants Kane there with him, and our ride—as in, yours and mine because I'm your escort—is waiting outside. We have to go."

She didn't want to leave Kane. She wanted to spend the rest of her life with him.

"I'll always come to you," Kane told her. "Nothing could keep me away."

Tears filled her eyes, and Ana had to blink quickly. "I'm holding you to that promise." One hundred percent, she was. Ana did not want to leave him. She didn't want Kane facing the threat without her. She wanted to grab Kane and run *with* him.

But...

She understood.

She did.

He was worried about her. He couldn't track Logan and guard her at the same time. Couldn't hunt and protect at once. She was leaving. The only reason she was leaving, though, was because she couldn't protect *him*. She didn't have fighting skills. Hadn't been trained by the military and special ops. Lethal fighting and operational deployment were not exactly her skill sets. So she would back away. She would allow him to focus. She would hate it with every breath in her body, but Ana didn't intend to make the situation harder on anyone.

"Come for me, Kane. I'll be waiting for you." Ana surged up onto her toes and threw her arms around him even as Kane was reaching down for her. He lifted her up. Kissed her frantically. Deep. Hard. Passionately.

"Jeez." A disgruntled exclamation from Tyler. "I'd tell you two that you should get a room, but, apparently, you had one."

Kane let her go. Slowly. Her feet touched the floor. Then he...

He reached into his back pocket. He wore jeans. A blue button-down. He pulled a wallet from his pocket and reached inside.

Kane handed her a worn, folded piece of paper. Voice gruff, he explained, "My mom—she was always big on me writing notes to people. An old-school stickler about things like that."

Ana frowned at the paper, turning it over in her hands.

"Thank you notes. Apology notes."

Surprised, her gaze rose to collide with his.

"I was serious when I said I'd write a note to the doc, apologizing for being an ass." A sheepish smile flashed on his lips. "My mom would haunt me forever if I didn't." The smile vanished. "After you got your new life two years ago, I wrote you a note."

Her grip tightened on the paper.

"Two years ago," he repeated. "You wonder how I felt then? It's in the note."

"A note you never sent."

"Yeah, mom would not be pleased with me."

Her lower lip wanted to tremble, so she clamped her lips together.

"I considered getting Gray to give it to you a dozen times. But then I always thought..." He rolled his shoulders in a shrug that was far from casual. "Some things are just better delivered in person. So I'd drive by your place every now and then, hoping to get a glimpse of you."

Tyler had backed away. She didn't spare him a glance.

"That's what kept me going. You. Glimpses of you." Kane clasped his hands behind his back. "I'd live and die for you, Ana."

She almost crumpled the note in her fierce grip. "Don't you *dare* do the dying part. I will be super pissed if you die on me."

"Fine. I'll live for you, baby, and I'll kill for you, too." His hand rose. Skimmed over her jaw. "See you soon, sweetheart. That's a promise."

Chapter Nineteen

ANA HAS TO BE SAFE. THIS IS THE BEST OPTION FOR HER safety.

Ana slipped into the backseat of a nondescript SUV. She didn't look back. Probably because she didn't know that he'd snuck down to the parking garage and was watching her from behind a large stone column like the freaking stalker that he was.

Tyler climbed into the back of the vehicle after her. The driver shot away, the brake lights flashing as they turned and then...

Gone.

Ana was gone again.

But Kane would get her back. This wasn't a forever gone.

He *would* get her back.

His phone vibrated again. The thing had been vibrating the whole time he'd been talking with Ana. Gray hadn't just been texting Tyler. He'd been sending his messages to Kane, too.

Kane pulled out his phone and swiped his finger across the screen. The most recent text jumped out at him.

Where in the hell are you, Kane? Call. Stat.

He called his friend. Put the phone to his ear. It was answered on the second ring.

"What the fuck?" Gray said by way of greeting. "I sent you ten messages!"

"Ana just left with Tyler."

"Oh." Then. "Oh." A pause. "You okay?"

Not even close. "What's our move?"

"Our move? Um, I'm currently in a car trailing Turner Mitchell. Looks like the guy is headed to his dojo. We had agents search his house and dojo while he was being held in custody."

Kane wasn't sure that search had been entirely legal, but he wasn't going to question the situation. For all he knew, maybe Gray had gotten search warrants. Whatever. He'd let his Fed buddy handle the legal side of things. That was Gray's job, after all.

"We searched, but there was no sign of Logan." Gray seemed damn disgruntled. "Not at either location. But maybe they're planning a meet-up right now. Maybe this is our chance to grab Logan. Turner isn't alone, just so you know. His lawyer is driving Turner. Kyle Sanchez? I think I mentioned him before."

Yeah, he had. Sanchez was the lawyer who was also connected to Logan. Check.

"Sanchez flew in from New York and started raising hell in order to get Turner released. Now they are heading fast and hard for the dojo. Arrival is imminent."

"Then I'll meet you at the dojo." His motorcycle had been stashed nearby, thanks to the Feds.

"Try not to come in with your motor roaring, would you? We're going for stealth here."

If stealth was what he was after, his buddy was talking to the wrong man. Rage poured through Kane's veins. He wanted to attack and destroy. Not pull some stealth BS.

"Kane?" A note of worry. "You okay?" Gray asked again.

"I'm not losing her a second time." Flat.

"Hell. You are *not* okay."

No, he wasn't okay. He was in the mood to kick the shit out of Ana's murderous ex.

Agenda items...

Track down Logan Catalano.

Destroy him.

Love Ana forever.

Done.

* * *

"You're doing the right thing, Ana." Tyler sat beside her in the back of the SUV. All focused and certain and, well, typical Tyler.

Tyler Barrett had always struck her as a very grown-up, very intense Boy Scout type. The good guy. A good guy with a spine of steel.

"You'll be safe. Kane and Gray can apprehend Logan, and soon, the danger will be over."

He was clearly trying to be reassuring. Only she didn't feel reassured. She felt sick to her stomach. "Why does it feel like I'm abandoning him?"

"You're not." Immediate.

It still felt as if she was. She got it—she wasn't a

professional. Or semi-professional or *anything* close to the super fighters all around her. "You were a Marine, too?"

"Yes." Just that. No more.

Her head turned toward him even as she continued to clutch the letter Kane had given to her. "You served with Kane."

A nod. "You're right about him. He's a good man. Has a heart as big as the rest of him. That 'Heartless' nickname? I've always thought it was pure bullshit. He can pretend to be cold, but if know him well, you get that ice never flows through his veins."

A lump threatened to choke her. She swallowed it down. After three attempts. "For two years, I thought he'd forgotten all about me." Then he'd come roaring back into her life on that big, black motorcycle of his.

"There are some people that you just can't ever forget."

She looked down at the letter in her hand.

Tyler leaned forward. He tapped the driver's shoulder. "Hey, Wayne. Hurry up and get us to the airport."

Ana unfurled the letter. Her fingers pressed over the creases. Had Kane really written her a note two years ago?

Dear Ana,

I'm sorry that I am not there with you right now. But at my core, I'm a cold-blooded bastard, and you need more than me in your life. I'll drag you into the dark, and you belong in the light. Hell, you are the light. At least, you are to me.

You told me that you were falling in love with me. When you said those words, all I wanted to do was grab onto you and never, ever let go—

A motorcycle raced past their vehicle, the engine growling. Her head whipped up. She looked to the left and caught a fast glimpse of Kane as he rushed by the SUV.

And all she wanted to do was chase after him.

Instead, she swallowed, and her gaze dropped back to the note.

When you said those words, all I wanted to do was grab onto you and never, ever let go, but I couldn't do that. You've been with a monster. You've been running. You've been scared. You need peace, and you need a normal life. Or as close to normal as you can get.

So I didn't grab tight to you. I didn't tell you that I loved you from the first moment you smiled at me. That I loved you when you curled up with me on the couch and watched all the old horror movies that made you shudder but kept you distracted from the real nightmare that was stalking you.

I walked away, fled the damn motel room, and because of that, you were hurt. I'm sorry, Ana. So sorry that you were hurt. I will do everything in my power to make sure that you never hurt again. When you hurt, I hurt.

I wanted to kill Logan. When I saw your blood, the world stopped. The only thing that pulled me back from the brink was you.

But in that moment, I understood how dangerous I truly was. You don't need more danger. You don't need to be dragged into the dark.

You need more light. You need the light to shine even brighter.

So I'm staying away. I'm doing what someone who loves you should really do...let you live the life you want. Let you have all the joy that you deserve.

I'm sorry that I'm not with you right now.

I'm sorry that I never told you that I love you.

But you deserve more than me, Ana. So much more.

I'm a liar. I'm a killer. I'm a man you should not have in your life.

And I am a man who will love you until I die.

Yours,
Kane

Her breath shuddered out. "Bastard."

"Uh, Ana?"

She carefully refolded the paper. "He loved me two years ago." Her head turned toward Tyler. "He loves me now."

"Yes, I figured that out." He ran a finger over the bridge of his nose.

"He's not going to find me when the danger is over."

A furrow appeared between Tyler's brows. "I'm sure that he is. He said he would."

"Kane Harte is a liar."

Tyler didn't argue.

"He said that he'd come for me—he said that just to get me to leave, didn't he?"

"I don't know." Tyler seemed genuinely uncertain.

Her shoulders squared. "He's your friend."

"Yes."

"You served with him in the Marines."

"Yes."

"You know where he lives."

"I—yes?"

She smiled at him. "Good. Then when the danger is over, you'll tell me exactly where to find Kane. If he won't come to me, I'll go to him."

His lips snapped closed.

"I'll go to him," she repeated with determination. "Because I love him, and I don't care if Kane thinks he's good enough for me or not. *I want him. I love him. I choose him.*" Always.

* * *

"TURNER and the lawyer just went inside the dojo." Gray glanced toward the small, squat building from his position on the opposite side of the street. A dark blue SUV waited near Gray, partially concealing his body. *How many SUVs do the Feds have at the ready?* But Kane didn't ask that question because Gray fired out, "They went inside about ten minutes ago. Got eyes on the front of the place and the rear. They went in, and no one has exited since then."

Kane assessed the perimeter. Large glass windows made up the front of the dojo's building, but through the glass, he could see no one. No sign of movement at all.

"They must have gone into the back office," Gray decided. "They hauled ass here for a reason." He shifted slightly. "I think that reason is Logan Catalano."

"You believe Logan is *inside* that building?"

Gray glanced his way. "It's certainly a possibility. Before Turner was released today, I gave him my number. Told him that if he wanted to stay alive, he'd call me the minute he put his eyes on Logan. That I would be willing to work a deal with him in exchange for Turner giving up that jerk."

Kane surged toward his friend as rage churned hard in his gut. "Turner tried to *kill* Ana, and you offered him a deal?" Fuck that!

"I'm after Logan. He is the end mission on this case. Logan Catalano is the man pulling the strings. He's the one we have to stop, and, yes, sometimes, you have to slither with the freaking snakes in order to get shit done. It's the way of the world."

It wasn't the way that Kane worked. "So you're just gonna stand out here and you're gonna wait for a call? That's the plan? If so, it's total bullshit. Turner is not gonna be calling you up and just offering Logan to you on a silver platter—"

The ringing of Gray's phone cut through Kane's snarling words.

Gray smiled at him. Then he lifted his phone and swiped his finger over the screen. "Grayson Stone." He'd put the call on speaker.

"You come in. Only you."

Gray blinked.

That wasn't Turner Mitchell's voice.

"Logan?" Gray barked. "Logan Catalano?"

"I see you outside, Agent Stone. You're rather obvious. So is your whole crew. You want me? You want to take me down so badly? Then come in. Only you."

Kane's entire body tensed. His head whipped toward the building. All of the gleaming glass windows stared back at him. Still no sign of any movement inside.

"Screw that crap," Kane growled.

Gray immediately swiped his left hand in the air, indicating for Kane to stay quiet. The black brace still covered his wrist and part of his forearm.

Sure, Kane got that Gray wanted him to settle down and shut the hell up. *Again, screw that.*

Kane took a step toward the dojo.

"If anyone else comes inside, I'll have to kill Turner. Not that I particularly mind the task. The man is a failure, after all. But I'll have to kill him. The lawyer, too," Logan added, almost as an afterthought.

Gray stepped into Kane's path.

Kane had already stilled.

"But maybe you don't care if they live or die," Logan mused. "I'm sure your friend...ah, Kane, I believe, would be quite happy to see Turner lose his life. That is him I see with you, isn't it?"

Kane didn't move. Not a muscle.

"And lawyers? I mean, come on, this one is as crooked as they come. Seriously, I'm speaking from personal experience." Laughter. "But, hey, what if they aren't the only ones inside? What if I have someone...*else* inside? Someone who is a friend to my sweet Anastasia?"

"Who else is inside?" Gray demanded at once.

"Come on in and find out." Laughter. "Only you, though. You come in—you come inside within the next two minutes, unarmed, alone, and we'll work out a deal. Otherwise, I think I'll have to start killing people."

A car door slammed.

Kane jerked at the sound, and he saw Emerson rushing away from a sedan.

"You tried to shut me out!" she accused as red stained her cheeks. She barreled toward Gray.

Kane reached out and snagged her, locking his arm around her waist and lifting Emerson off her feet. She elbowed him and twisted her upper body to stare at him as if he'd lost his mind.

"Oh, is that the lovely Dr. Marlowe? Now it's just a party." Logan's voice was oddly delighted. "Do tell her how much I enjoyed our sessions. Maybe we'll be chatting again. Soon." A beat of silence. "Two minutes and counting, and then people start dying." He hung up.

Kane released Emerson. She staggered forward as soon as her feet hit the pavement again. "What is happening?"

Gray tightened his grip on the phone. He glanced toward the dojo. "Agent Johnson!"

A young guy with light brown hair hustled toward Gray.

"Trace this number." Gray rattled off the number that had appeared on his screen. "I want to know who owns the phone."

"On it." Johnson sprinted away.

Gray tucked the phone back into his pocket even as he kept staring at the dojo.

"Don't do it," Kane fired immediately. "It's a trap." Obviously. "You go in there, and you die." He believed that with utter certainty—and that was why there was no way he was gonna let his friend step inside that dojo alone. Alone and unarmed? Oh, hell, no.

"I'm a federal agent." Gray moved to the side, making his whole body visible as he removed the shoulder holster that he'd been wearing. He placed it on the hood of the SUV. *To show Logan that he's removing his weapon.* "If I don't go in, people will die. I can't let that happen." He rolled back his shoulders. The brace on his broken wrist was clearly visible. "It's not who I am."

Yeah, right. Kane knew exactly who Gray was. His friend was the true-blue hero. Always had been. The guy would sacrifice himself to save the world.

And I'd burn it to ashes if it meant I could protect the people I love.

"You can't go inside." Emerson grabbed Gray's non-broken hand. Held tightly. "Is that what you're thinking? You're going in there, alone? No way. You *can't.* You know Logan wants you dead! I told you before that he was after revenge."

"He has at least two people in there with him." Gray frowned down at her hand. "Maybe even a third individual. He said something about Ana's friend." An exhale. "I go in, unarmed, alone, and we make a deal. I can get the others out safely."

"No!" Emerson was clearly horrified. "You go in and you *die!* No one will be safe in there."

Kane nodded. "Damn straight. Listen to the shrink."

But Gray shook his head. "I know the risks. I also know my job." A deep breath from Gray. "I go in alone—

Forget that shit. He was done arguing. Kane pulled his fist back and slammed it into Gray's jaw. He didn't pull the punch, not even a little bit.

Emerson screamed. "What are you doing?"

Gray crumpled. Guy had a glass jaw. Normally, Gray could defend himself from a punch pretty well. This time, there was no defense, probably because Gray hadn't expected the attack.

Kane grabbed Gray's phone even as Emerson crouched over Gray. He dialed back the number that had just called.

"What the fuck?" Logan snarled when he answered.

"Change of plans, asshole." Kane didn't identify himself. If Logan was inside, he'd see Kane. Kane was standing there, after all, big and bright as day. "I'm coming in. You want a deal? You talk to me. I come inside. You let the other two bastards go. If you really have one of Ana's friends in there, you let that person go, too. If that doesn't work for you, then, hey, how about this option? How about I send in a swarm of federal agents, and they can shoot up the place? That good for you?"

Gray let out a groan as his eyelashes fluttered.

"Because I'm not Gray," Kane bit out each word. "I don't care about following rules. I don't care about Turner or the lawyer. All I care about—"

"Is *my Anastasia*?" Logan finished quietly.

"She's not yours." Rage nearly choked him.

"We'll see about that." Mocking. "I'd had other plans for you but...come inside. Now. *You and Gray*. Get your friend off the ground. Come inside, and we'll make a deal. Come inside!"

Something hit Kane from behind. Not something, someone. He turned and realized Gray had just slammed his shoulder into Kane's back.

"Asshole, that was a low blow!" Gray snapped.

Actually, it had been an uppercut.

"Come inside," Logan bellowed, "or I will slit their throats right now!"

Gray stared at Kane. Kane stared at Gray. Then they looked at the entrance to the dojo. They squared their shoulders. And started to advance.

So this is what it feels like to walk straight into a trap.

But...

Gray snatched the phone from him. "Proof of life," he barked. His jaw was dark red from the punch. "Give us proof of life right the hell now. You want us inside so badly? Then let me talk to Turner. Or the lawyer. Or Ana's friend—"

"Zuri?" Laughter from Logan. "I'm afraid she can't come to the phone right now. She's all tied up. And you will talk to *no one* else. Not Turner. Not the lawyer. Not until you get your asses inside. I want to see you both. Face to face." More rough laughter. "You know what? I think the two minutes are up. Time for me to kill a bastard."

Once again, the line went dead.

"Uh, Agent Stone?"

Gray whirled on the brown-haired agent who'd approached him. "What, Johnson?"

"It's, ah, I traced the number, sir. Like you asked. The phone that called you? It's...it's registered to a Zuri Harris."

Gray's head sagged forward. "This just went from bad to clusterfuck status."

Kane knew there was no choice. They were going in the dojo.

Chapter Twenty

"May I borrow your phone?" Ana asked.

Tyler frowned at her. They'd just arrived at the airport. They were still outside, right next to the vehicle.

"I need to call my friend Zuri." Her fingers strummed nervously at her side, playing a tune on a harp that wasn't there. *Get control. Everything is going to be okay.* At least, she hoped things would be all right. "I want to tell her that I'm leaving town."

"No, Ana."

Yes, Tyler. "She'll be so worried about me! The shooting at my house must have made the news. Please, Tyler, I'm sure you have some burner phone somewhere close by." Didn't all these government types have untraceable phones somewhere? "Let me use it. Let me tell my friend that I'm okay. Just that I'm all right so she won't worry. I can't just vanish on her without a word." She had to let her friend know that she was safe. Otherwise, Zuri would worry herself to death.

Zuri and my clients. Ana would need to get someone to

cover her music therapy sessions. She'd need someone to take over the yoga classes. She'd need someone to—

Take over my life.

Because she was leaving everything behind. Again.

Tyler reached into his pocket. "Burner," he muttered. "I do happen to have one. Make it fast, all right? Do not mention you're at the airport. Say nothing about me."

Yes, yes, she got it. Ana dialed quickly. Her breath held as she waited for Zuri to pick up the call. Was her friend at the restaurant? Probably, but Zuri usually had her phone nearby even when she was working. The phone rang once.

Twice.

And—

The phone was answered. Only no one said a word. Maybe she had a bad connection. "Zuri?" Ana prompted, frantic because she didn't have much time. "Zuri, I need you to listen."

"No, my Anastasia. I need *you* to listen."

The phone nearly slipped from her fingers when she heard Logan's voice. "Logan?" She grabbed for Tyler's hand.

He'd already spun back toward her.

"Your boyfriend is dead, Anastasia. He's a dead man walking right now." Laughter. "And Zuri will be dead soon, too. Unless you do exactly what I say. Do you understand me, Anastasia? Are you *listening* to me?"

"Put it on speaker," Tyler snapped.

"Kane's not dead!" Ana yelled at the same instant.

"Boom, boom," Logan taunted. "The bigger they are, the more pieces they explode into."

Her eyes widened in horror. "Bomb!" Ana yelled at Tyler. "There's a bomb! Get Kane! Call him—call Gray, call—"

Crap, she had Tyler's phone! He couldn't call when she had his phone gripped in her hand. Did Tyler have another one on him? A regular, non-burner phone? Or was he just using the burner while he was moving her to a secure location?

The driver of the SUV ran up to them. He threw his phone to Tyler.

"Don't hurt Kane, please," Ana begged. "You don't have to hurt anyone!"

"Too late for him." Logan was smug. "Too late, too late."

No, no, no! "Let Zuri go," Ana pleaded. "You don't even know her. Please, don't hurt her, don't hurt Kane, don't hurt anyone! Don't!"

"Get that sweet ass home right now, Anastasia. *Right the fuck now.* If you come to me, then maybe I'll spare Zuri. Or maybe you'll just find her dead body dumped near your harp. Get away from any guards. No one but you comes in the house, understand? Go *home.*"

Fear and fury battled within Ana. "You hurt Kane, you hurt Zuri, and I will *kill* you."

"*Boom, boom,*" he taunted, and the line went dead.

She leapt toward Tyler. "Stop Kane! Whatever he's doing, stop him! Please, please!"

Tyler had the phone to his ear.

She was still clutching his burner, so she started dialing frantically on it. Calling Kane. He'd given her his number the first night he'd come to Gulfport and stayed at the house with her. Made her memorize it. Had Tyler called Kane or Gray? Ana dialed and waited and prayed and she—

* * *

GRAY'S PHONE WAS RINGING.

They were right at the glass doors of the dojo. Gray's phone was ringing.

And Kane finally saw movement inside. The faintest movement. He squinted. Something was on the floor.

Someone?

About ten feet away from the windows, someone was sprawled on the floor.

Kane's phone rang, too. Fuck. He ignored it, just as Gray was ignoring his ringing phone, too.

Gray reached for the door. He hauled it open, and the bell above the door gave a bright and happy jingle.

Kane felt the weight of his gun pressing into his back. Hell, no, he hadn't gone in without a weapon. He'd never even pretended to remove his gun. As for Gray, Kane knew his buddy had a backup weapon strapped to his ankle. Gray always had a backup.

Gray walked over the threshold. "What the hell...?" he began.

The phones had stopped ringing.

Stopped for a moment and then...Kane's phone rang again.

And in that same instant—

"Two men down," Gray bellowed. "It's Turner and the lawyer—both bleeding and unconscious. Shit. *Shit!*"

Kane still held the door open. He started to rush fully inside even as Gray dropped to his knees near the fallen men. Kane took a step—

"*Get out!*" A terrified, feminine scream.

He glanced over his shoulder, following the sound of that scream.

Emerson raced toward them. She clutched a phone in her hand. *"Get out! Tyler says there is a bomb in there! Get out!"*

But...

If there was a bomb...

Kane's head whipped toward Gray. Horror covered Gray's face. But...but Gray wasn't staring at Kane. Gray was staring above him. At the bell above the door. Kane looked up. He saw the wires shooting out from that bell.

He still held the door open. He'd grabbed it after Gray entered, preventing the door from closing. Preventing the bell from ringing a second time.

Tricky bastard. The first ring armed the bomb. The second—it will make it explode, won't it? Only the bell hadn't chimed a second time. Not yet.

Not. Yet.

"Get out!" Emerson screamed.

It was too late for that. Kane remained exactly where he was. "Emerson, don't take another step!" Angry, sharp. He didn't look back to see if she followed his command.

He kept his eyes on Gray.

Neither of them were experts on demolitions. Not by a long shot. But they'd both seen the damage bombs could create. And in the course of their missions, Kane had picked up some knowledge that had saved his ass a time or two.

"It's armed, isn't it?" Kane asked Gray.

Gray nodded. "I think I armed it the minute I opened the door."

That was Kane's suspicion, too.

"I didn't check—I should have looked up—*so fucking sorry.*" Rage and guilt twisted in Gray's voice.

"I caught the door before it could swing shut." Kane was still holding that freaking door even as he felt sweat slide down his back. "And that is going to buy you time."

"Kane..." Gray leapt to his feet and advanced toward him.

"No." Kane shook his head. "Do not come closer to me." A quick exhale. "Are the two men still alive?"

"Yeah, yeah, stabbed to hell and back, but I think they're both breathing. For now."

"Find another way out. See if the back door is clear. You can drag them out if that works."

Logan isn't inside the dojo any longer. Tricky SOB. He'd been there before, clearly, in order to stab the lawyer and Turner, but he'd made an exit. He'd escaped without alerting the Feds.

Had he been watching from nearby? We thought he was in the dojo, but he had another way out, and he was out there, had to be very close by, waiting and watching and taunting until Gray and I came inside.

Without a word, Gray turned. He pulled the backup gun from his ankle and disappeared into the back area of the dojo.

Kane remained where he was. The bomb was above his head. For all he knew, it could go off at any moment. Especially if Logan was still close, watching, playing with them. If he was close, then Logan could trigger the bomb remotely. In that case, it wouldn't matter if that stupid bell above the door chimed again or not. The bomb could go off, and Kane would be blown straight to hell.

His phone rang again.

* * *

"He's not answering!" Ana knew she was practically screaming but she couldn't help herself. People turned and gaped at her, but she ignored them. Her entire world was falling apart.

Tyler caught her arm. "I reached Emerson. Gray gave

me her number. She had them in sight. She was going to get them. They'd just entered Turner's dojo—she was trying to stop them."

"He's not answering!"

Tyler gave her a light shake. "I reached Emerson."

His words registered this time.

"Gray gave me her number because he's working with her on this case. She had them in sight. She was running toward them. The, uh, the line went dead."

Ana shook her head. "Kane...?" His voicemail had picked up again. She could hear it coming from her phone's speaker.

"I need you to come inside the airport with me," Tyler told her. "The plane is waiting. My job is to get you out of here. To take you to a safe place."

"Kane is my safe place," she whispered.

The faint lines near Tyler's mouth deepened. "You need to get on the plane."

"Is Kane okay?"

Tyler swallowed. "They were—they'd opened the door and gone inside Turner's dojo. I got that part before I lost Emerson."

No, no, no. She tore away from him and scrambled around the parked SUV. The driver was just standing there, looking helpless, so Ana swiped the keys from his slack grip.

"Wait!" A sharp cry from the driver. Wayne, his name had been Wayne.

"Get your asses in!" Ana yelled at Wayne and Tyler.

But Tyler lunged after her. His fingers clamped around her wrist. "Ana, what are you doing?"

She looked at his hand. Then his face. She could see worry and fear in his eyes. He cared about Kane. About

Gray. And both men—*no, no, stop it. They are not dead.* "I'm going to Kane."

"Ana, you were supposed to go to a safe house. That was the plan."

New plan. "I'm not going anywhere until I know that Kane is safe." Her breath sawed in and out. "Logan has Zuri. He has Zuri, and he might have killed Kane. There is no way I'm getting on a plane right now. I'm not leaving the people I love to die."

She'd only been willing to leave because she thought her departure would *help* Kane. Protect him. Stop him from being worried about her so that he could focus on catching Logan.

That plan had been blown to hell. *Like Kane? Has my Kane been blown into pieces?*

No, no, no! "Kane is going to be fine." She jerked her hand from Tyler's. "I know a shortcut to get us to Turner's dojo." That was where Tyler had said Kane was. That was where she'd be. "Get in the vehicle or get left behind. Your only options."

They got in the vehicle. Tyler rode shotgun.

Wayne jumped into the back.

Ana drove. The SUV's wheels squealed as she raced away, and even as she drove, she was yelling at Tyler, "Call Kane again! Keep calling—get him! *Call Kane!*"

KANE'S PHONE wouldn't stop ringing.

Maybe that's the bastard calling me. Taunting me. Telling me that my time is up.

But Kane didn't move. He kept holding that door.

Because maybe he could have a few more moments.

Maybe he could stop the bomb from going off. Maybe Gray could get out. If he kept the door in the exact position. All he had to do was not let that bell chime once more.

Gray appeared again. He grabbed Turner and heaved him up. Tossed Turner over his shoulder. "Fucking hell," Gray snarled as he flexed his brace-covered wrist. "Like I needed that." He rushed away.

Kane realized he was barely breathing.

Gray ran back into his line of sight again just—seemingly—seconds later. "My team is at the back door," Gray told him, voice flat, expression unyielding. "Bomb squad is on the way. There is no sign of Zuri Harris here. If Logan has her, he stashed her someplace else."

Kane glanced up. He could see the red light on the small bomb. Such a small device. But one that he knew could cause so much damage. With a soft exhale, he looked over at his friend again.

Gray grabbed the other man's arm—using his non-broken wrist for most of the work— and began hauling him away. That was...the lawyer. What had been his name? Sanchez. Kyle Sanchez. A trail of blood followed behind Kyle. And then...

Gray was gone.

The two vics were gone.

Kane's phone wasn't ringing any longer.

Once more, he stared up at the small bomb. He'd seen bombs before. In other places, other times. In a café in Paris. In a hospital that had become a nightmare scene. Other times, other terrible memories rolled through his head. As a Marine, he'd seen so much violence. Too much. He'd never been able to escape it.

Now, here...the bomb was right above him. And time was running out.

He wondered if Ana had read his note.

He was so glad his mom had made him always write those freaking notes. Because if he didn't make it out of that place, Ana would know how he'd felt. She would know that she'd been his everything. He'd lived for her. He'd die loving her.

"Bomb squad will be here in minutes, understand?" Gray was back. Hurrying toward him. "I'm not going to leave you. I'll be right here the whole time, and we will figure this shit out together. We've done it before. We can do it again. Just another survival story for us, am I right?"

Maybe.

Unless...Kane had to voice his worry. Because he needed Gray to get the hell out of there. "If Logan has a remote detonator, he could blow it at any point. Doesn't matter if I hold this door open or not."

"Don't say that." Gray took another step forward when the jerk should have been backing away. "Why in the hell are you going to put that negativity into the universe? There's *no* remote detonator. Say it with me. There is no—"

The red light flashed to green. "There is a remote detonator," Kane rasped. "Run, *now!*" Maybe it was a remote detonator. Maybe the bomb had just been equipped with a timed delay so that if the door didn't close, the bomb would still go off after a certain amount of time.

Either way...

Fucking green.

Gray had seen the flash to green, too. Only Gray wasn't running toward the rear of the dojo. Gray hurtled toward him as Kane remained on the threshold of that damn building. Gray's body hit Kane. They flew over the threshold and landed outside.

And the building erupted. Fire. Glass. Chaos.

Hell.

Chapter Twenty-One

"KANE."

He couldn't hear anything.

"Kane!"

But he could see Gray's mouth moving. His friend leaned over him, and Gray's lips were clearly forming Kane's name over and over again.

Blood dripped onto Kane. Blood from Gray. His friend was bleeding and cut and he was shaking Kane. Gray could stop that crap any minute.

"Kane!"

The bellow finally broke through to Kane's ears. Sounds rushed back to him, a big gush, like a dam breaking. The back of Kane's head throbbed sickeningly—probably from where he'd slammed down onto the pavement in front of the dojo. And then Gray's heavy ass had fallen on top of him.

Kane had cushioned the fall for the bastard. That was what you did for a friend. Cracked your skull open so your friend would be alive.

"You're okay!" A wild smile curved Gray's lips.

"Sonofabitch, you're okay!" He hauled Kane up and hugged him.

"No!" Emerson's sharp voice. "He could have a broken neck or a spinal injury! You *both* could have severe injuries! Stop! Stay still until the paramedics can get to you!"

Kane wasn't staying still. Fire was bursting in the air above Gray. Plus, something was...broken beneath Kane. He reached down and found the shattered remains of his phone.

"That was Tyler and Ana calling," Emerson hurried to explain as she crouched next to them. Gray had blood and ash and cuts all over his face. Emerson was right beside Gray, and she looked completely pristine. Not a hair out of place. Dress without a wrinkle. "Ana knew there was a bomb inside. She was trying to save you."

Ana.

His heart thudded hard in his chest. He shoved Gray out of his way and climbed to his feet. He also almost immediately fell on his face. Emerson caught him—tried to, anyway—and she nearly slammed down under his weight.

"Umph!" She held him tighter. "What part of *neck or spinal injury* did you miss?"

Other people rushed around them. Cops. Feds. Maybe even the promised bomb squad personnel. Everything seemed a bit of a blur to Kane. He *thought* that two EMTs— or perhaps paramedics?—crowded around him, too. Huh. Perhaps things were more than a bit blurry. *Definitely blurry.* Had he been knocked unconscious for a time? Kane feared he had.

Emerson backed up to give the paramedics more room.

Hard hands reached for Kane before he could fall on his face or even his ass. He may have fought those hands because... "Where the fuck is Ana?" Ana had to be all right.

He needed to be told she was safe. On her plane. Flying far, far away from this hell.

Glass crunched beneath his feet. Dark smoke billowed. Red and orange flames raced up the walls of the dojo.

"Grayson, are you all right? How's your wrist?" Emerson's worried voice. She coughed, waving at the smoke in the air. "Oh, no, you're bleeding...a lot."

"Do not dare vomit on me," Gray shot back. "Or faint. And the wrist is still freaking broken. Though, actually, it's probably *more* broken than before. I swear, I felt more bones snap."

At least, Kane *thought* that was Gray's reply. But the paramedics—*definitely* paramedics—had closed in around him. One had grabbed hold of Gray, too.

The next thing Kane knew, he was in the back of an ambulance. A siren was screaming somewhere nearby, and he curled his fingers around the arm of the guy trying to shove a needle into him. "Put that in my vein, and it will be the last mistake you make," Kane gritted out.

The paramedic's eyes got very, very big.

"Where in the hell is Ana?"

The man swallowed. "I have no idea who Ana is or where she is."

"Find someone who knows." Then... *"Gray!"* Kane bellowed. *"Gray, where the hell is my Ana?"*

Because Logan was still out there. Logan and his traps, and terror clawed apart Kane's insides. *I just need Gray to tell me that she's safe. I need him to tell me that Ana is okay. That Tyler took her far away. That Logan can't ever touch her. That's what I need Gray to say.*

"Sir, you need to calm down," the paramedic advised him. "I can give you something to help calm you down and ease your pain." The man came at Kane with the needle again.

So Kane snatched the syringe from his hand and tossed it.

"That is not cool," the man snarled. *"I'm trying to help you."*

"He's a real shit patient," Gray declared. "Sorry about that." Then Gray was there, leaning over Kane. A bandage had been slapped on Gray's forehead. The bandage was already turning red. "You're gonna have to write that man an apology note," Gray chided. "What would your mama say?"

Kane grabbed Gray's shirtfront. *"Ana."*

"She'd say Ana—"

"Tell me that Ana is safe."

"I'm safe, Kane."

That voice—Ana's voice.

He tossed Gray the same way that he'd tossed the syringe. In the next heartbeat, Kane was bounding out of that ambulance. Swaying a bit, but bounding, and Ana was right there. His beautiful Ana. He grabbed her, pulled her into his arms, and felt her softness against him. He buried his face in her hair. Drank in her scent.

Ana. Ana. Alive. Safe. In his arms.

She's supposed to be on a plane. She isn't supposed to be here. He would let her go. In a moment, he would. Kane would tell her that she had to go to the safe house.

In a moment.

Once his hands could manage to let her go.

"You're a terrible patient," Ana mumbled.

He still didn't let her go. Her arms were around him, too, holding on tightly. Maybe even tighter than he held her.

"I called you," Ana said.

He made himself let her go. Not completely. Just eased up enough so he could stare down into her face.

"You didn't answer." She blinked away tears. "I thought you'd died on me."

He kissed her. Had to do it. Kissed her deep and hard. Kissed her with all of the wild emotions coursing through his veins. Fear. Fury. But most of all, love.

He loved her so much. So insanely much.

He pushed her back. "You have to get the hell out of here." His gaze whipped around. Landed on Tyler. "Why is she here?" His buddy had been given one job. One very important job. Fly Ana to safety. *Not* bring her into hell.

"Ana's here because she drove the vehicle," Tyler responded.

What?

"I had to make sure you were okay." Ana's soft response.

His gaze jumped right back to Ana.

She winced. "You're bleeding. I'm pretty sure you're going to need more stitches."

No, what he needed was her. But first—first he needed to wipe Logan Catalano from the face of the earth. "Go get on the plane, Ana." His fingers curled around her waist.

But she shook her head. "I can't."

"Ana…"

She wet her lips. "He has Zuri. He wants me to come to him. If I don't, he'll kill her."

What. The. Hell?

"I'm not leaving you. I'm not leaving Zuri. I'm staying. I'm fighting."

They were *both* fighting.

* * *

261

ANA'S HOUSE WAS DARK. The windows had been boarded up in the front. Yellow police tape covered the pretty, wraparound porch.

Cops were everywhere. Cops. Feds. Bomb squad members.

Gray and his team had taken over the house next door—Mrs. Shirley's place. Ana's sweet neighbor had been quite stunned when the team of armed officers had appeared at her door. A female agent had spirited Ana's neighbor away to a new, safe location, and Gray and Tyler had immediately accessed the footage from Mrs. Shirley's doorbell camera.

There had been no footage of Logan or Zuri on that camera.

But...

Zuri's car was parked behind Ana's house.

"How did he get here?" The question came from Emerson. "Gray, you had eyes on the dojo. You said he never left. Turner Mitchell and Kyle Sanchez went inside. They were attacked. That means that Logan *had* to be there. So how did he get out? Without anyone seeing him?"

Ana wrapped her arms around her stomach. She wanted to hear this explanation, too. Her gaze kept darting to Kane. A bruised and scratched and slightly blood-covered Kane. A Kane who looked exceedingly dangerous and exceedingly pissed.

A Kane who is alive.

"I've got people pulling up schematics for the block and businesses around the dojo," Gray replied. He stared out of Mrs. Shirley's side window, with his eyes narrowed. "I think there must have been a tunnel or hell, some kind of air duct or some shit, that connected to the businesses on either side of the dojo. If he'd been prepared—and clearly, he was—

262

then Logan could have escaped that way. I believe the bastard was close by. I think he was watching us—at least for part of the time—and he made his getaway while we were trying not to get blown to hell and back."

Ana pulled in a deep breath. "But where was Zuri?" Ice seemed to encase her skin. "Did he have her in my house the whole time?"

Gray glanced back at her. "Have you gotten proof of life?"

Ana bit her lip. "No."

"Then we don't know that Zuri is alive in your house, Ana. And I am not sending you in there. I'm not letting you walk inside so that I can watch the whole place explode around you." His gaze flickered to Kane. "We've been there, done that routine already. I'm not making the same mistake again."

"You *saved* those two men," Emerson pointed out, tone sharp. "If you hadn't gone in the dojo, Turner and the lawyer would be dead right now. Even removing the *bomb* from the equation, their wounds were so severe that the paramedics said if they didn't get immediate attention, they would've died."

"Still might be their fate. They're in critical condition," Gray bit out. "For all we know, they'll both be dead soon."

"Ana isn't going in that house," Kane said. Adamant. "Not happening."

This was the same argument they'd had on the furious rush to their current location. Ana threw him a glower. She got that he was worried. She was completely terrified herself, but there was no way she would leave Zuri alone with Logan. "I am not letting my friend die."

"She could already be *dead*," Gray snapped. "No proof of life, remember?"

"If you believed that Zuri was dead, you would have already ordered your team to storm the door of my house." Ana wasn't backing down. "You think she's alive. You think there's a chance she's alive, anyway. That's why we're all here right now. You're holding your men back because if Zuri is alive and they rush in there, Logan will kill her. You know he will."

Gray nodded. Then, voice grim, he told her, "Or maybe the sick freak has the place wired. I send in my team, and I watch a whole lot of good people get blown to hell. So, yes, I'm sitting here, I'm running over every option I have, again and again, and the number one thing that comes back to me is *we need proof of life.*"

Gray had tried to call Zuri's number several times already. There had been no answer. But his agents had confirmed that Zuri's phone *was* currently inside Ana's house.

"The only way we are going to know if Zuri is alive—I have to go in the house," Ana said. "I can see her with my own eyes."

"No." From Kane.

"No." From Gray.

"No." From Tyler.

"I can go in." From Emerson. "Me, not Ana."

Everyone whipped their heads to look at her.

"I can." She nodded. Her hair slid lightly over her cheek. "Or I can at least go to the porch. I don't have to actually step foot inside the house."

"That's a shitty idea," Gray barked. "Absolute shit."

But Emerson shrugged. "Logan doesn't have me on his vengeance list. I think he'll talk to me. I'm not saying he'll come out of the house, but if he's there, I can get his focus on me for a bit. I can either get him to give us proof that Zuri is alive..." A slow exhale. "Or I can at least distract him long enough for some of you to sneak in the back door—*not get blown to pieces in the process*—and maybe you can take him out."

"Not happening." Gray pointed at her. "If you try that shit, I will cuff you to a chair in here."

Emerson's shoulders stiffened. "It might not be the best plan ever, but it's an option. One with minimal risk. Put a bulletproof vest on me. I'll go no closer than the porch—or, you know what? I'll stay off the porch. I'll remain on the sidewalk near the porch. I won't climb up the steps. I'll call out to him. Logan knows me. I think he even trusts me. If he's in that house, he will talk to me once he sees me. I can get you proof that Ana's friend Zuri is alive or..." An exhale. "Or like I said, I can at least distract him so that one of you can sneak in the house and get close enough to apprehend Logan."

"It's not—" Gray began.

"It's a solid idea," Tyler interrupted.

Gray rounded on him. "What the hell?"

"She's his shrink." Tyler waved toward Emerson. "She knows him. She knows how he thinks."

"And he doesn't hate her," Kane muttered. "He'll talk to her, if he's in there. We need this." He pointed to one of the agents milling around. "Get her a bulletproof vest."

"No." Gray shook his head. "She can't do it. She'll fuck it up. *No.*"

Ana saw the flash of pain on Emerson's face. But the flash was quickly hidden.

"I won't fuck this up," Emerson retorted. Brutally polite. "I want to help. That's all I've ever wanted to do."

"If she doesn't go in the house," Ana spoke slowly, "then

265

she won't be breaking the rule that Logan gave to me. He said that only I could go in."

"I won't be in." Emerson nodded. "I'll leave that part to whoever we think can get in the back without making a sound and alerting Logan."

Gray's right hand fisted. Released. Fisted. The left had been encased in an even bigger brace than before. The man probably needed an actual cast for his broken wrist, but Gray had refused to be taken to the hospital. He'd said no one would sideline him.

The tension in that room was so thick that it felt suffocating. Ana wanted to scream. All of these people—these good people were putting their lives on the line because of Logan and the threat he posed.

When would the nightmare end? When would it ever stop?

But she knew.

When we make it stop.

Gray's nostrils flared as he glared at Emerson. Then, grudgingly, each word coming like the growl of a beast, he ordered, "Get Dr. Marlowe a bulletproof vest."

"Get one for me, too," Kane added immediately.

"I need one," Tyler said.

Ana raised her hand. "Can I get one, too?"

"Fuck," Gray snarled. *"Fuck."*

But Kane curled his hands around Ana's shoulders. He tugged her toward him. "You are not getting anywhere near Logan."

"'Better safe than sorry,'" she quoted. "Isn't that how the saying goes?"

"You're better alive than dead," Kane returned. "That's how the freaking saying goes."

She did like that one better.

Chapter Twenty-Two

"Logan!" Emerson kept her hands up as she neared the edge of the sidewalk. She wasn't going onto those steps that led up to Ana's home. She'd given her word to Grayson, and she intended to keep that word. "Logan, it's me! It's Dr. Emerson Marlowe!" She could feel eyes on her. The Feds. The cops. The cops were behind her, with their parked patrol cars at the edge of the property. Feds were with them. Just as there were Feds hidden at the house next door. Hidden *behind* Ana's home. Hidden pretty much everywhere.

Grayson was watching her. Grayson was also talking in the small earpiece-slash-transmitter that he'd insisted she wear.

"Do not get on those steps, you understand me, Emerson?" Grayson snarled.

She barely controlled a wince. She wanted to tell the man to trust her, but she also didn't want to give away the fact that she was wearing an earpiece. So she kept her gaze on the front of the house. Yellow police tape flapped in the wind, and the smashed windows had been boarded up. "Logan, I know you're in there!"

Traffic was being diverted from the immediate area on Grayson's command. The whole place was eerily quiet, except for the crashing of the waves on the nearby beach.

Emerson tried again, shouting, "Logan, I'm here to help you!"

The front door opened. A squeak of sound.

Emerson held her breath.

"I didn't ask to see you, Dr. Marlowe." Logan's voice drifted to her. Amused. "I wanted my Anastasia."

He was just out of sight. The door had only opened a few inches. Precious, precious inches.

"Ana...Anastasia is close by," she promised him. "But she's not coming in. At least, not until I have proof that her friend Zuri is alive. You have to give me proof."

Silence. And then—

A woman's scream.

Emerson lunged forward.

"Don't you dare get on that step," Grayson snapped in her ear. "Don't you do it."

A woman appeared at the door. A gun was shoved beneath her chin. Emerson immediately recognized the photo Grayson had shown her of Zuri Harris just moments before.

Right height.

Right weight.

Hair.

Eyes.

Face—

Logan jerked the woman back. "Happy? She's alive. For now."

Another scream from inside.

Emerson's foot pressed to the bottom step.

"What in the sweet hell are you doing?" Grayson demanded. "Hold your position. Keep him focused. Kane is at the back of the house right now. He's going in. Insisted on being the one to lead the charge. All you have to do is keep Logan distracted. Stay where you are. Do you hear me? *Stay there.*"

Her breath shuddered out.

"I don't want to see you, Dr. Marlowe," Logan informed her, petulant and demanding at the same time. "I want Anastasia. If she's not here in the next five seconds, her friend Zuri dies. Be a dear and relay that message for me, will you? Either Anastasia comes in or Zuri goes out in a body bag."

"Is there a bomb here?" A stark question that burst from Emerson. "Are you just going to blow up Anastasia if she rushes inside?"

He laughed. "To do that, I'd have to kill myself. I'm not planning to die today."

IF SHE'S NOT HERE *in the next five seconds, her friend Zuri dies.*

She'd heard her friend scream. And thanks to the tiny earpiece that Grayson had given Emerson, Ana had been able to hear every word that Logan and Emerson exchanged. Grayson had been broadcasting the conversation on a speaker inside of Mrs. Shirley's house.

And as soon as she heard the *five seconds* part...

Ana ran for the door.

"No, Ana!" Grayson bellowed.

She didn't stop.

One of the Feds tried to grab her arm, but she ducked, then elbowed him. She ripped open that front door, and she ran toward her house. Jumping over the azalea bushes, rushing beneath the long, twisting branches of the oak trees. Branches weighed down by swaying Spanish moss.

Her breath heaved in her lungs and then, "I'm here!" Ana yelled. "Don't hurt Zuri!"

Emerson whirled around. The Feds near the street—those hunkered down with the cops—sprang up, and she knew Grayson had given them a command to stop her.

Ana ran faster. The bulletproof vest she wore bumped against her chest and back.

Kane was at the rear of her house. No, no, Kane should be *inside* the house by now. Kane who was so big but could move so quietly. He'd insisted on going inside to take out Logan.

And she was going to make certain that she held Logan's attention so that Kane could get close enough to subdue the other man.

"Ana!" Emerson's eyes were wide. "You shouldn't be here! Go back!"

Gunfire erupted. It came from the house, and Emerson jerked, her body shoving forward, right before she screamed. Emerson fell to the ground, but she rolled, twisted, and gasped.

"Not like the shot killed her," Logan taunted as his voice carried easily to Ana. "That's what bulletproof vests are for, am I right, Dr. Marlowe? To keep you alive when you're shot. But I *can* kill you. I can aim for your head, where you have no protection from a bullet. And I will, unless Anastasia gets her ass inside. *Now.*"

Was Kane already in the house?

Ana climbed the first step.

Another bullet exploded from the house. It hit the ground near Emerson.

"Don't move, Dr. Marlowe! The invitation wasn't for you! It was just for Anastasia!"

Ana climbed the second step. "Send Zuri out, and I'll come in with you."

He smiled even as most of his body remained concealed behind the partially open door. "Why in the hell would I want to do that?"

"Because Zuri hasn't done anything to you." Emerson had said Logan was focused on the eye-for-an-eye mentality of revenge.

But then again, Emerson hadn't done anything to Logan, and he just fired at her. A shot that he'd deliberately aimed to hit the bulletproof vest. And the second bullet had hit the ground near Emerson.

He hadn't killed Emerson.

Zuri appeared in the doorway. Logan had shoved her forward. Tears tracked down Zuri's cheeks. "Ana?"

Ana rushed up the last two steps. She hurtled toward her friend. Put her arms around Zuri and held tight.

"Say goodbye, Anastasia," Logan ordered her.

Her gaze jumped to him. A shadowy form behind Zuri. He still had his gun, and it was aimed right at the back of Zuri's head.

She choked down her fear. "Goodbye, Zuri."

"Ana?" Zuri's nails bit into her.

"Run to the cops, Zuri. Go, now." She shoved Zuri. Felt her friend's nails tear into her arm, but then Ana positioned herself right in front of Logan. Between Logan and Zuri.

Zuri would get away. Her pounding footsteps told Ana that she was escaping.

And as for Ana...

Logan reached out. Curled his left hand around her neck. He hauled her into the house. Slammed the door shut behind her.

"My sweet, sweet Anastasia." His handsome face twisted with his fury as the fingers of his left hand tightened around her throat. "I've missed you, you lying bitch."

* * *

"Kane, I know you can hear me." Gray eased out a hard breath. "Ana is in the house, and your ass better be in there, too." He'd wanted to go in the back of the home himself, but Kane had insisted on doing the job.

Tyler—hell, Gray knew that Tyler was supposed to be watching Kane's six. Were they both in the house? *They'd better be.*

"Zuri is secure." Gray could see her with the cops. The cops also had Emerson. *The bastard shot Emerson.* "Logan is armed with a gun, but I'm thinking you know that." His teeth snapped together. "Suspect is armed and dangerous. Defend yourself."

As if he didn't already know what Kane intended...Why Kane had been so adamant that he had to go into the house...

Logan Catalano is a dead man.

Gray just didn't want the guy to drag anyone else down with him on his way to the grave.

* * *

Ana shouldn't have been in the house.

She should never have left Gray's side.

But she was there, and Kane didn't need Gray's voice in

his ear telling him that fact. He could see her. Logan had her pinned between his body and the closed, front door. The bastard had a gun to Ana's side.

And he was saying—

"You're gonna pay for what you did, Anastasia. I've waited a long time for this."

"I don't love you, Logan." Her voice rasped. Almost like she'd been choked.

Was the bastard choking her? Kane couldn't see the front of Ana's body. Logan blocked his view.

"I-I never loved you," she gasped.

Logan jerked back from her, as if he'd been burned. "What?"

"Don't be surprised." Clearer. Stronger. There was no fear from Ana. "I'm sure you figured this out long ago." She remained near the door. "But in case there is any doubt, let me be completely honest. I don't love you. I love Kane Harte. And when you're back in prison, I will be living my best life ever with him."

"No!" Logan took another step back. "No, no, you won't, because I am going to kill—"

Kane attacked. The gun was angled away from his Ana, and Kane knew he had to seize the moment. He lunged forward, and he swept out with the knife he'd gripped in his right hand. One slice to the back of Logan's right leg. Down low, near the ankle.

The man screamed and whirled even as he sank toward the floor.

Kane drove his knife into the bastard's gut.

Logan jerked. Blasted his gun.

The bullet went wild. And Ana—she launched at Logan's back. She slammed into him, hitting with her fists, but Logan shook her off. Ana fell, sliding across the floor

273

toward the harp and it's broken strings. Strings that had been ripped and partially destroyed in the drive-by.

Kane pulled back his knife and prepared to slice the Logan's throat right then and there.

It's what you do to your enemies, isn't it, Logan? You often slice their throats. You shoot them. You blow them up. You kill. And that's what I am going to do to you. Kill you.

"Kane!" That fierce shout didn't come from Ana.

She was on the floor, grabbing for her broken harp.

The shout had come from Tyler. Tyler who had trailed Kane into the house. "Kane, step back!" Tyler roared. "I've got my weapon on him. *Get back!* We're taking him into custody."

Ah, that was Tyler. The Boy Scout. True blue until the end.

Blood dripped from Kane's knife and hit the floor. Logan was still crouched a few feet from the front door. Blood pooled beneath him because that was what happened when your Achilles tendon was severed. A brutal attack to take down prey.

You're not running away. You're not getting away at all this time.

Kane's grip tightened on the knife.

But Tyler's left hand grabbed Kane's shoulder. "I said get back. That's an order from a US Marshal. We're taking the perp into custody."

And there, on the floor, with blood all around him, Logan began to laugh. "I'll get out!" he yelled.

Ana climbed to her feet. Something twisted in her hands.

"I'll get out again, and I'll keep coming." Logan's hand darted down his body. Went toward his boot.

Do it, bastard. Kane would bet his life that the sonofabitch had a knife in that boot.

Do it. Reach for whatever weapon you have. I'll end you and have a perfect self-defense claim. Do. It.

Kane waited. Waited...

"Kane," Tyler warned. "Don't—"

Logan let out a guttural cry. He leapt up, putting his weight on his left foot, not the useless right, and he brought up a small knife. A small and squat knife with a fat, thick, sharp blade, and the bastard shoved it toward Kane.

But Ana jumped on Logan. She threw her body on top of his before he could get to Kane. And she wrapped—*what the hell?*—she wrapped harp strings around Logan's throat and tightened her grip on them—on him—with all of her might.

Logan's tongue jerked out. His face purpled. He grabbed at the strings and clawed at his throat.

"Ana!" Tyler's roar. "Ana!"

Logan dropped the knife. He drove his elbows back, and he hit Ana. He shoved back his whole body and slammed her into the door.

Her grip slackened on the strings.

But Kane was there. He'd leapt forward the instant that Logan had pulled his elbows back to hit Ana. He wrenched the prick forward.

The harp strings fell to the floor, and Kane proceeded to pound the ever-loving-hell out of the bastard who'd turned Ana's world into a nightmare. Over and over, his fists connected with the creep. Logan's face. His chest. His already bleeding stomach.

Down, down the former mob enforcer went.

And as he hit Logan, Kane saw—

Ana, in a cheap motel room, with blood soaking her side.

Ana, terrified near a shark tank. Eyes wide. Lips trembling.

Ana, near the ambulance as smoke billowed from the dojo. She'd reached for Kane—

She reached for him right then. Right there. Her fingers skimmed over his back. "Kane."

His fist froze mid-air.

"We're clear in here," Tyler barked. "Stand down, Kane. Stand the hell down, Marine. That's an order!"

Kane blinked. He...wasn't a Marine. Not any longer.

Once a Marine, always a Marine.

Tyler had kicked away the knives—Kane's knife. Logan's knife.

Logan was out cold.

So much blood.

"Gonna need an ambulance," Tyler said. He had a transmitter in his ear, too. They all did.

"Suspect is down," Tyler snapped.

Kane's gaze collided with Tyler's.

"Suspect is down," Tyler repeated. He exhaled. His voice softened as he added, "I've got him, Kane. It's done."

It wasn't done. Logan was still breathing.

But Ana threw her body against Kane's. She wrapped her arms around him. She held him as if her life depended on the embrace. She'd just seen him beat Logan again and again, and she was *hugging* him after what he'd done?

"You saved me. You protected me."

Kane blinked. He pulled back. Frowned down at her. *Shit. I was talking out loud.*

"I would have killed him for you in a heartbeat," she whispered. "I understand. *I understand.* I love you, and we don't have to cross this line. He's done. *Done.*"

The front door flew open. Almost slammed into Logan's crumpled form.

"Damn!" A sharp exclamation from Gray. "Someone played hard."

Kane just grunted. As if he knew any other way to play.

"Who needs medical treatment?" Gray demanded.

Only the man on the floor.

Gray checked Logan for weapons. He signaled for the paramedics. They rushed inside, even as Ana kept holding tightly to Kane, and he kept holding just as tightly to her.

When the paramedics touched Logan, his eyes flew open. He jerked upright. Only for Gray to shove him right back down. "Oh, yes, we will be restraining your ass," he swore.

Logan's wild eyes whipped around the room. Landed on Ana. Ana held in Kane's embrace. "I'll get out!" Blood poured from his busted lips. "I'll get out again. Should have...should have ended me...I'll come back...I'll—"

"Hey, asshole." Gray's calm voice.

Logan's attention jumped to him.

"My team says they found your fingerprints in the abandoned truck. Fingerprints. DNA. All kinds of delightful pieces of evidence in the stolen vehicle. Come on, you remember the truck I'm talking about—it had a dead body inside? You know, the man you killed? The dead guy littered with the bullets that will probably match those in the gun you used here?"

A gun that had already been bagged and tagged as evidence.

"Got a fun fact for you." Gray nodded grimly. "Mississippi has the death penalty. Think you'll get it at the trial? My money says you will. You're also going to be placed in one nightmare of a prison. No psych transfers for you. Just a fast trip to your own, private hell."

Logan's mouth dropped open. Blood-soaked. Beaten. He tried to surge up—on his one good foot.

Kane shoved Ana behind him.

But Gray was the one who slammed his fist into Logan's jaw and sent him slumping right back down to the bloody floor. "Let's get some restraints here, people!" Gray blasted. But, Kane caught it when, voice lowering, Gray growled to Logan, "That was for shooting Emerson, you prick. Just so you know, I'm not even close to being done with you."

Chapter Twenty-Three

"He locked me in the trunk of my car." Tears poured down Zuri's cheeks. "I had just arrived at the restaurant. You know I always arrive before everyone else. He came up behind me. Grabbed me. I tried to fight him, but he was too strong."

Ana held her friend's hands. Their foreheads pressed together as they huddled in front of Ana's house.

The crime scene. The chaos scene.

Logan was being loaded into the back of an ambulance. All of the color had left his face—he'd looked ashen, probably from the blood loss. And the beating.

And me nearly strangling him to death with broken harp strings.

"I was in that trunk for hours. He...he told me what he was doing." A shuddering breath from Zuri. "He left me in the trunk while he met those men at th-the dojo. Turner's dojo. He was inside when they arrived. He'd gagged me, tied me up, and I couldn't get out. He disabled the trunk release lever right in front of my eyes. I couldn't get out!" she said again. "I banged and banged, but no one heard me. I knew he was going in there to kill them, he told me that he was. I wanted to stop him, but I couldn't. And then...then he was back. I don't even know how long he was gone. He opened the trunk to look at me. There was blood on his clothes, and he told me that he'd tied up loose ends."

Tied up loose ends. By that, Ana knew Logan had meant that he'd stabbed Turner Mitchell and the lawyer, Kyle Sanchez. He'd also left a deadly trap for Kane and Gray.

Kane.

"He was waiting for something when we were parked near the dojo." Zuri backed away a bit. "When he had the trunk open to check on me, he kept looking to the sky like he should see something."

An explosion?

"And when he didn't, he got mad. He hit some black device he had, and then he slammed the trunk shut, and I-I heard a big *boom*. Felt like the world was exploding."

Not the world. Just the dojo.

But when I thought Kane was in the wreckage, I thought for sure my world had exploded.

Her gaze darted to the left. She found Kane watching her. He was talking to Gray, with Tyler standing close to them. She knew Kane was giving his statement to the other Feds, the ones wearing dark suits. But Kane's gaze burned as it pinned her.

"I was in the car that whole time, and I-I think he was killing people."

"They aren't dead." Emerson appeared at Ana's side. A very subdued Emerson. One who no longer wore a bulletproof vest.

Ana had removed her vest, too.

"Turner Mitchell and Kyle Sanchez are in ICU. They

aren't dead." Emerson's lips pulled down. "At least, they aren't dead yet.

Zuri's breath left her in a whoosh. "I want to go home. Can I *please* go home?"

Emerson nodded. "You can. There are just a few questions we need you to answer first."

Zuri pulled her hands from Ana's grip. Wet tear tracks lingered on her cheeks. "That's the ex, huh?" She jerked her thumb toward the ambulance. The rear doors were closed. Two uniformed cops waited outside the vehicle. Ana knew a Fed had been stationed inside with Logan.

"That's him." Ana's voice was grim.

"I like the new boyfriend way better," Zuri told her. "*Way* better."

Ana blinked. Her lips began to kick up. Leave it to Zuri to find a bright spot in the middle of this madness. "I like him way better, too."

"Thanks for saving me," Zuri told Emerson. "I don't know who the hell you are, but—"

A gunshot rang out. From *inside* the ambulance. Ana's head turned toward the sound. Her heartbeat seemed to stop. Every single moment seemed too slow as she watched those rear ambulance doors fly open.

Logan—Logan was there. With a gun. *How the hell had he gotten another gun?*

He looked at her. Aimed the weapon.

This can't be happening. Can't. Why won't he just stop?

No bulletproof vest. She'd taken it off.

She'd—

Another gunshot blast.

One blast.

Two.

Three.

All the bullets hit Logan, and he fell. Not back into the ambulance, but right onto the ground.

Uniformed cops swarmed. Ana didn't move. For a moment, she couldn't even breathe. Then, slowly, her gaze swept the area.

Kane had a gun up and still aimed at Logan.

Gray was armed, too. His weapon pointed at Logan's slumped figure.

And Tyler? His face was ice-cold as he held his gun and gazed at Logan.

There were lots of shouts. Lots of jumping into action. The Fed who'd been in the back of the ambulance leapt out, with his left shoulder bleeding. General chaos ensued.

But Ana knew, even as the first responders went to work on Logan, she knew that he was gone. Three shots. By three men who knew how to kill. Who'd fired first? Did it even matter?

Her breath slowly expelled. Then she inhaled. Exhaled. *In and out.*

Time picked up again.

"OhmyGod!" Zuri shuddered. "He's...he's dead, isn't he? *Dead.*" There was horror in her voice. And relief.

Ana understood. She felt the same way. Horrified. Relieved. Scared to the soles of her feet. And...Her gaze darted back to Kane.

He was watching Logan. Not moving.

He fired first.

She would have bet her life on that fact.

* * *

"No choice," Gray announced to everyone and to no one. Just saying the words. "Couldn't let the man fire that gun at a crowd. Federal agent in the ambulance should have damn well known better than to have an unsecured weapon back there. Hell, I *thought* Logan was restrained. Thought he was down for the count. You severed his Achilles tendon, for shit's sake. Not like he could go running off with that kind of injury."

Logan would never be running anywhere again. Kane knew his bullet had torn its way into Logan's heart. He'd always been a little faster on the trigger than Gray.

"It was mine," Tyler said from beside him. "My bullet took him out."

"The hell it did," Kane denied. "It was mine."

"Bullshit," Gray called. "Even basically one-handed, I fired faster than both of you bastards. It was my bullet. I'm sure of it."

Tyler shrugged. "We don't miss," he noted simply. "None of us." A pause. "Ana is safe now. No more running. No more hiding. She gets her life back."

Logan's body had been loaded into the back of the ambulance. Was someone doing chest compressions on him? Cute, but that wasn't going to help.

"What do you think she's gonna want to do with that life?" Tyler asked.

Before Kane could answer, Ana was there. She threw her body against his. Ignored the gun he held. Ignored the men next to him. She wrapped her arms around him, and she held him in a fierce grip.

"Yep," Tyler sighed. "That's pretty much what I thought she'd do. Invite me to the wedding, will you? My Esme loves a wedding."

Ana wasn't turning away because of the violence Kane carried. She wasn't afraid of him. Wasn't desperate to get away. Instead, she'd strangled a man with harp strings in order to help Kane.

And now, the monster from her past was dead.

Ana tilted her head back. She stared straight up at Kane, and she told him, "I love you."

His friends were watching him. Hell, reporters might be pulling up now, too. So much for keeping the scene under wraps. But Logan was dead. There would be no more need for secrets when it came to Ana.

And Kane wasn't going to hold back with her. Not ever again. When she'd gone through that door at her house...

Dammit, Ana, that had not been the plan!

His heart had stopped.

His world had stopped.

I'd live and die for you, Ana. I'd kill for you, too.

He had, in fact.

"I love you, too," he told her.

Ana smiled at him. A big, beautiful grin that lit her eyes. "I know."

He bent to kiss her because, yes, she did know. The woman knew everything about him now. No secrets. No lies. She knew all of his dark places. And she loved him still.

He was one lucky SOB.

His Ana. His sweet, determined, willing-to-fight-to-the-death Ana. She held his heart in the palm of her delicate hand.

Chapter Twenty-Four

"You can go back to New York."

Ana nodded.

"You can go back to being Anastasia Patrick again. Playing with the Philharmonic," Grayson told her as he stood near the desk in the small, unassuming office at the Gulfport police station.

But she winced. "I doubt they held my spot." For two years? Highly unlikely. "Pretty sure I've long since been replaced."

Grayson leaned his hip against the side of the desk. "You can go back home, Ana. Big city, bright lights. Get back to all the performances that I know you enjoyed before. You don't have to hide anymore. You can go back into the spotlight." He folded his arms over his chest. "We were able to trace Logan's steps, thanks to the cooperation we received from Turner Mitchell and Kyle Sanchez."

She knew those two men had been chatting a ton with the Feds. Turner had been desperate for a deal. Both he and Kyle had also been pissed that they'd nearly been murdered. So they'd turned and were feeding as much evidence as they could to Grayson and his team.

"A ton of lawyers from Kyle Sanchez's New York firm are now in custody. They are the ones who paid the psych transport guards to look the other way long enough for Logan to escape. The lawyers helped him to get down here. Hell, they even helped uncover your new identity and location for him. Logan had a ton of cash sitting in an offshore account, and he was happy to throw money their way."

Probably cash he'd earned for his mob hits.

"For the right price, those New York lawyers were willing to do whatever he wanted." Gray sent her a hard smile. "Now they can do whatever *they* want in prison. Because that's where they are going to be for years."

She pressed her palms to the tops of her jean-clad legs. "I'm not going to have to look over my shoulder any longer?"

"You are safe. The threats to you have been eliminated. Like I said, you can go home."

Because all the bad guys who'd worked for Logan in that law office had been arrested. Because Logan wasn't a threat. Because New York was supposed to be safe for her again. All wonderful things to know. But Ana exhaled slowly. Then she smiled at him. "This is home."

Grayson blinked.

"I like the sound of the water crashing into the shore. I like working with my music therapy clients. I like sitting on the porch and seeing the glow of the moon reflected on the water." She rolled back her shoulders and stopped pressing her palms to her jeans. "This is my home, and I don't want to go back. I just want to go forward."

"Forward." A pause. "With Kane."

"You knew I loved him two years ago."

"Yes." No fake denials from Grayson.

"Did you know that he loved me back then?"

"I suspected that he did. With Kane, it can be hard to tell, but...when he asked that you have his house—then I knew. He was trying to give you everything that he had, even when he didn't think he could be in that home with you."

Her heart ached. She'd come to this meeting alone. Finishing up paperwork. Giving final statements. Doing the whole tying-up-loose-ends routine.

Logan was dead. They'd called his time of death as soon as the ambulance had arrived at the hospital, but she was pretty sure he'd died when the bullets had been fired at her home. Ana knew that ballistic tests had been performed. Three bullets had been pulled out of him. All three had gone into his heart.

Which one hit first?

She knew.

Zuri was doing better. Still jittery. Still having nightmares. A week had passed, so it was early days. Emerson had been talking with Zuri a lot. Helping.

Ana hated to think of her friend trapped in the darkness of a trunk. Terrified that she might be killed any moment. She *hated* that her own past had brought such horror to Zuri's life.

But Zuri was safe. She was strong.

A survivor.

We both are.

Grayson raised his brows. "If I know Kane, he's probably been carrying around an engagement ring for you...oh, I'd say he's been carrying around a ring for two years now."

She shook her head. "Impossible."

"He's not really '*Heartless*' Kane Harte, you know."

She'd never liked that nickname.

"It was just that his heart belonged to you. So he didn't waste time with anyone else."

Ana blinked. "I think that might be the nicest thing you've ever said to me."

His brows notched up a bit higher. "Really? That's the nicest? Then, obviously, I need to step up my charm game."

She stared up at him. "I'm going to hug you."

He opened his arms.

She shot into them. Hugged him tight. "Thank you for helping me."

"You don't need to thank me. It's my job."

No, it was more than that. "Thanks for being Kane's friend, too."

"That's not a job," he returned without missing a beat. "That's a way of life. Sometimes, it's also a struggle."

Smiling, she eased back.

"I'm going to be his best man, too," Grayson informed her. "Just you wait and see."

"He's not going to ask me to marry him. I'm sure we'll...date first." They had just gotten back into each other's lives. Oh, wow, had it only been a few days before? No way Kane would be all-in on a wedding yet. No way.

"If he asks, what will your answer be?" Grayson cocked his head to the side as he waited for her response.

But Ana just smiled. Because the answer wasn't for Grayson. Her answer would be for Kane.

* * *

A MASSIVE, immovable object waited in her driveway. And

Ana wasn't just talking about the big Harley that blocked her from reaching the back of her house.

Kane perched on the edge of the Harley's seat, with his long legs sprawled before him. His arms were at his sides, the white t-shirt he wore putting up a courageous fight to fit around his muscles. A cap—this one with the logo of a local baseball team on the top—pulled low over his head.

Ana parked her Jeep, stared over the row of happy ducks on her dashboard, and smiled at Kane. She really loved that immovable object.

She hopped out of the Jeep. Rushed toward him.

He blinked, then smiled, and her breath left her body because that was the sexiest, most beautiful, *most real* smile she'd ever seen Kane give.

She hurried to him. He stepped away from the bike. Opened his arms. She went right into them. And Ana heard him mutter, "That's the dream I had for so long."

Surprised, her head tilted back. He stared at her with *so much love.* It almost hurt to see because the emotion was so powerful. She swallowed. Twice. And backed away.

His hands fell to his sides.

"Grayson said I could go home. That I'm safe."

Kane waited.

She should say something else. But, hold on, was that a small box on the seat of his Harley? A small, white box? It had been blocked by his body before, but now she could definitely see it.

No, no way. Kane is not going to ask me to marry him right now.

"Are you going home?" Kane asked, voice ever so careful.

Her attention whipped right back to him. "Like I told Grayson, I am home."

"Are you sure?" He swiped off the ball cap. Put it behind him. Near the white box. "Maybe the house has bad memories for you now."

Because bullets had broken her windows.

Because Logan had trapped her friend inside.

Because Logan had died at the edge of the property.

Yeah, okay, she could see where the place might need some serious sage work, but it was still hers. And his. *Theirs.* "This house gave me peace when I needed it the most. I'm not going to let Logan take away my peace. Not ever again. I'm staying here, and I thought you might want to stay, too." *Will you stay? With me?*

He stared at her. Seemed to eat her alive with his eyes. But he didn't say a word. Not one single word.

"Kane?"

He reached back. Knocked the cap to the ground. But Kane picked up the white box. He thrust it toward her.

Is this a ring? With shaking fingers, Ana opened the box. And she saw—

There was no ring inside. In fact, Ana was pretty sure she was staring at the yellow, plastic head of a duck. Just like all the ducks that lined the dashboard of her Jeep.

"Noticed that you collected those," Kane told her. His voice seemed extra gruff. "Thought you might like that one. See, uh, Ana, I have this thing...I notice everything that matters to you. I notice the candy bars you like to eat."

Her head snapped up.

"I notice the movies that make you smile. I notice your dreams—like when you say you want to live at the beach. I notice the way you move your fingers when you're in deep thought—like you're strumming your harp. I notice all the details when it comes to you. Big and small. Because you are what matters most to me."

Ana realized that maybe—perhaps she wasn't noticing the details enough with him. She pulled the small duck from the box.

The duck was holding a harp. And wearing a white wedding dress.

Laughter sputtered out of her even as joy and love filled Ana. "Where on earth did you find her?"

"Was not easy, I can guarantee you that. She's a custom job. One of a kind."

Her gaze collided with his once more.

"Just like you," Kane told her. Then he exhaled. "Ana, will you—"

"Yes."

He blinked. "But I didn't even ask—"

"Kane?"

"Yes, Ana?"

"You love me."

"More than anything in the world."

She dropped the box and held her duck like the treasure it was. Screw giving her a ring. She loved that damn duck. "Will you marry me?"

"*I* was asking," he began.

She waited.

"Yes," he rasped.

"Yes," Ana said. Her smile went from ear to ear. She was so amazingly happy. She clutched the duck and stepped toward Kane.

But...

Something rattled in her precious duck.

Ana frowned.

"False bottom," Kane explained. "She is a really, really special duck."

Sure enough, when Ana twisted the bottom of the

duck's dress, a small opening appeared. And a gleaming diamond ring waited inside that hidden bottom.

He notices everything about me. Her breath sawed in and out. "Kane." Ana cleared her throat. "How long have you had this particular duck?"

"A pretty long time," he confessed.

"And the ring? How long have you had it?" No way could Grayson have been right. Her head tipped back, and she held her breath as she waited for Kane to say—

"That was my grandmother's ring, Ana. I've had it for most of my life." He squared his broad shoulders. "But I've been holding it, meaning to give it to you, ever since we met. Well, probably the day *after* we met, if you want the truth. Took me that long to haul it out."

"No."

"Yes."

A tear leaked down her cheek.

He immediately wiped it away. "We can get a different ring. Or if you don't want to get married, we don't have to do it. We can live together. We can date. We can do anything you want."

"We're *getting* married. As fast as we can. I love the ring. Don't you dare get me anything different. And I love *you*." She rose onto her toes. "I love you. Forever."

He scooped her up. The way he always did. Held her so easily with that fierce strength of his. He kissed her. Soft. Sexy.

Sweet.

Her badass hero.

Her protector.

Her Kane.

Her heart.

Epilogue

EMERSON HAD SEEN ANA LEAVE GRAYSON'S temporary office. The other woman had practically flown out of there. Ana had looked happy. And intent.

Emerson knocked lightly on the now closed door. Grayson had been chillingly polite to her ever since Logan Catalano's death. They really needed to talk. To break the ice between them. Especially if they were going to be working together in the future. *Which we are.*

"Come in," Grayson called in response to her knock.

Sucking in a breath and schooling her features, Emerson opened the door. She put a bright smile on her face. "Good news," she started, determined to be positive, "I've gotten the approval to work with—"

"Shut the door. Then come closer." He sat behind his desk. He had put on a pair of glasses. She hadn't realized he wore glasses. They made Grayson look extra sexy, dammit. As if he'd needed any extra help. But the glasses gave Grayson a whole smart and gorgeous vibe that really worked for him.

Who am I kidding? Everything works for Grayson.

She shut the door. Her heels tapped on the floor as she advanced.

"How's the bruising on your back?" Grayson asked as he studied her.

"Gone." It was. The bruising from the bullet had long since faded. "How's your, ah, wrist?"

He sported a cast now, one that he sent a glare toward. "Broken. In multiple places."

Obviously, he was not happy with that situation. "A broken wrist is better than being dead." She didn't actually remember him thanking her for that life-saving moment, either.

His glare turned toward her. "Speaking of being dead... you realize, of course, that Logan could have killed you."

So they were going to talk about this, huh? Jump right to it? Fair enough. "I was wearing a bulletproof vest. If he'd wanted me dead, he would have just shot me in the head. Logan had the opportunity. The man is—was—an excellent shot."

Grayson rose from his chair. His hands flattened on the top of the desk. "You think telling me that Logan could have shot you in the head...you believe that's a good idea right now?"

She could not read his mood. Sure, he was pissed. But there was more at play. Emotions that went way deeper. "I've upset you."

"You have no idea what you've done to me."

She had to bluff her way out of this situation. "Well, too bad." She tapped her way to the edge of his desk. She should probably invest in some shoes that were less noisy. Unfortunately, she loved heels. "Because I've been told that I'll be your new partner for the foreseeable future."

"No fucking way."

That response was hardly encouraging.

"Has dear mom been pulling strings?" he taunted. "Got the senator to force you into the FBI?"

She wasn't going to take his very obvious bait. "I think I proved that I was willing to risk my life in order to help someone. I take this job seriously."

"You're not a Fed, Emerson."

"No, I'm not."

"You have zero field experience with the Bureau."

Not true. She'd been in the field when she got shot in the back.

"You don't know how to handle yourself in dangerous situations." His eyes scorched her.

"Right. I don't." His hands were on the top of the desk. She put hers right next to his. Not touching. But so very close. "And that's why I have you, partner."

Behind the lenses of those glasses, Grayson blinked.

"You're going to train me to handle dangerous situations. And I'm going to help you profile killers."

"I *know* how to profile killers."

"Then with my help, you should be able to take down twice as many of them. Win, win."

His gaze dropped to her mouth as she said, *Win, win.* He shook his head. And then he responded, "Fuck. *Fuck.*"

Obviously, they would have a glorious partnership. She extended her hand toward him.

He did not take it.

Emerson sighed. "You're going to be difficult, aren't you?" Her fingers wiggled.

"You have no idea."

THE END

Up Next...

You had to know this one was coming...want to see Gray and Emerson team up again? Team up, face danger, and maybe fall in love along the way? Let's have a battle and see just which person is better when it comes to mind games...

WHEN HE DEFENDS is the next Protector and Defender Romance.

Up Next...

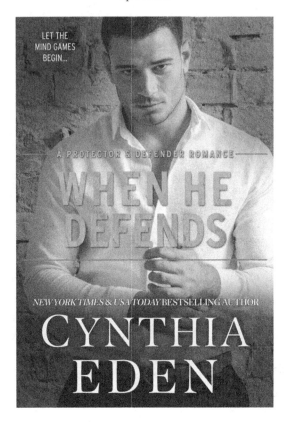

LET THE MIND GAMES BEGIN...

A PROTECTOR & DEFENDER ROMANCE

WHEN HE DEFENDS

NEW YORK TIMES & USA TODAY BESTSELLING AUTHOR

CYNTHIA EDEN

He didn't want a new partner, especially not *her*.

FBI Agent Gray Stone knows killers. As a top profiler at the Bureau, monsters are truly his business. So he absolutely does not need to be paired up with the infuriating—and gorgeous—Dr. Emerson Marlowe. But her mother is a senator with far too much power, and, all of a sudden, Gray finds himself on training duty, a duty that includes way too many hours and way too much temptingly close contact with Emerson.

He doesn't play well with others. In fact, he doesn't play at all.

What's he supposed to do with a sexy shadow? One who is just as good at mind games as he is? One who is smart and funny and...*dammit.* Emerson has practically no field experience, and the last thing Gray wants to do is put her in harm's way. He may not want to work with Emerson, but he will *not* let anyone hurt her. So when a new case goes sideways and a killer gets chillingly close, Gray has to come up with a new training plan.

New rules: She follows his orders. She does exactly what he says. And she does not get in the way.

Except Emerson can't follow orders to save her life. She does whatever she wants, and the woman is one hundred percent in his way. In his way. In his mind. In his dreams. And, maybe, just maybe, the infuriating Emerson is even working her sneaky way into his heart. But danger is growing around her, danger that doesn't seem to just be coming from their work at the FBI. A stalker has eyes on Emerson, a predator who is well-acquainted with darkness and pain. A perp who wants Emerson to suffer.

To protect his new partner, Gray will have to let his own darkness come out to hunt.

No one turns Gray's partner into prey. No one terrifies Emerson. No one hurts her. Ever. Gray stops playing the good guy, and he goes all in on protecting her. Protecting and defending—that's his way of life, but this time, the defense is personal. Emerson is *his*—uh, his partner, of course, and, hell, maybe a whole lot more. Gray has always kept his inner darkness on a tight leash, but when Emerson is threatened, his control shatters. He will claim her, he will protect her, and he will put the perp who threatens her in the *ground*.

Author's note: Grayson "Gray" Stone has spent far too many years playing mind games with other people. This time, he's the one who will see his life spiral out of control as he falls hard for a partner he never expected. Forced proximity, danger, desire, opposites fiercely attracting...oh, get ready for all the fun things. Did I mention the steam? Because there is plenty of it in this romance.

Author's Note

I love a protective, fierce hero (and I hope you enjoy them, too!). The bigger they are, the harder they fall...and Kane certainly fell hard for Ana. Thank you so very much for taking the time to read this Protector and Defender Romance! I am incredibly grateful to you for choosing this book.

I've had so much fun writing about this group of former Marines, and I can't wait to bring you Gray's story next. His friends warned Gray previously that, one day, he would meet a woman who was even better at mind fuckery than he was...and, that day is here. Gray will face off with Dr. Emerson Marlowe in WHEN HE DEFENDS.

Thank you, again, for taking the time to read this book. If you have time, please consider leaving a review for WHEN HE FIGHTS. Reviews help readers to discover new books —and authors are definitely grateful for them! (Trust me— we are super, super grateful!)

If you'd like to stay updated on my releases and sales, please join my newsletter list. Did I mention that when you sign up, you get a FREE Cynthia Eden book? Because you do!

By the way, I'm also active on social media. You can find me chatting away on Instagram and Facebook.

Until next time...wishing you lots of wonderful reads and happy days.

Best,

Cynthia Eden

cynthiaeden.com

More Books By Cynthia Eden

Protector & Defender Romance
- When He Protects
- When He Hunts
- When He Fights

Ice Breaker Cold Case Romance
- Frozen In Ice (Book 1)
- Falling For The Ice Queen (Book 2)
- Ice Cold Saint (Book 3)
- Touched By Ice (Book 4)
- Trapped In Ice (Book 5)
- Forged From Ice (Book 6)
- Buried Under Ice (Book 7)
- Ice Cold Kiss (Book 8)
- Locked In Ice (Book 9)
- Savage Ice (Book 10)
- Brutal Ice (Book 11)
- Cruel Ice (Book 12)
- Forbidden Ice (Book 13)
- Ice Cold Liar (Book 14)

Wilde Ways
- Protecting Piper (Book 1)
- Guarding Gwen (Book 2)
- Before Ben (Book 3)
- The Heart You Break (Book 4)
- Fighting For Her (Book 5)
- Ghost Of A Chance (Book 6)
- Crossing The Line (Book 7)
- Counting On Cole (Book 8)
- Chase After Me (Book 9)
- Say I Do (Book 10)
- Roman Will Fall (Book 11)
- The One Who Got Away (Book 12)
- Pretend You Want Me (Book 13)
- Cross My Heart (Book 14)
- The Bodyguard Next Door (Book 15)
- Ex Marks The Perfect Spot (Book 16)
- The Thief Who Loved Me (Book 17)

The Fallen Series
- Angel Of Darkness (Book 1)
- Angel Betrayed (Book 2)
- Angel In Chains (Book 3)
- Avenging Angel (Book 4)

Wilde Ways: Gone Rogue
- How To Protect A Princess (Book 1)
- How To Heal A Heartbreak (Book 2)
- How To Con A Crime Boss (Book 3)

Night Watch Paranormal Romance
- Hunt Me Down (Book 1)
- Slay My Name (Book 2)

• Face Your Demon (Book 3)

Trouble For Hire
• No Escape From War (Book 1)
• Don't Play With Odin (Book 2)
• Jinx, You're It (Book 3)
• Remember Ramsey (Book 4)

Death and Moonlight Mystery
• Step Into My Web (Book 1)
• Save Me From The Dark (Book 2)

Phoenix Fury
• Hot Enough To Burn (Book 1)
• Slow Burn (Book 2)
• Burn It Down (Book 3)

Dark Sins
• Don't Trust A Killer (Book 1)
• Don't Love A Liar (Book 2)

Lazarus Rising
• Never Let Go (Book One)
• Keep Me Close (Book Two)
• Stay With Me (Book Three)
• Run To Me (Book Four)
• Lie Close To Me (Book Five)
• Hold On Tight (Book Six)

Bad Things
• The Devil In Disguise (Book 1)
• On The Prowl (Book 2)
• Undead Or Alive (Book 3)

- Broken Angel (Book 4)
- Heart Of Stone (Book 5)
- Tempted By Fate (Book 6)
- Wicked And Wild (Book 7)
- Saint Or Sinner (Book 8)

Bite Series
- Forbidden Bite (Bite Book 1)
- Mating Bite (Bite Book 2)

Blood and Moonlight Series
- Bite The Dust (Book 1)
- Better Off Undead (Book 2)
- Bitter Blood (Book 3)

Mine Series
- Mine To Take (Book 1)
- Mine To Keep (Book 2)
- Mine To Hold (Book 3)
- Mine To Crave (Book 4)
- Mine To Have (Book 5)
- Mine To Protect (Book 6)

Dark Obsession Series
- Watch Me (Book 1)
- Want Me (Book 2)
- Need Me (Book 3)
- Beware Of Me (Book 4)

Purgatory Series
- The Wolf Within (Book 1)
- Marked By The Vampire (Book 2)
- Charming The Beast (Book 3)

• Deal with the Devil (Book 4)

Bound Series

• Bound By Blood (Book 1)
• Bound In Darkness (Book 2)
• Bound In Sin (Book 3)
• Bound By The Night (Book 4)
• Bound in Death (Book 5)

Stand-Alone Romantic Suspense

• Waiting For Christmas
• Monster Without Mercy
• Kiss Me This Christmas
• It's A Wonderful Werewolf
• Never Cry Werewolf
• Immortal Danger
• Deck The Halls
• Come Back To Me
• Put A Spell On Me
• Never Gonna Happen
• One Hot Holiday
• Slay All Day
• Midnight Bite
• Secret Admirer
• Christmas With A Spy
• Femme Fatale
• Until Death
• Sinful Secrets
• First Taste of Darkness
• A Vampire's Christmas Carol

About the Author

Cynthia Eden loves romance books, chocolate, and going on semi-lazy adventures. She is a *New York Times*, *USA Today*, *Digital Book World*, and *IndieReader* best-seller. She writes romantic suspense, paranormal romance, and fun contemporary novels. You can find out more about her work at www.cynthiaeden.com.

If you want to stay updated on her new releases and books deals, be sure to join her newsletter group: cynthiaeden. com/newsletter. When new readers sign up for her newsletter, they are automatically given a free Cynthia Eden ebook.

Made in United States
North Haven, CT
31 July 2025

71210813R00176